Whiskey Jack's Secret

By
Randall Probert

Whiskey Jack's Secret
by Randall Probert

Copyright © 2018 Randall Probert

All rights are reserved. No part of this book may be reproduced or transmitted electronically in any form without written permission from the publisher or author.
For more information, address Randall Enterprises.

www.randallprobertbooks.net
email: randentr@megalink.net

Art and Photography credits:

Front and back cover art ~ Robin Fraser, Newry, ME
Smithsonian Castle, pg 58, Wikipedia, cc. Brian Pirwin
Elinor Smith photo, pg 198, Wikipedia
Author's photo, pg 272 by Patricia Gott

Disclaimer:
This book is a work of fiction, but it does contain some historical information.

ISBN: 978-1986008679

Printed in the United States of America

Published by
Randall Enterprises
P.O. Box 862
Bethel, Maine 04217

Acknowledgements

I would like to thank Amy Henley of Newry, Maine for her help typing this and for the many revisions. I would also like to thank Laura Ashton of Woodland, Georgia, for her help formatting this book for printing, and Robin Fraser of Newry, Maine, for the sketches on the front and back cover.

More Books by Randall Probert

A Forgotten Legacy

An Eloquent Caper

Courier de Bois

Katrina's Valley

Mysteries at Matagamon Lake

A Warden's Worry

Paradigm

Paradigm II

A Quandry at Knowles Corner

Trial at Norway Dam

A Grafton Tale

Train to Barnjum

A Trapper's Legacy

An Esoteric Journey

The Three Day Club

Eben McNinch

Lucien Jandreau

Ekani's Journey

Whiskey Jack Lake

Life on the Little Black River

Flores Cartel Goes to Maine

Marquis

Whiskey Jack Lodge

Whiskey Jack's Secret

Chapter 1

"It would be a nice story of two world leaders here in our home to pass on to our grandchildren, if we had any," Rascal said.

"Yes it would be. And who's to say we won't have any?" Emma said and then continued, "I think it is time we start making a family Rascal. Come on, I mean now," she looked at Anita and she was smiling.

Anita watched as Rascal and Emma walked arm in arm back inside. She stood on the platform a while longer looking out across the lake. She was overwhelmed with emotions that had been building up for a long time and now after this week with the President of the United States and Canada's Prime Minister here and sharing with them their plan for uniting the two countries before telling anyone else, her eyes suddenly reddened and she began to cry with both joy and sadness.

She wished Silvio could have been here also. She was missing Silvio and at the same time she knew she had never been so happy.

She wiped the tears from her face and looking across the lake she said, "I do love and miss you, Silvio, but I have never been so happy. I wish I could tell you how much Rascal and Emma mean to me. They are my family now." She wiped the tears away again and went back inside.

Emma had her clothes off and was in bed while Rascal was still pulling his pants off.

As they lay on their backs, Emma said, "You know Rascal, I was thinking maybe it would be a better idea if we waited to get pregnant until after your operation. And plan it so the baby would be born in . . . let's say March."

"So that would put it at June. I think maybe you're right."

"So, we agree we wait?"

"Yes, we'll still have to be careful."

Anita splashed water on her face. Then she went to the kitchen to start supper.

****

At supper Emma said, "No matter how often we have steak, it always tastes so good. This is just how we like it, Anita. A little pink inside."

"It is good, Anita," Rascal added.

"Do we have anyone coming next week to hunt?" Rascal asked.

"No."

"Maybe we should call Jarvis and see if they still intend on coming for Thanksgiving."

"Why don't you call him after supper, Rascal?"

While Emma and Anita were picking up and cleaning the kitchen, Rascal, with some difficultly, telephoned Jarvis. "He said they were planning on coming, and their son Herschel was discharged from the Army last week and he'll be coming also."

"That'll be good, we haven't seen Herschel for several years now," Emma said.

Afterwards they sat in the living room and listened to the evening news on the radio. Rascal asked, "What are we going to do with the plaques that the President and the Prime Minister gave us?"

"I know," Emma said, "we could put them on that wall." The back wall had space and there needed to be something there. "Go get ours, Rascal. And you also, Anita."

"You want my two with yours?" she asked, rather surprised and pleased.

"Of course, Anita. You're family."

When they came back she had them hold them up against the wall so she could see how they looked. "Up a little higher. About eye level. That's good. Perfect. I'll hold 'em, Rascal, so you can see."

Rascal wasn't much for interior decorating. "They look fine to me." Then he swapped with Anita so she could see.

"I think they look real good there," Anita said.

"Will you hang 'em tomorrow Rascal?"

"Well, I was planning to trap, now that next week will be empty and we're all caught up for winter."

"That's okay, Anita and I can do it."

They set the plaques on the table and sat back in the living room. "Are you going up to Ledge Swamp in the morning?" Emma asked.

"I don't think so."

"Bear?"

"Bear is one reason and it's a long walk up and back around the swamp."

"Do you really think Bear would bother you?"

"I really don't know. Trapping nuisance beaver up there is one thing. But I think he claims the swamp as his. If it were later in the season I would."

Anita was listening to all this about a bear and wasn't really understanding. "I have overheard you two talking about a bear. What's this all about?"

They told Anita everything and she burst out laughing. "You mean Rascal, you play with a bear?"

"It's more like I'm his plaything."

"Do you suppose that is all he was doing when he buried your traps? I mean he didn't make any offer to hurt you, did he?"

"No, he didn't, and maybe that's all he was doing. But all the same I won't go up until I'm sure he has hibernated.

"Everything we have told you, Anita, about Bear must stay here. If people were to hear about him people would come here just to see him. And we don't want that."

"I won't say a word."

****

The next morning Rascal said goodbye and hiked out behind the cabin. He set two traps on either side of the road close to his trap line trail and then two on the beaver dam and then he circled to the left, back to his trap line trail. He set traps along the trail until it turned sharply back towards the lake. He cut across country back to the beaver flowage and both traps had been pulled into the water.

He was there until dark pulling in beaver and skinning. He had four and only two were skun. With the three he had taken a week ago, so they would have beaver meat for their two guests, he decided he had taken enough. He put the two hides and beaver in the root cellar and he would take care of them tomorrow.

"How'd it go, Rascal?" Emma asked.

"I set what I wanted and caught four beaver. After supper I'll go up to the cabin and finish skinning two of them and put them on drying boards.

There weren't any electric lights at the cabin now and he had to work with a lantern.

****

At the breakfast table the next morning, "I'll tend what sets I made yesterday and then go out where we hunt and down the Jarvis Trail."

"Anita and I are going to take the train to St. Jean and get a turkey and some wine. Would you like some brandy or something?"

"Yes, a fifth of good brandy. You make the choice.

"I'll put up the red flag for you on my way out. You two ladies be careful."

"We will," they both answered.

He decided to set one trap on the dam for beaver. He

hadn't thought to bring along any food, so he was counting on eating beaver. He had picked up a bobcat in one of the first sets, and in the next five along his trail to the corner he picked up five martin. He reset everything and headed for the flowage.

The trap was gone and he built a small fire before pulling it in. And much to his surprise he pulled in another extra large beaver. He set some meat to roasting while he finished skinning and then he put everything in his pack basket. He would wait for evening or tomorrow to cut away the meat to be canned.

After he had eaten his fill of roasted meat, he left the martin, bobcat and beaver in the root cellar and headed for the Jarvis Trail. There he set two cubby sets, hoping for at least another bobcat or lynx. Out at his hunting glade he set a trap a hundred yards along the glade on both sides of the road and both sides of the glade—four traps in all.

Those behind the cabin he would leave and tend the following day and the new sets he would check tomorrow afternoon.

The train was pulling out heading south as he walked across the field to the lodge. Emma saw him coming and waited for him.

"How'd it go?"

"Pretty good, picked up another beaver, one bobcat and five martins."

"That is good."

"Yeah, but remember I haven't trapped since we began the lodge."

"Still, it's good."

"Can you and Anita can the beaver tomorrow?"

"Sure."

"Did you get everything?"

"Yes. We were able to buy a turkey that a local farm had killed that morning and plucked. He brought four into the grocery store."

"Thank goodness for that. I hate plucking turkeys."

"Can you carry it down stairs and put it on ice?"

"What if we left it out for a while? I think the temperature is dropping."

"That'll work."

****

Rascal and Emma slept a little longer the next morning. They waited for daylight which didn't show until almost seven. "Hey you," Emma poked him in the ribs with her elbow. "It's a good thing we don't have any guests. Come on it's time to get out of bed, Rascal."

"Okay."

He had cut off all the beaver meat the evening before and Anita and Emma had filled seven quart jars and then set them on ice in the cold storage room. While Emma and Anita were making breakfast Rascal started the fires in the wood stoves. It wasn't cold enough yet to use the fireplace.

That morning behind his cabin he picked up another, larger bobcat, a fox and a fisher. He wasn't going to tend out to the Jarvis Trail and the glade, but since he was done by noon he decided to go out and Emma wanted to go also.

There were wolves in both traps on the Jarvis Trail. "Those are almost the same color as a fox, Rascal. Their fur sure is pretty."

"They are at that. Catching these two makes me wonder if a pack of wolves have moved in."

"Could these be dangerous, Rascal?"

"They're much smaller than the gray or timber wolf, but if you had one cornered they might be. I doubt if either of those two would weight more than fifty pounds."

She watched as Rascal shot the wolves in the ear and she was beginning to feel sorry for them. He reset both traps and carried both animals out to the road. One under each arm. Emma carried the axe and pistol. "We'll leave these here and pick 'em up on the way back."

They checked the two traps on the right side of the glade first. "Hum, nothing has been to either one."

Then they went down below the road on the left and nothing had been near those sets either. They crossed the glade to the other side and that first trap was untouched and the next one. They crossed the road and the last two sets had not been touched.

Rascal took his hat off and was scratching his head and he noticed Emma had pulled her pants down and was going pee. "Em, not here. The smell of your pee will keep the animals from coming close. You'll have to go about a hundred feet away, up through the hardwoods."

"Oh, all right," she pulled her pants up and hung on to them and ran up through the trees.

When she was back she asked, "Does the smell of pee really make that much of a difference?"

"It sure does. All animals mark their territory with pee. The smell tells other animals that this territory is theirs. Or it can be used to entice a mate during the mating season. Like moose or deer."

They walked back and picked up the two wolves and headed for home. "Will the wolf hides be worth much?"

"Ordinarily no. But the color of these two should bring a good price."

****

That night it snowed a couple of inches and by daylight the temperature had dropped to zero. "Another night like this and the ice on the lake will be strong enough to walk on," Rascal said as he slid his chair back away from the table.

"I hope you have better luck today," Emma said as Rascal opened the door to leave.

Behind the cabin he picked up another fox, two raccoons and two huge male fishers. He pulled all of those traps and headed for the Jarvis Trail. He had two more raccoons there and in the two traps below the road on this side of the glade he had two martins, with bright orange fur on the throat and chest.

He crossed the glade and had two fisher cats. "This is beginning to pay off," he said aloud.

Above the road and on that same side he picked up a huge male lynx. As he was crossing the glade to the other side he noticed cat tracks in the deer trail and set a cubby set ten feet to one side of the trail. In his last two traps, he had two smaller fisher cats.

As he was walking home he was thinking that normally after doing so well in a few short days he would pull his traps and not over trap. But it would probably be a couple of years or more before he had the chance to trap again. And by then the fur animals will have moved back in.

"How much longer are you going to trap?" Emma asked.

"I was going to set up the farm field, but coming in this afternoon I thought better of it. One of these nights we're going to get enough snow to make it too difficult to trap, let alone hike through the snow. I'll pull up everything tomorrow."

****

Daylight was a long time coming the next morning. Anita was up first and she had a pot of coffee making and the smell of fresh coffee drifted into their bedroom and Emma and Rascal weren't long getting up. Anita had poured herself a cup and was standing looking out the window at the frozen lake when Emma and Rascal walked in. "It'll snow before dark. Look at those dark clouds. They're heavy with snow," Anita said.

"I think I'll skip breakfast and head out and start pulling traps. I should be back shortly after noon," and he closed the door and headed for the Jarvis Trail.

He picked up a red fox and another raccoon and pulled the traps. In the glade he picked up three more martin, another red fox, a fisher cat, a bobcat and in the cubby set next to the deer trail he had a female lynx.

He was loaded down heavy with the lynx resting on his

shoulders between his head and pack basket. As he stepped onto the old road it started to snow and by the time he was back at the lodge it was coming down in blizzard form.

"Well, you made it back just in time. How'd you do?" Emma asked.

"Really good. There was fur in each trap. They must have been trying to hunt for food before the storm arrived so they could hold up for a couple of days if they had to."

"Are you hungry?"

"I could eat the bark off a dead tree, I'm so hungry. I'll put these in cold storage and wait to skin them at the cabin after the storm breaks."

During the night the wind started to blow down the lake and come daylight the ice was swept clean and the snow was piled up at the dam bridge. It was packed so hard Rascal could easily snowshoe across staying on top. It was difficult to judge how much had fallen, it was so windblown.

Once he had all of the fur pelts on stretchers, he shoveled snow around the cabin and he made sure the water pipes had been drained and all containers were empty. After lunch he filled all of the wood boxes in the lodge and then he sat down in the living room with the newspaper.

By midafternoon the temperature had warmed and the snow was settling. But at 7 o'clock that evening, a cold arctic chill blew down the lake and all night long they could hear the lake making ice. Sometimes there was a loud creak that ran up the length of the lake.

"I wonder what city folks would think, Rascal, if all of a sudden they could hear a lake making ice."

"I don't know if they would even know what the noise was. If you didn't know I suppose it could be rather unsettling."

"I like lying here with you Rascal and listening to it.

"Not to change the subject, but I hope we hear from the President's doctor soon, so we can make plans," Emma said.

Chapter 2

Thursday morning the train stopped and Jarvis and his wife and son stepped off. "Brrr, that wind is cold."

"You getting soft, Jarvis, since you retired?" Rascal gibed.

"Well—just an observation. There are times, though, when I look back on my career and wonder how I ever stayed out in the elements for days at a time. Looking back on my life now, it seems more like a previous life that I remember."

"Well, I doubt if there'll ever be another Jarvis Page."

"Thank you, Rascal. As soon as we have unpacked we have some news to tell you."

"You know where the rooms are; help yourselves. Then we'll have a pot of coffee and a few of this morning's donuts."

They all sat at the table and Anita poured the coffee and then sat down with them. "It's good to see you again, Anita. I hope you're well," Rita said.

"I have never been happier."

"Anita is part of our family now," Emma said.

"How did you like the Army, Herschel?" Rascal asked.

"I did. But I changed my mind when I received a letter from home." He let it hang there for a few moments before continuing. Everyone was looking at Jarvis and Rita, and waiting for him to continue. "Dad said that Marcel Cyr had transferred to southern Maine and this area was going to be held open until the beginning of the fiscal year, next July, and if I wanted to be a game warden in this area, all I had to do was say the word. So now I'm home until July."

"That's great news, Herschel," Emma said.

"Yes, it is," both Rascal and Anita said.

"What are you going to do until July?"

"I haven't gotten that far yet. I'll pick something up," Herschel said.

"When do you expect to hear from Washington?" Jarvis asked.

"'We're not sure, but we hope it is soon so we can start planning," Rascal said.

"Will you go with Rascal, Emma?" Rita asked.

"Yes."

"What about you, Anita? Will you stay here by yourself?" Jarvis asked.

Before she had a chance to answer, Emma said, "No, she won't have to. We'll find someone to stay here with her and help with the upkeep."

"And then there's the farm that will have to be looked after," Rascal added.

"Herschel could help you out, maybe."

Rascal looked at him and Herschel said, "Sure, I wouldn't mind spending some time out here. How long are you talking?"

"I wouldn't think it would be more than two months, maybe three at the most."

"I could do that all right. Just let me know when you want me."

"As soon as we know, we'll call you."

"Now, gentlemen, us women have to start preparing dinner," Emma said and stood up.

"Jarvis, are you or Herschel wanting to go hunting?"

"Yeah," Herschel said. "I am, but not today. It's too cold. Maybe tomorrow morning."

"Whenever I come here now, it's difficult to think of Whiskey Jack without remembering the village and the people. I miss the village and the people," Jarvis said.

"I understand how you feel, Jarvis. The three of us feel the same."

"I think my most enjoyable times were when I was here early enough to join you, Silvio, Jeters and Jeff for coffee and donuts," Jarvis said and he took another sip of his coffee. "And of course there was the time when you and I, Rascal, were standing on the dam when Emma shot that deer that was eating her lettuce."

Rascal almost choked and spit up his coffee, then he looked square at Jarvis and grinned.

Jarvis smiled and said in a low voice, "Well I'll be to go to hell, you did, didn't you. But how on earth did you do it? I think I know why, but how did you do it?"

Rascal began grinning and he was about to say something when Emma said, "Rascal will you carve the turkey? Jarvis, Herschel come sit down, everything is ready."

Jarvis stood up, thinking Emma had just spoiled a good story. And one she too would probably like to hear—but not appreciate.

As they were sitting down Emma opened a bottle of wine and began filling glasses. Herschel looked questioningly at his dad. Jarvis saw the look on his son's face and knew what he was thinking. He ever so slightly shook his head 'no.' And then he looked at Emma and smiled. She too knew what he was thinking.

Just then it occurred to Jarvis that they each had a secret that they didn't want the other to know.

The meal was as good as it always was and everybody ate too much. "There's pie and some sharp cheese for dessert. Would you rather have it with coffee later, maybe for supper, or now?"

They all wanted to wait. "Okay, why don't you men help Anita and I take care of this food then we all can sit in the living room and talk."

The wind was still blowing and the temperature was still too cold to venture outside. Rascal put more wood in the fireplace and in the ram-down heater upstairs.

The men were just getting in the way in the kitchen so

Emma had them clear the table and then sit down in the living room. Then in a few minutes Anita, Emma and Rita joined them with a plate of cheese and a bottle of good brandy.

"I'll say one thing, this is sure a quieter place to sit and converse with friends than when it used to be a cafeteria—more relaxing," Jarvis said.

"This is more like home to me now," Anita said, "than even the cabin Silvio and I had. But I sure do miss all the people. They were good people."

"When do you expect to hear from Washington?"

"We have no idea. I hope President Cutlidge doesn't forget. I suspect he's a busy man," Rascal said.

The brandy was awful good along with the cheese, but soon everyone was sipping brandy and had stopped eating the cheese.

"How are the fur prices looking, Jarvis?" Rascal asked.

"Real good. The Ontario fur markets are wanting as many beaver pelts as they can get. Otter has shot up, as well as martin, bobcat and lynx. Did you trap?"

"I set out a few behind the cabin, the Jarvis Trail and out in the glade. Did pretty well actually. It'll be a week or so before everything is dry."

"How many pieces do you have?"

"Forty two, and maybe two pounds of castor."

They stayed up late talking. Mostly about the days gone by and the people who once lived in the village. One glass of brandy was enough for each of them and they changed to sipping coffee with hot apple pie.

"The wind has stopped blowing," Emma said.

"If it isn't blowing come daylight I would like to go hunting," Herschel said.

"We'll go out with you, son." He looked at Rascal and said, "The glade?"

"That should be as good as any. I'm going to fill the stoves and then go to bed." They all agreed that was a good idea.

****

Rascal, Jarvis and Herschel left the lodge at daybreak and walked out to the glade. Rascal told Herschel where to sit on the rock so he could watch the crossing and he and Jarvis hiked up to the beech grove. Rascal pointed to all the fresh deer tracks. They had pawed the entire area under the tree looking for nuts.

Without saying a word, Jarvis knew what to do. They spread out and started walking slowly back towards the road. The main trail was already packed solid with deer tracks and the deer had wandered back and forth in the glade looking for bough tips that had blown from the trees and branches.

A pine martin came running from Rascal and up a cedar tree near Jarvis and then it began screaming. It was a weird sound and as used as Jarvis was to the woods, hair on the back of his neck felt like it was standing up.

He walked over to the tree and kicked it. The martin climbed to the top and began screaming again. Jarvis shook the tree and the martin had had enough. It jumped to a nearby tree and disappeared.

Jarvis smiled and before continuing on, he stood up straight and stretched. "Yeah, this was a great life."

Herschel was enjoying himself immensely. He was being accepted as an equal and no longer just a kid. There were red squirrels chattering and scolding all around him. They were making so much noise, it would be difficult to hear a deer walking in this dry snow. He thought about throwing a snowball at the one behind him, but that wouldn't do either. He would have to watch the crossing closely as he knew he would not be able to hear a deer coming down the glade.

There was movement. About a hundred feet up the glade, something was moving the cedar tree branches. And then he saw a huge buck rubbing his neck on a tree. The buck stood still and turned his head to look behind him, and then he continued walking towards the road. Herschel patiently waited until he was near the road and he had a clean shot at the throat.

When Jarvis heard the one shot he stopped and listened for another. When there wasn't another shot, he smiled happily and moved on. He had missed out on so much of his kids' growing up. There had not been many times in the past when he had had enough time to go hunting with his son.

Rascal also knew where there had only been the one shot that it was probably a good one. Both men arrived at the downed buck at the same time. Herschel already had the innards pulled out. He wiped the sweat from his forehead and left a bloody streak from the blood on his hands. He didn't care, though. He was that happy with his prize and that his dad was there with him. "How many points, son?"

"Twelve." Herschel was so excited he had a difficult time to keep his knees from shaking.

"That is a nice deer, Herschel," Rascal said. "Look how fat it is." Rascal opened the stomach to see what it had been eating. "Clover, apples and beech nuts."

Rascal carried the rifles and Jarvis and Herschel dragged the deer back to the lodge. "We'd better weigh this, Herschel. I think you'll be surprised."

Rascal pulled the deer up with the rope and pulley hooked to a scale. When the scales stopped bouncing the needle rested at 248 pounds.

"How about we take the heart and liver to the kitchen and fry up a mess of onions with heart and liver," Herschel said.

"Do you suppose Bear is hibernated, Rascal?" Jarvis asked.

"I'm not sure. I didn't see any of his tracks and this is the first appreciable amount of snow in what's been a fairly mild fall. If he hasn't, you can be assured he'll find that gut pile."

"What do you suppose he would weigh, Rascal?"

"Last spring I would have guessed about four hundred; now it wouldn't surprise me if he might be heavier than five hundred."

"I sure would like to get a bear like that," Herschel said.

At the same time Rascal and Jarvis said rather loudly—which jumped Herschel—"No!"

He stopped dragging and looked at them both and asked, "What, is he a pet or something?"

"Or something," Jarvis said. He knew he couldn't leave it like that so he continued. "Bear is a special sort of bear, son," and then he told Herschel all about him.

"Have you ever tried to play with him, Rascal?"

"No, I'm not sure how he would react. He's a wild animal and we don't try to encourage him to be anything but."

"Aren't you concerned that one of your hunters might shoot him?"

"We do not allow any bear hunting here."

"Does he play with anyone else besides you?"

"No, and he never offers to harm anyone that is with me. You can't be telling people about him because we do not want people coming out here to watch the bear who plays with me. Do I have your word, Herschel?"

"Yes, not a word."

After eating his fill of deer heart, liver, onions and fresh biscuits, Jarvis pushed back away from the table and said, "For the life of me, I don't understand why you three aren't as big as a flour barrel. I couldn't eat another bite. You know maybe you three should come to Beech Tree for the winters and open a restaurant. I can assure you you'd have a full house every meal."

"Thanks for the compliment, Jarvis, but we're all pretty happy right here," Emma said.

"It was an idea."

"Emma," Anita said, "If you don't need me for a few days I'd like to leave with the Pages and visit my sister for a few days."

"Sure, you go ahead, Anita, and tell your sister we said hello."

"I was hoping you'd say to go ahead. I packed my bag

this morning."

Jarvis and Herschel left the table and dragged his deer out to the platform. The engineer blew the steam whistle that he was a half mile out. Just enough time to go inside and get their bags and say goodbye.

"Herschel, when we know for sure when we'll be leaving I'll be in touch with you."

"Okay," and he waved goodbye.

Chapter 3

"I always hate to see them leave," Emma said.

"They're good people. And I'm glad Herschel is going to be the game warden here."

"And it's a good thing if you don't poach anymore, Rascal. I think Herschel has a lot of his father in him."

It was cold standing on the platform. "The wind is starting to blow again," Rascal said.

"Will you help me pick up the kitchen and the dining table?"

"Sure."

Later after everything was put away they sat on the sofa next to the fireplace and Emma turned the radio on. Then they snuggled together listening to the news and then music.

Emma leaned against Rascal and he put his arm around her. She liked this closeness. "We have had such a busy year and now suddenly it's all over and it's just you and me, Rascal, and the stillness."

****

Each day until Anita returned five days later, Rascal worked with the fur pelts. Taking them off the stretchers, pulling out the hair knots and brushing them. He found lice in two of the martin pelts and washed them with strong soap and restretched them. When they dried the lice were gone and the fur was so clean they each shined in the light. Two days after Anita's return he said at the supper table, "The fur pelts are already to take to Beech Tree. We can leave on the afternoon train."

"Will you be okay, Anita, alone for two days?" Emma asked.

"Sure, you two go ahead."

Rascal called Jarvis to let him know he and Emma would be coming in on the afternoon train with the fur pelts. "We'll come straight from the train station. I hope you'll still be open."

"I'm open until 5 o'clock every day."

It wasn't a long trip to Beech Tree and there was less snow. "Let me see what you have, Rascal."

"I'm going to go talk with Rita," Emma said.

"These are the best looking fur pelts you have ever brought me, Rascal. And these red wolves are so much redder than anything I have ever seen. They are certainly pretty."

"I caught both of them on the Jarvis Trail."

"I'll give you $5 extra apiece for the wolves. How's an even $1,200.00 sound?" Jarvis asked.

"That sounds good to me."

"Have you heard anything from the doctor in Washington yet?"

"No but the president said I probably wouldn't hear anything until the middle of December."

"Well, the middle of the month is almost here."

****

They had supper with the Pages. Herschel was there also and he and Rascal talked a lot about what he would have to do. It would be mostly keeping the roofs cleaned off and that meant at the farm also, the wood boxes full and anything Anita might need.

They were dressed for the weather and after supper they walked to the hotel. It wasn't far. "After that big meal, it feels good to walk off a little of it," Rascal said.

"We should sleep good tonight."

The train left on schedule the next morning. The conductor Tom Whelling took their ticket stubs and said, "I believe there is a mail bag for you this morning, Rascal. When I have finished gathering these ticket stubs I'll go back to the freight car and bring it up for you."

"Thank you, Tom."

There were only a few passengers going on to Lac St. Jean and the conductor was back with the mail bag and gave it to Rascal. "Thank you again, Tom."

"Are you going to open it?" Emma asked.

"We might as well wait until we're home." The engineer blew the steam whistle for the half mile warning.

They stepped onto the platform before the train had stopped. Tom signaled to the engineer that he was clear to leave.

Anita met them at the door. "Welcome back." Rascal handed her the mail bag while they took their coats off. "There is a lot of mail in here, this bag is heavy."

"Well, let's see. Is there any hot coffee, Anita?" Rascal asked.

"I'll get it."

"Nonsense, Anita, I'll get it for all of us," Rascal said.

Emma started screaming with excitement and shouting. "It's here, Rascal! It's here! The letter we have been waiting for from Dr. Rollin!" She was shaking all over with excitement.

"Open it, Em, I'll be a minute with the coffee."

"It's from Dr. Rollin himself. I'll read what he has to say:"

Dear Mr. Ambrose,

I have recently talked with President Cutlidge about the wounds you received in France during the Great War. I am sure Doctors Hanson and Langford did all they were able to at the time. But medicine has had many advancements since then.

After talking with President Cutlidge about your condition, I am convinced that our orthopedics team will be able to help you greatly.

"Oh, isn't that good news Rascal?" Emma said.
"It's what we have been waiting for. Is there anymore?"
"Yes he continues:"

> Your first appointment, Mr. Ambrose, will be at 1000 hours on the morning of January 8th. The president informs me it takes 5 days by train from Beech Tree, wherever that is, to Washington. If I were you I would plan on 7, considering the time of year. If you arrive early, there will be accommodations for you and your wife on the hospital grounds. Simply inquire at the front registration desk. Make arrangements for at least 6-8 weeks, depending on how fast you recover.
>
> I have enclosed some additional information about the complex here at Walter Reed. Please telephone me as soon as possible so that I can have everything scheduled for your arrival. Call this number at Bethesda, Maryland, Walter Reed Hospital 43396 and ask to be connected to my office.
>
> Dr. Rollin

"Well there it is Rascal, now all we have to do is be there and don't be late. I think you should probably make that telephone call now."
"Will you, Em. I'll talk with Dr. Rollin but I'd prefer if you make the call and talk with the operators."
"Okay, let me finish my coffee and unpacking."
Emma did make the call. She had to go through eight different telephone operators to reach Walter Reed Hospital in Bethesda, Maryland.
"Good morning this is Doctor Rollin's office."
"Good morning I'm Emma Ambrose and I'm calling for

my husband, Francis. We received a letter this morning from Dr. Rollin asking that we telephone him immediately."

"Certainly, Mrs. Ambrose, we have been expecting your call. I'll connect you."

"Thank you. Rascal you can talk with Dr. Rollin."

"Good morning, Mr. Ambrose. I understand you prefer to be called Rascal."

"Yes sir."

"As my letter stated you are to be here on January 8th for an initial examination in my office at 1000 hours. My office is on the first floor. Just ask the receptionist at the front desk. She'll give you directions to my office.

"I understand you'll be traveling from somewhere in Maine, so I would allow six or even better seven days travel. If you do arrive early we can accommodate you in the hospital's comfort ward.

"Do you have any questions, Mr. Ambrose?"

"Not that I can think of now, but I'm sure by the time we arrive they'll be questions."

"Good, then I look forward to meeting you and your wife. President Cutlidge has told me much about you."

Rascal hung up the phone and said, "You know, Em, it's amazing, talking with someone over a spindly wire that stretches all the way to Washington. I wonder if we could talk with someone in California?"

"I don't see why not, Rascal. It is marvelous though, isn't it?" Emma agreed.

Anita began laughing and said, "If Silvio was still with us, he'd object to it and say something like, 'Why would I want to talk with someone so far away.'"

"Today is December 14th, Rascal; that gives us a little more than two weeks before we have to leave. I'm going to start making a list of things we need to take with us. And no, Rascal, you're not going to take along your pack basket."

"I think I'll go see how thick the ice is. I'll have to cut ice before we leave." He went down behind the dam and cut a hole with his ice chisel. There was a foot of good black ice.

After lunch he went down with his ice saw and ice tongs and he started at the hole he had already chiseled and cut two parallel lines about fourteen inches apart for about thirty feet. The ice saw cut through the ice easy enough, but once there was water on the ice, footing was very slippery. He slipped twice and now his legs were wet. But this was not anything unusual. In the past years, every time he cut ice for the warm months he always slipped and fell down and by the end of the day he was usually wet.

After he had the blocks out of the hole and sitting on the ice he went up and started the bulldozer. While it was warming up he went inside and changed into dry clothes.

The crawler worked really good hauling the ice up to the cellar. He loaded as much ice in to the bucket as he could. He had to make three trips. For now he piled the ice next to the cellar door. The last trip he had to work using the one headlight on the bulldozer for illumination.

The next day he banked the cabin again with more snow and the hen house also. He was having to use the kerosene heater now to keep the chickens warm. In the afternoon he snowshoed out to the farm to make sure it was all shut up for the winter and no bear or raccoons had gotten in.

That night at supper Emma said, "Rascal, I think we should make train reservations now and not wait for the last minute. I think we should go into town tomorrow."

"Why don't you and Anita go and I'll stay here this time."

"That'll be good," Anita said, "We can stay at my sister's house also."

****

"You go ahead, Anita, and I'll finish up my business here and then I'll be up to your sister's house."

"Good afternoon, Emma," Greg Oliver, the station

master said. "What brings you to town today?"

"I need to make reservations for Rascal and me to Bethesda, Maryland. We need to leave here on the 31st."

"All the way to Bethesda, Maryland, you say?"

"Yes, Greg."

"Okay, without any delays it'll take the most of five days. Would you like sleeper berth accommodations?"

"Yes."

"That'll be extra."

"That's okay, Greg."

Greg was busy for several minutes checking all the time schedules and transfers. "Okay, Emma, the S&A will take you as far as Portland where you'll transfer to the B&M line that'll take you to Boston, transferring there to Penn Central, and in Philadelphia transferring still on Penn Central and direct non-stop route to D.C."

"Can you write that all down, Greg. It sounds a little confusing."

"Certainly, but if you need any help along the way, just ask the on-board conductor. He is there to help passengers.

"I'm assuming you'll be wanting meals also?"

"Yes."

"Okay, traveling with private sleep accommodations in first-class travel, and it's a little more expensive."

"How much, Greg, for both of us?"

"I'm also assuming you'll be wanting return travel?"

"Yes, but we don't know when that'll be."

"That won't be a problem, Emma. I can simply make these tickets out for return travel also. If that is what you want, Emma, that'll be $450.00 each; now that includes your return trip."

Emma handed Greg $900.00.

"Thank you, Emma. It's none of my business, but why are you going to Bethesda?"

"Rascal is going to have his leg and hip fixed."

"Is Anita going to stay at the lodge by herself?"

"No, Herschel Page is going to stay with her."

From the ticket office Emma had just enough time to buy Rascal some traveling clothes. She already had what she would be needing. She hoped.

By the time she arrived at Bertha's house she was exhausted. After supper the three women sat up a long time chatting.

Rascal decided, for nothing better to do, to start the bulldozer again and after it had warmed up he decided to pack down the farm road. He had to make several passes back and forth. The lag tracks were not very wide. When he had finished he was pleased with the job; when the temperature dropped overnight, the packed snow would be almost as firm as ice.

And that worked so well he did the same to the hen house and then across the dam to the log cabin. The wind had blown all the snow off the roofs so he wasn't concerned with that.

That evening after supper he telephoned Herschel Page at his folk's house. "Hello, Herschel. Emma and I will be leaving the Beech Tree station on the 31st. Would you plan on being here on the 30th? We'll have to take the afternoon southbound."

"That'll be fine, Rascal. I'll see you on the 30th."

****

The next morning when the train pulled to a stop at the platform, Rascal was still asleep. Emma and Anita, before stepping off the car, noticed that there was no smoke in the chimney. Her first thought was that Rascal had been hurt. They rushed inside and when she opened their bedroom door, Rascal was still in bed albeit awake and stretching his arms. He looked at Emma and grinned. She couldn't help it, she began to laugh so hard Anita came in to see what was the matter. "Silvio used to sleep in late like this sometimes when he had had too much brandy before going to bed."

"I didn't have a drop, Em. I promise."

"What time did you go to bed?" she asked.

"Oh, 9 o'clock or so."

"You've been sleeping for almost twelve hours."

"Guess I needed it." Then he told her what he had been doing the day before.

"I think you better get up and start the fires. Anita and I will make breakfast." As she left the bedroom she was still laughing and shaking her head.

"Anita, I think it is a good thing that I am going to Washington with him."

One day Rascal was carrying the blocks of ice into the cellar and burying them with sawdust and Emma and Anita went for a walk along the farm road looking for a Christmas tree. It had been agreed to earlier that the three of them would enjoy each other's company and a roast chicken dinner and no presents. But a decorated tree the two women did insist upon.

They made popcorn garland and paper chains, with pine cones for ornaments.

Emma was more excited about their trip to Washington than Rascal. To him it was only another day where he would have his leg fixed. For Emma it was a journey that she thought would never be possible. She had never been much further from home than Beech Tree or Lac St. Jean in Quebec. A whole new world would be opening for her. One she hoped she was ready for.

A cold wind blew in from the northwest and when the wind stopped blowing, it began to snow. A gentle storm of dry snow flakes that seemed to slowly drift down to the ground. On Christmas morning there was a new blanket of snow and everything was so pretty. The sun was out and the sky was indigo blue.

They stayed inside the lodge all day, not venturing outside for any reason. They were happy being together and enjoying a roast chicken dinner and then sitting near the fireplace sipping a glass of wine and talking like loving friends and family do.

****

True to his word Herschel arrived on the morning train with practically everything he owned. He even brought his guitar that he was learning to play.

Rascal walked with him around the buildings of what used to be the mill, the log cabin and hen house. Emma said, "Here's four hundred dollars for two months. We're not sure when we'll be coming back. If it runs over two months we'll square up with you then."

Emma already had everything packed in the suitcases. After lunch they all sat around the table drinking coffee and talking. Rascal put up the red flag and came back and poured himself another cup of coffee.

"There's the half-mile signal. I'll write and tell you how we're doing," Emma said.

"I can't see where you two will have any problems," Rascal said.

The train was coming into view now and slowing down.

Rascal and Emma disappeared inside of the passenger car and Anita was feeling happy, knowing they trusted her this much to take care of things. She wouldn't let them down.

Chapter 4

The southbound from Beech Tree was scheduled to leave at 6:00 a.m. sharp, so they had to be up early. There was a breakfast car so they would not have to eat at the hotel. And like country folk everywhere Rascal didn't need an alarm clock or someone to wake him. He always seemed to know, even asleep, when he had to get up. Emma was used to rising early and this was not an inconvenience for her either.

"Just take a seat anywhere folks. Breakfast will be served at 6:30," the conductor said.

When the train was up to full speed Emma said, "Wow, Rascal, this train goes so much faster."

Rascal knew Emma had a grand adventure in front of her. She was going to see things that she had until now only read about in magazines, newspapers and books. And he was excited for her.

The half hour before breakfast went fast and they were seated next to a window so they could watch the countryside as they rode through. Their meals had already been paid for up front, so they both went for seconds. "I didn't think I was this hungry," Emma said.

"It's good food, but not like home cooking," Rascal said as he smiled.

It was just getting dark when the train stopped in Portland. Emma had seen a lot of country so far, but they transferred immediately to the B&M. Here they had their own berth. The conductor escorted them to their accommodations and said, "The dining room will start serving in a half hour. If you need anything, pull this cord here and I or one of the others will be here as soon as we can."

"Thank you," Rascal said.

"Isn't this nice, Rascal? Our very own room abroad a train. I would never have believed it."

"This is much nicer than trying to sleep in one of those stiff upright seats."

****

It was dark when they went through Boston, only stopping long enough to allow more passengers to board. Again the food was good, but not like home. "This food reminds me of the food we were served in basic training." But they had all they wanted.

Rascal went right to sleep when they lay down for the night. Emma was so excited still, she got up and sat by the window watching the lights pass by. She had never before stopped to think how big the United States was, and this was just the first day. Eventually she crawled in beside Rascal and fell asleep.

Emma was like a child on Christmas morning. She didn't want to miss anything. She was awake before daylight and she crawled out of bed and sat at the window. They were only a few miles out from the New York train station where they would switch trains again. The expanse of this great city was unbelievable. She shook Rascal awake. "Rascal, wake up. Rascal, we're almost in New York City. Don't you want to see it? Come on, Rascal, get up; we have to switch trains here. Come on, get up," and she pulled the covers off him.

She dressed hurriedly and sat by the window. There was a knock on their door and Rascal opened it. "Good morning folks," Henri said. "I just wanted to let you know we are ten minutes out from the New York terminal. And it is my understanding you'll be transferring to the Penn Central."

"Yes, that's right. And thank you."

"Wow, I never expected service like this," Emma said.

Breakfast wouldn't be served until they were aboard Penn Central's train. "Rascal, I just can't believe that New York is so big, so spread out. I'd be afraid if I were here by myself."

When they arrived at the terminal there were so many other trains. "All heading in different directions, Mrs. Ambrose," Henri said. "New York is the commercial hub of the nation and from here goods are shipped all over the country."

"I've seen so many wondrous things so far on this trip."

"Just wait until you see Washington, D.C., Mrs. Ambrose. It's the prettiest and cleanest city I have ever seen."

Henri walked with them over to Penn Central Station and helped them find the right train. "Thank you, Henri, for your kind generosity," Rascal said.

"Maybe I'll see you on your return trip."

"I hope so," Emma said.

There are more people, Rascal, in this terminal than there is in all of Beech Tree. I wouldn't have believed it myself if I weren't here."

"I hope breakfast is soon," Rascal said. "I'm hungry."

They boarded the train and were shown to their room. "The train has an hour delay this morning folks, but the dining room will be open in half an hour. Is there anything else I can help you with?" Samson asked. "If there is, just ask for Samson."

"Thank you, Samson."

When he had left and closed their door, Emma said, "You know, Rascal, that is the first black man I have ever seen or met. I'm beginning to sound like I have lived a sheltered life."

He hugged her and said, "I wouldn't be a bit surprised if we don't see a few more things that we have never seen."

"I need to walk around some, Em. Let's walk the length of the train and see what there is. These rooms are getting a little cramped."

They met Samson at the front end of the car. "You folks going for a walk?"

"Yes, Samson, we need to stretch our legs and we need some fresh air."

"I was on my way to inform you folks that there has been a delay of about four hours."

"Oh, what's the problem?" Emma asked.

"Twenty miles south of here a section of rails is being replaced. We can't wait on the main line as another train will be coming in from the west and we would be in the way. So we have to wait. And since this is the busiest terminal in the country you'll be asked, required to stay on board," Samson saw the disappointment on Emma's face. "Of course I could go with you as a chaperone."

Rascal smiled and said, "That would be good. We just need to stretch our legs a little outside of the cubical."

They followed Samson outside and onto the platform. There were several other trains there also. Some were just arriving while others were departing.

"I have never seen anything like this. I have never imagined anything that would come close to this," Emma said.

Inside the terminal there must have been a thousand people or more, all moving about like ants. "This sure isn't Beech Tree," Emma said.

"Is that where you are from? And where is Beech Tree?"

"Beech Tree is a small town in northwestern Maine, but we live at Whiskey Jack," Rascal said.

"You sure have funny names for your towns in Maine. How many people live in Whiskey Jack?"

"Just Em and me and an older woman who works for us."

"You mean there are only three people in the whole town?" Samson asked disbelievingly.

"Well, Whiskey Jack really isn't a town anymore. It was a wilderness village alongside the S&A railroad. The only way in or out is by rail. The village grew up because of the Hitchcock Lumber Company. When the lumber was cut off the company moved and the buildings were burned, all except for a hotel which we own now and turned it into a fishing and hunting lodge," Emma said.

"And the three of you live there all by yourselves?"

"Except during the fishing and hunting seasons," Rascal said.

"This is the first time I have been out of the state of Maine, except for Canada."

"And now you folks are going to Washington, D.C.? Boy is that a change."

"It sure is," Emma said.

Samson took them outside to see what they could of New York. "Wow, I never imagined New York could be so big. This is New York, isn't it, Samson?"

He chuckled when he answered her, "It sure is, ma'am. What you can see from 34th St. and the grand entrance to the Penn Central terminal. There's a whole lot more of the city you can't see from here, ma'am."

"I'd be lost out there, Rascal. And look at all the people. How many people live in New York, Samson?"

"Somewhere over six million."

"Looking at all this now makes me homesick for Whiskey Jack," Emma said.

****

They returned to the train but not before looking at the locomotive engine. "Wow," Rascal said, "that is four times the size of S&A that goes through Whiskey Jack."

"How many cars does the S&A pull?" Samson asked.

"Five, sometimes seven."

"This engine is pulling seven passenger cars, two sleeper cars, two dining cars, a tender with water and coal and twenty freight cars. The trains that go west from here will pull more cars and the locomotives are bigger still.

"Come, we'd better get back aboard," Samson said.

Once back inside their berth, Rascal asked, "Samson, we're both from the wilderness of Maine and we are unfamiliar with the ways and customs—let's say in this part of the world. Is it proper or expected to leave tips for those onboard who make our journey more comfortable?"

"All I can say there, Rascal, is that some do, some don't."

"And you'll be going all the way to Washington with us?"

"Yes sir."

"Good," They left it at that and Samson went back to work.

"This is being quite an education isn't it, Rascal?" Emma said.

"It sure is."

After a three and a half hour delay, the engineer blew the steam whistle, warning all passengers that it was leaving. Arriving trains were blocking any view there was of New York now. They sat back to relax.

****

There was another six-hour delay just south of Wilmington, Delaware, for some strange reason—the rails on the train trestle spanning Delaware Bay. "Is this the ocean, Samson?" Emma asked.

"No, it's the northern end of Delaware Bay. Have you ever seen the ocean, ma'am?"

"No."

"You have haven't you, Rascal?"

"How do you know, Samson?"

"You walk with a limp; you're traveling to Washington from Beech Tree, Maine, so I have to assume you are going to Walter Reed Hospital in Bethesda. So that means you were in the Army and probably during the Great War in Europe."

"You'd make a great detective, Samson. And yes, I spent too much time on the ocean in slow-moving ships."

"You two should treat yourself to some Chesapeake seafood while you're in Washington. Better yet, take a side trip to the Bay."

They finally arrived a day and a half early. "How far is Bethesda from here, Samson?"

"Come with me. I'll get you folks on the right bus. Remember this is the Silver Springs terminal. Bethesda is not too far from here."

Samson found them the correct bus which would take them to the hospital. "Hello, Harry," Samson said. "These good folks are going to Walter Reed. Will you take care of them? They have come all the way from Beech Tree, Maine."

"Sure thing, Samson. Hop aboard, folks, we leave in two minutes."

Emma turned to Samson and hugged him and kissed his cheek. "Thank you for your help, Samson."

"Sure, ma'am; it won't nothing. I was glad to do it."

"Samson, here comes the part where I don't know if I'm right or not, but here's $10 for a tip."

Samson took it and asked, "When will you folks be going home?"

"We're not sure, maybe six weeks."

"I hope to see you on your return. Six weeks, huh, that must be some operation. Good luck to you, Rascal."

They climbed on board and Harry closed the door.

As they rode along Emma said, "Are you getting nervous, Rascal?"

"Not nervous exactly, I'll just be glad when this is all over, and to tell you the truth I can't wait until we're home."

"I'm nervous," Emma said. "In these last five days I've seen things that only existed in magazines and newspapers. And now here we are, Rascal, we're part of it. I just wasn't expecting all of this. I guess I didn't know what to expect."

"We're here, folks. Follow this walkway and it will take you to the admission center. When you are inside walk straight across the lobby and the desk; people you will want to talk with are right there."

"Thank you, Harry," Rascal said.

The bus was overloaded. People were having to stand in the aisle between the seats. Thank goodness it had only been a short ride.

As they followed the walkway, Emma asked, "Are you nervous now?"

"Apprehensive would be a better word."

"You be apprehensive; I'll be nervous."

A black attendant at the door held it open for them and said, "Welcome to Walter Reed Hospital, folks."

"Thank you," Emma replied.

Just as Harry had said the reception desk was straight ahead.

"Good afternoon, how may I assist you?"

"I have an appointment with Doctor Rollin on the 8th," Rascal said.

"Then you must be Mr. Ambrose."

"Yes, ma'am. I know we are a day early but Doctor Rollin said that would be okay."

"Yes, he told me the same thing. If you'll have a seat an orderly will be with you soon to show you where to go."

"Thank you." They found a seat and Rascal said, "I have a knot in my stomach."

"Me too. This sure isn't like home is it?"

Before Rascal could answer a young well-dressed black orderly stopped in front of them and said, "Mr. and Mrs. Ambrose?"

"Yes," Rascal managed to say.

"Good afternoon. I'm Jeters Arsenault."

Before he could continue both Rascal and Emma burst out laughing. "Please excuse us, Jeters, we are not laughing at you. Back home we have a good friend who goes by Jeters. Jeters Asbau. It isn't a common name and I guess all of the anxiety just came out. And you can forget Mr. and Mrs., this is my wife, Emma, and I'm Rascal."

It was Jeters turn now to laugh, and that broke the ice. "I finally meet someone who has a stranger name than mine. If you'll follow me." He was still laughing.

They left that building and walked to the second building to the right. "This is like a dormitory for service men and women's family if they should need a place to stay while their spouse is recovering from surgery and therapy. There is a room on the first floor that was recently vacated." It was a corner room at the far end of the hall with two windows.

"Now I'm here to help you both. This is a large complex and at first it can be confusing trying to navigate your way around without help. Emma, while Rascal is in recovery and-or therapy, if there is anything you need just go to the admission's desk and ask for me.

"Perhaps after dinner this evening you would like a tour of the grounds."

"We would like that, Jeters. When is dinner?" Emma asked.

"Around here everybody uses military time—1800 hours or 6 p.m."

Jeters left and closed the door and they both lay back on the bed. "Suddenly I'm exhausted, Rascal."

"Well, in the last six days we have traveled over seven-hundred miles."

"Home seems so far away now," Emma said.

****

Jeters Arsenault waited for them to finish eating and then he took them on a tour of the Walter Reed complex.

"I had no idea this would be so huge," Rascal said. "I was expecting a hospital building."

"Where did you receive your injury, Rascal?" Jeters asked.

"In France during the war."

"Excuse me for asking, but you two talk with a definite accent. Where is home?"

"Whiskey Jack, and we and a woman who works and lives with us are the only residents," Emma said.

"Is Whiskey Jack in Maine?"

"Yes about ten miles north of Beech Tree." Again Jeters began laughing.

"I'm sorry. I'm not laughing at you. It's just—well, just that you seem to have a funny of a name as I and you two and an old woman are the only residents in a town called Whiskey Jack," he began laughing again and then added, "North of a town called Beech Tree. I'm sorry if I hurt your feelings. I surely didn't mean to."

Rascal said, "That's okay, no harm done."

"What do you two do in Whiskey Jack where you have to hire another woman? Make whiskey?"

Emma said, "We own and run a fishing and hunting lodge."

Then Jeters wanted to know why it was called Whiskey Jack. "And where exactly is it?"

"Its' almost half way between Beech Tree and the Quebec border in the western mountains of Maine."

"And the only way in to Whiskey Jack is by the St. Lawrence and Atlantic Railroad. There are no roads," Emma said.

"It sounds like wilderness."

"It is, and we love it," Rascal said.

After Jeters had finished the tour he walked with them back to their room and said, "Remember, if you need anything while you are here ask for me at the front desk."

"We will," Emma said.

"Goodnight."

****

After breakfast the next morning Rascal and Emma took a walk around that part of the city. "Rascal, have you noticed how all of the streets here are paved. What a marvelous idea. No dust or mud, and paved sidewalks, so you don't have to walk in traffic."

"Someday probably all of the roads all over this country will be paved."

"There are so many stores and shops and places to eat. It's a good thing I'm not a shopaholic. I do think, though, that we should bring back gifts for Anita and Herschel," Emma said.

"I think that would be a good idea."

Instead of eating at the cafeteria they decided on a seafood restaurant not far from Walter Reed.

"I doubt if we could get a bottle of wine."

"Very doubtful."

"Here's a platter of seafood for two. Let's try it, Rascal."

It took several minutes before their food was ready. In the meantime they had several cups of weak coffee. The platter was wheeled in on a small cart.

There were shrimp, clams, fried oysters, snails and Chesapeake crab. "Have you ever eaten snails or oysters, Rascal?"

"No, but I have heard they are good."

Halfway through the platter Emma said, "This is all so delicious."

"Even the snails and oysters?" Rascal asked. They had to have directions how to eat the crabs.

"Even the snails and oysters."

Later as they were walking back Emma said, "We ate so much I don't think we need supper. We'd both blow up I think."

Chapter 5

At 10 o'clock Jeters showed Rascal and Emma where Dr. Rollin's office was and then he left. "Come in. You're punctual. I like that. Come in and sit down. I must say coming from the wilderness mountains in Maine, you two sure do have friends in high places.

"I have reviewed your medical records Mr. Ambrose—"

"Please, call me Rascal."

"Okay, Rascal, I have reviewed your medical records. The bullet did not hit bone, it severed tendons and muscles. We have a new machine that is called an x-ray machine and with that we can take pictures of your insides. And we need to do that now. My assistant nurse Paula will take you to a changing room. You'll need to take off all of your clothes. She'll give you a johnny to put on. Then she'll take you to the x-ray lab. It'll only take a few minutes to take the shots and then maybe a half hour to develop them.

"I'd prefer if you would stay out here, Mrs. Ambrose."

"Emma, please."

Rascal followed nurse Paula into another room and pulled on the johnny. "We'll start with you lying face down on the table."

Nurse Paula shot two views, then one on his side and two more lying on his back.

"Okay, Rascal, you can get dressed and join your wife. When these are developed I'll bring them out to Dr. Rollin."

Forty minutes later Dr. Rollin was back in his office and nurse Paula gave him the five x-rays. "The surgeon who will be performing the operation is Doctor Charles Hynley and he will be joining us momentarily."

When Dr. Hynley did join them he introduced himself and he and Dr. Rollin looked at the x-rays. "If you two would step up here I'll show you what these x-rays are telling us."

"You see this line here, that is where the bullet scraped the iliac or hip bone. The bullet took a chip out from the edge, but I don't think that has been your problem. It looks like the bullet was deflected and tore tendons and cartilage. I'll know more once I have opened you. You see these knots or buckling? This, I think, is your problem. I'll have to detach the tendons, straighten them and reattach them, clean up and repair the cartilage, and in six or eight weeks you'll be a new man."

"When can we get started, Dr. Hynley?" Rascal asked.

"Tomorrow morning at 0900 hours. That will require that you be admitted now."

"Will I be able to stay with him, Dr. Hynley?" Emma asked.

"Probably it would be best if you didn't. Dr. Rollin will have to give him a thorough examination and there are tests that will have to be performed.

"If you were here at 0730 tomorrow, well, then you would have a few minutes with him before the nurses started to prep him for surgery."

"I'll be okay, Emma. Maybe Jeters will show you around some more."

Emma kissed him and left. She met Jeters near the admission desk. "Are you alone today, ma'am?" he asked.

"I guess I am until tomorrow morning. Will you join me for lunch, Jeters? I'm hungry."

In the cafeteria everyone turned to look when they walked in. They stepped in line with a food tray. Then they chose a table and sat down. "Why are they watching us, Jeters?"

"You don't know, do you?"

"No."

"Most whites haven't yet accepted my people as equal as the Constitution says. And to most people a black man having lunch with a white woman is not acceptable. Someday it'll change. I hope. But not yet. If you prefer, we can leave."

"Certainly not," she said loud enough for all to hear. "Enjoy your lunch, Jeters, I'm going to."

Jeters smiled and said, "I like your spirit, ma'am."

"Are you worried about Rascal?"

"A little. I hope the operation won't make him worse."

When they had finished eating, Jeters said, "If you will be okay by yourself, ma'am, I have my duties I must get back to."

"I'll be okay, Jeters. I'll walk around the grounds. How old are you, Jeters?"

"Nineteen, Ma'am."

"How long have you been working here?"

"Three years. I would love to get into medicine, but I do not have enough money yet for school. Someday though. In the meantime, I work here and save my money and I pick up a little knowledge here and there while I am performing by duties."

"You have a great attitude, Jeters, and I think you'll make it. Don't stop trying."

Emma looked at the clock, and knew Rascal would be in the operating room. She decided to wait in the waiting room outside the operating room. There were magazines there but she was too nervous to read anything.

There were many thoughts going through her mind. The biggest one was, *What if he isn't any better, but worse.* And then on the flip side, *What if he was like new again, would he want to become a game warden.* She knew he would make a good one, much like Jarvis Page, and he would enjoy it. But—she knew he would be gone for days at a time without any word, like Jarvis had done. And she didn't want that.

She was wearing herself down with worries. Then four

hours later Doctor Hynley came out from the operating room. Emma stood up and asked, "How is he, Dr. Hynley? Will he be okay?"

"He'll be just fine, Mrs. Ambrose. The surgery took a bit longer than I first thought but there were no complications. The nurses will be bringing him out shortly to the recovery room. You can sit with him there if you wish. When he awakens, tell him I'll stop by before dinner and explain to you both what I did."

"Thank you, Dr. Hynley." Emma sat down and waited.

The door opened and Rascal was brought out on a bed with rollers. The nurses rolled him down the hall to the recovery room. "If you wish, ma'am, you can wait in here with your husband."

"Thank you."

"Would you like anything?"

"No, no thank you. I'll be fine."

Emma was relieved that the operation was over and Dr. Hynley was surely encouraging, but she was mentally exhausted. An hour later Rascal opened his eyes only briefly and then closed them again. Then a little while later he opened them again and asked, "Em, Em, are you here?"

"I'm right beside you, Rascal."

"Why can't I move my head? I can't move anything, Em." Panic was beginning to sweep over him.

"It's alright, Rascal. The nurses said they couldn't risk you moving, so they secured you to the bed to keep you still. You'll have to remain like this for twenty-four hours."

Dr. Hynley walked in then, and he heard the last part of what Emma had said. "She's correct, Rascal; we just need to keep you as still as possible."

"How did it go, Doc?"

"Superbly. There was more damage to the tendons than what I could see on the x-ray, but I was able to fix that. I also smoothed out the bone on your hip. When you heal and after your therapy you probably will not have that limp anymore."

"I'm hungry, Doc."

"That's understandable. For supper you'll be given some chicken broth but no solid food until tomorrow evening. This was a very classic operation, Rascal. If you do as your therapist says you won't have any problems at all. She will be checking in on you tomorrow morning."

"Now, if you don't have any more questions, I must prepare myself for another operation. Good day."

****

The next morning the same two nurses changed the dressing covering the incision. There was a little blood seepage but not bad. Two days later his bed was fixed so he could sit up and eat. "I sure would like some strong black coffee and some beaver meat to eat." The two nurses were shocked. Emma only smiled.

"I'm afraid you'll have to wait to eat beaver until we get home." Again the two nurses looked surprised.

The nurses changed the dressing every morning and after that first morning there had been no sign of seepage. "This is healing nicely, Mr. Ambrose."

"Just call me Rascal."

"And you probably have come by the name rightfully so," one of the nurses said. "Next week, Rascal, you will start therapy."

He had been flat on his back now for four days. At night, memories of France and recovering from those wounds, oftentimes kept him from a restful sleep. He was anxious to start his therapy.

On the morning of the twelfth, the day he would start therapy, he was awakened early by someone gently shaking his shoulder. "Come on, Rascal, wake up."

Whoever it was had a sweet voice. "Let me sleep a little longer, Em."

Again she was trying to shake him awake. "Em, let me sleep."

Then in a sterner tone to her voice she said, "Private Ambrose you are addressing a Lieutenant."

Rascal thought for sure now he was having another nightmare about being wounded in France. He opened his eyes so the nightmare would stop. But—but there was a lieutenant standing beside his bed with her hands on her hips. He looked at her again and shook his head and wiped the sleep from his eyes and looked at the lieutenant again. "Lieutenant Belle? You mean we never left France? Boy, have I been having one hell of a dream."

Just then Emma came in and stood beside of Belle, "Em what are you doing in France?"

"Hello, Belle. What are you talking about, Rascal?"

"I think I awoke him when he was dreaming he was back in France."

Emma sat down on the bed beside him and said, "Rascal, you are at the Walter Reed Hospital and you were operated on a week ago. Do you remember?"

"Then why is Belle here in her lieutenant's uniform?"

"Rascal," Belle said, "my husband and I moved to Bethesda two weeks ago. He's studying to be an orthopedic surgeon and I was reinstated in the reserves. I am in charge of your therapy."

"Are things clearer now, Rascal?" Emma asked.

"Now—yeah, but when I recognized you, Belle, in a lieutenant's uniform, my mind must have played tricks on me—'cause I thought sure this was France."

"So are we okay now, Rascal?"

"Yes."

"Good, then before you can have breakfast we need to get your leg moving." She removed the restraints from his legs and began bending each one gently. "How does that feel?"

"Good. My right one feels awful weak and lame though."

"That's to be expected. Remember how it was in France at first?"

"Yes, it came back slow."

As she was working with his legs she said, "You must know someone in high places to get referred to Walter Reed and Doctor Hynley and his surgical team so fast."

Before Rascal could answer her, which he didn't want to tell her who, Dr. Hynley walked in, "And how is our patient doing this morning, Lieutenant?"

"We have just started."

"I understand you two know each other from France."

"Yes Sir, Lieutenant Belle was my therapist there also."

"I understand you are recovering quite well from the operation. Do what the Lieutenant tells you and do not overdo it."

"I'll see to that, Doctor Hynley," Emma said.

He left and all was forgotten about friends in high places. Emma and Belle helped Rascal out of bed, to stand, and then to sit in a wheelchair. "You have a good breakfast and we'll start work at 1000 hours for an hour and again at 1500 hours for another hour."

Emma pushed him in the wheelchair to the elevator and into the cafeteria. After a good breakfast of scrambled eggs and bacon and coffee Rascal wanted to go outside even if only for a minute. "This sure doesn't seem much like the middle of January, does it."

"The air is raw, but not as cold."

After a few minutes, Rascal said, "Okay, I guess I've had enough of this fresh air for now."

At 1000 hours Belle returned to Rascal's room. "How are you doing now, Rascal?"

"Better, I had a good breakfast and we went outside for a while for fresh air."

"We're going to do the same exercises as earlier and then again in the afternoon. Before you put any weight on it or walk, you'll need to loosen those muscles and tendons. We'll go slow, but if the pain is too much, just say so."

Belle spent the hour doubling up first one knee and then the other one. "Let me move this leg, Rascal. I only want the muscles to loosen."

"You never did say how you found your way here."

"We had a hunter last fall that knew someone that might be able to help." She accepted that explanation without asking more questions.

"Does this cause any discomfort in this leg?"

"It doesn't hurt, but that leg feels more tired than the other one."

"Well this is enough for now. We'll continue in the afternoon."

"Would it be alright if Em pushes me around in the wheelchair? I hate being confined to this room."

"No problem, only ask one of the nurses to help Emma to get you in and out of the chair. An under no circumstances are you to put any weight on it. Okay?"

"Okay."

"I can help you now, Emma, if you would like."

"Yes."

As Emma was wheeling him down the hall he was thinking how long the healing and therapy process was before. But then he was also healing from two gunshot wounds. Maybe this time the process won't take so long. He hoped so.

"I hope she doesn't ask any more questions about who helped us get me here."

"I don't know if it would be wrong to tell her the truth or not. I surely wouldn't want to get on the wrong side of President Cutlidge. We probably won't ever hear from him again."

"Probably not; he's a busy man," Rascal added.

At two o'clock it was another hour of Belle moving his legs and knees back and forth.

****

For the next two days his therapy was Belle moving his knees back and forth, only now she was doing both legs at the same time. Like pedaling a bicycle. And he was doing most of the work now. "Your muscles are getting stronger."

Five days after the operation, in the morning Belle took him out to the swimming pool. "There are parallel bars in the water Rascal and we'll wheel you out into the water until you can hold onto the bars. First though I have to put on my bathing suit. Emma can help you into yours. I'll be right back."

Five minutes later she was back. She was in front of him ready to catch him if he should fall, but she wanted him to do the work himself. After he was standing she asked, "How does that feel?"

"It feels good to stand up."

"What about your leg?"

"Oh, that. I can surely feel my weight on it, but it isn't hurting yet. This water is warm like bath water."

"It is supposed to be, so it will help to loosen stiff muscles. The water will displace much of your weight. Now try walking while holding onto the bars. One step at a time. That's good. The water will get a little deeper, probably up to your chest. How do you feel now?"

"Okay."

"Good. Every day there'll be less and less water until you can walk the full distance of the bars. It'll be a little at a time though."

"Emma, you can come in also if you want to swim. The water is warm," Belle said.

"I would but I don't have a swimsuit."

"Go in your underwear, we're alone in here. There won't be anyone else coming in."

"I can't swim, but I would enjoy the water." She took her clothes off and waded out. "You're right, Rascal, this is just like bath water." She walked along with Belle as Rascal worked his way back and forth between the bars.

"See if you can keep walking, Rascal, without stopping." He did, but slowly.

After an hour Emma pushed the wheelchair out between the bars and Rascal sat down and then the two women pulled him back and out of the water. While Belle was massaging his bad leg, Emma took her underclothes off and slipped into her blouse and skirt. "I'm going to have to get me a swimsuit."

"I can pick you up one tonight, Emma, after I leave here," Belle said.

****

Each day the water level in the pool was dropped two inches. Not enough to notice, but it required a little more weight to be transferred to Rascal's legs. Instead of therapy three times a day, Belle had changed it to twice daily. She didn't want him to overexert his capability and tear a muscle or tendon. That would set him back another six weeks.

With more weight being transferred to his legs, his right leg was hurting more. "This is only natural, Rascal. Do you remember your therapy in New York? You were beginning to doubt you'd ever be able to walk again. But you worked through the pain, didn't you.

"That's all you are doing now, Dr. Hynley was very specific about your therapy. He doesn't want you recovering too fast. If you go slow then your muscles and tendons will become strong enough to support your full weight.

"Are you ready to walk the bars two more times?"

Emma was enjoying watching Belle work with Rascal. She had a certain kind of determination that wouldn't let Rascal fail. She was very good with what she was doing.

When they had finished for the day, Belle said, "I have tomorrow off, so another therapist will be assisting you, Rascal, Betty Jones. And Emma would you like to spend the day with me and see a little of Washington, D.C.?"

Emma looked at Rascal. He grinned and said, "You've earned it, Em, go and have fun. You have been cooped up inside here for three weeks now. I'll be just fine."

"I'll meet you here, Emma, after breakfast."

For the rest of that day Emma was so excited she had a difficult time staying in one place more than a few minutes. All the while Rascal was watching her and happy Belle had asked her to spend the day touring Washington.

Rascal was still having to sleep in his hospital bed and once in a while Emma would join him and snuggle close to him and go to sleep with her head on his chest. Belle had said one more week and he could leave his hospital room and bed and stay with Emma in her room.

Emma was awake before Rascal the next morning and she let him sleep while she washed up and dressed.

She woke Rascal and sat on the bed and said, "Come on Rascal or you'll miss breakfast." He had to shave while sitting in the wheelchair. At first it was pretty awkward, but after a few days he got used to it.

There was a knock on his door and Betty Jones came in. "I see you're already up and ready."

"Yeah, Em said I'd miss breakfast if I didn't get up."

Just as they were finishing breakfast, Belle walked in the cafeteria and came over to their table.

"Where will we be going, Belle?" Emma asked.

"We can take a transit bus from here that'll take us into the city center. From there we can take a taxicab to visit some of the monuments and memorials. The bus will be here soon, so we should probably go outside and wait. The drivers have a schedule they must keep."

Emma kissed Rascal goodbye. "Have fun, Em. Enjoy the day." He watched as the two left the cafeteria feeling happy that Belle was showing her around the city. He knew there was a lot to see. As much as he would have liked to go along, he was more concerned with his therapy.

Just as he was finishing his coffee nurse Betty Jones walked over to his table. She was rather stout with a hoarse voice to match. But she had been attentive to Rascal's needs and a really nice person.

"Okay, Rascal, time to get you into your swimsuit and hit the pool. Belle said you are doing very well."

The water was now at knee level and not really supporting much of his weight and he had to use more leg muscles and effort to move his legs through the water. "You're doing good, Rascal. How's your leg?"

"It's more tired than pain."

"Are you saying you want to rest?"

"No, it was only a statement."

After forty-five minutes of walking back and forth nurse Betty said, "Now we are going to do something else. I presume you can swim."

"Yes."

"Good, this time when you reach the end of the bars I want you to swim towards the other end. I'll be beside you if you should need any help."

****

"Where are we going first, Belle?"

"I thought we should go to the Washington Monument first. From the top we can pretty much see all of Washington."

Emma had no idea what the monument was. They left the bus terminal in a taxicab and were taken to the monument, or at least as near as it could drive.

"Is that it, Belle, an obelisk?"

"Yes."

"How on earth are we going to get to the top?"

"Well there are stairs, or we could take the elevator, which will cost us each fifty cents."

"I'll pay the fifty cents, I guess," Emma said.

They were the only ones going up. "I'm a little nervous about going so high, Belle."

"You'll be okay."

At the top when they stepped off the elevator a party of four were going down. "How do you feel now, Emma?"

"Okay, I guess it was just the feeling of going up."

They could look out over the city from all four sides. "This is a beautiful city. It must really be beautiful in the spring and summer."

There was a plaque there with information about the monument. Construction actually started in 1818 but because of the Civil War, work was delayed. It was finally completed in 1888.

"The roads here, Belle, are all paved. What a great idea. No dust or mud every time it rains."

There were informational brochures there that Emma took and put in her purse.

"You know, Belle, looking at the city from up here you wouldn't know that it was winter. Back home there probably is three feet of snow on the ground and three feet of ice. What a difference."

"Yes, but you have to understand, Emma, that you are a long ways south of Whiskey Jack."

"Where to next, Belle?"

Belle pointed to another monument. "That's the Lincoln Memorial."

Once they were at the bottom of the Washington Monument they started walking. Even in the cool weather there were several already there at the Lincoln Memorial. "Belle, he seems so life like."

"He does, doesn't he. I understand that there is a great likeness to the real President Lincoln. Before this was built in 1914 this whole area was a swamp. It had to be drained before they could start. It was finished in 1922."

"How do you know all of this, Belle?"

"The first thing Richard and I did when we moved here was to take a guided tour of Washington."

Emma picked up more brochures and then they were off again. "Where to this time?"

"Something really special, "The Castle," the Smithsonian Institution. It's a wonderful museum. Richard and I agree we could spend a full day there."

"How big is it?" Emma asked.

"As big as it needs to be. I'm not saying that in a sarcastic way. There are plans to add on as is required to display more exhibits."

"I have never heard anything about it or seen any articles in the newspaper. Is it new?"

"There are of course new exhibits each year and additions to the original building have been constructed. It all started with a British scientist, a James Smithson. He died in 1829 and left his estate to a nephew, Henry James Hungerford, who had no children. And when he died in 1835 the estate was passed to the United States to create an institution for knowledge in Washington, D.C.

"It took ten years of haggling, but finally in 1846 President James Polk signed the legislation. Mr. Smithson had insisted that it be called the Smithsonian Institution."

"I am beginning to realize living at Whiskey Jack how much out of touch we are of the rest of the world."

"You sound sad, Emma."

"Maybe in a way. This whole trip has certainly been an eye opener. I have seen so much that I never knew anything about."

"Are you saying you'd rather not live in Whiskey Jack?" Belle asked.

"No, that's not what I mean. I wouldn't trade what Rascal and I have or the way we live for the entire world. It's only I'm realizing how much there is that I do not know anything about.

"Once Rascal has fully recovered, we are planning to start another family and I will make sure they are not left behind, no siree."

"I'm happy for you, Emma, that you have decided on another family," Belle hugged her then and said, "I'm hungry. There are food concessions in the bottom level."

****

After eating they spent the rest of their time in the museum. The art gallery, antique household devices—some of which Emma was familiar with—some of the older exhibits she could remember seeing stored in her grandparents barn. There were gem and rock exhibits, currency from all corners of the world, flags, horse drawn carriages, the Wright Brother's airplane, old automobiles.

"I could spend a week in here, Belle. I hope there'll be time so Rascal can come to the Institute."

Rascal found swimming very relaxing and once he had stopped he could notice the difference with his leg muscles. In the afternoon nurse Betty had him swim again. This time she did not see the need to be in the water with him. He was doing just fine.

Just as he was walking out of the shallow end of the pool Emma came walking in. "How was your day, Em?"

She told him all about the monuments and the Smithsonian Institution and about almost every display they had seen.

"What have you been doing for therapy today?" she asked.

Rascal told her about swimming without any help and how good he was feeling. But nurse Betty had said that according to Lt. Belle's directive he was not to try walking on his own yet.

"It sounds like you have made some real progress, Rascal."

"Yes I have, and I can't wait to get home."

"You know, in spite of all the wonderful things I have seen here, I miss home also."

After supper that evening Emma placed a, ". . .collect call to Whiskey Jack Lake operator."

"Yes, that's correct, Whiskey Jack, Maine. Our telephone number is 052. My name? It's Emma Ambrose."

"This may take a few minutes, Mrs. Ambrose, so stay on the line. Don't hang up."

Five minutes later Anita answered. "All is fine at home. Herschel has cleared snow off the lodge, sawyer building, sheds and everything at the farm, and he has been doing some ice fishing behind the dam."

"I told her we shouldn't be here much longer and that I would call again when we knew for sure when we'll be leaving."

"Sounds like they have everything under control back home," Rascal said.

The next morning Belle said, "You have had five weeks of therapy and you are coming nicely. I'm going to have you walk between the parallel bars and I want you to put all your weight on your legs. Use the bars to steady yourself."

He stood up from the wheelchair on his own and grabbed the bars.

"Now just stand there for a few moments. How does that feel?"

"I don't feel any pain in my leg, only both legs feel tired."

"That's understandable. Now walk, slowly." He did and Belle stayed beside him just in case. He made it to the end and turned around and walked back.

"Now how do you feel?"

"No pain."

"Good, I want you to walk back and forth five more times. Take your time, there's no need to hurry."

While he was doing that she pulled up a straight back chair and when Rascal had finished walking she had him sit in the chair and began massaging the muscles in both legs.

Emma joined them in the afternoon.

"How do you feel now, Rascal?"

"Okay."

"Good, I want you to walk back and forth between the bars ten times. Now don't hurry."

Halfway through, the door to the therapy room opened and a man in a dark suit entered. Everyone turned to look at him.

Just as Lt. Belle was about to ask him what his purpose was, Emma stood up and walked over to meet him and said, "Hello, Mr. Butler," and Emma shook his hand. "What are you doing here?"

Lt. Belle knew who Raymond Butler was, but she couldn't understand what he was doing here. Or how Emma knew him.

"I'm on official business, Mrs. Ambrose. And how are you, Rascal?" he asked.

"Coming along. I'm able to walk on my own now."

"Only a short distance," Belle added. She still couldn't figure out the connection.

"I have an official request from the president. Prime Minister Kingsley from Canada will be here on Wednesday and that evening the president would like to invite you and Emma to dinner. Canada's Ambassador to Great Britain will be there, as will the United States Ambassador to Canada, and the vice president and his wife.

"The president would like to know now if you can attend."

Belle couldn't believe what she was hearing.

Emma answered "Mr. Butler, we would be happy to attend."

"Good, here is your invitation and you will need this to pass through security at the White House. The dinner is at 7 p.m. and I will be here at 6 p.m. to pick you up. Don't be late."

"We'll be ready, Mr. Butler."

With that Mr. Butler left. No one spoke for what seemed a long time. Rascal and Emma were looking at each other, and Belle with her mouth open was staring at them both.

Belle spoke first, "Okay, who in the hell are you two? I tried to look at your medical file, Rascal, to see how it was that you were able to see Doctor Rollin. Not just anybody can walk in and get an appointment. You were obviously referred to Rollin by someone in high places. Dr. Rollin wouldn't let me see your file. Now! Now the head of the Secret Service comes in and you two already know him. And the President of the United States invites you to dinner with Canada's Prime Minister Kingsley. I say again, who are you?"

Rascal and Emma looked at each other and Emma said, "We have to tell her something, Rascal. We owe you that much, Belle."

"Last November the president and the prime minister spent some time at our lodge. Mr. Butler came up in the spring and set everything up. That's how we know him. The retired game warden in Beech Tree was the president's personal body guard and guide for the trip. I was the prime minister's guide. He brought his own security. They had a good time, enjoyed Em's and Anita's cooking and they each shot a nice buck," Rascal said. He wanted to leave it there, but Belle pushed on.

"Why were they there, Rascal?"

Emma answered now. "They were discussing something that will have some great changes for this country. And that's all we can tell you, Belle. We're sworn under penalty of law."

"But I have an idea that if you listen to the news, it won't be long before the entire world knows," Rascal added.

"Are you sure you're not some deep undercover spy or something?" Belle said jokingly.

"No, I'm just a back-woodsman, hunter and trapper."

"Oh my God, Rascal! I don't have a thing to wear."

"Hah, hah," Rascal laughed.

"Don't laugh too much, Rascal, you don't either. We both are going to have to buy some suitable clothes.

"Belle, can you help me? I haven't any idea what we should wear," Emma was almost panicking now.

"Sure, I'd like to help. I'll have nurse Betty fill in for me tomorrow and we girls will go shopping.

"There is a men's store across the street from a ladies apparel shop."

"Did you bring enough money, Em, to buy us some fancy clothes?"

"I brought enough."

"Now, Rascal, we need to get to work on your leg muscles. No more walking this morning. We may do some more in the afternoon. Right now I think we should concentrate on toning up your muscles."

Back in their room after lunch Emma asked, "How do you feel now, Rascal? I mean your legs."

"I don't think I'd want to hike up to Ledge Swamp and back, but there is only a little pain, after I have been exercising."

"Well, don't overdo it."

****

Nurse Betty was happy to fill in for Belle. She liked Rascal's backwoods character, and his name, she thought, was funny.

Belle and Emma took the transit bus into the city and took a taxicab to Kernon Square. They went to the ladies' shop first. "I have no idea what kind of style dress, or how fancy, Belle. I'm out of my league here."

"Well, it's best not to be overdressed. My guess is the dignitaries who will be attending, the men will probably all wear expensive dark suits and the women will probably dress to match their husbands. Stiff and proper, if you get my meaning. You and Rascal are not part of their crowd and you should not try to dress as if you were. Can you wear pumps?"

"I can but I haven't for a long time."

"Then you must practice."

Emma started laughing as they walked across the street. "You know I am a wilderness wife, but now I am *really* feeling like a country bumpkin."

"You'll be okay, Emma."

When they entered the shop Emma was amazed with all the beautiful garments. Belle took the lead and discussed what kind of an affair that Emma would be attending without saying too much.

"I think I know exactly what you are looking for. Follow me."

They followed the saleslady to an array of evening gowns. The first one she pulled out was a flowing gray print. Emma took one look at it and said, "I hope it'll fit; that's what I want."

She went into the dressing room and in a few minutes she came back. "I love it. How does it look, Belle?"

"How do you feel in it?" the saleslady asked.

"I feel wonderful."

"You look elegant, Emma, but I think you will need shoes also."

She tried on a pair of matching two inch pumps. "I'll have to practice walking in these, but they do feel comfortable."

"Good so far, Emma. With a dress like that you are going

to need a jacket or coat. Do you have something? Not gaudy or flashy," Belle said. "I have a nice rabbit fur jacket that'll come down to your waist."

"I'd like to try it on."

"It fits wonderfully and this fur is so soft."

"Do you have an evening purse, ma'am?" the saleslady asked.

"No I don't." She looked at Belle and she nodded her head slightly.

"If this is a formal affair, I would suggest something in black."

"Okay, hats," Belle said.

"Over here." The saleslady reached for a popular style.

"No, not that one," Emma said and picked up another and tried it on and turned to face Belle. "What do you think?"

"It should match your gown, but I like the style. You have good taste, Emma."

The saleslady found a gray hat that would match the gown. A feather tulle hat. "The hat should not sit squarely on your head, ma'am. Here, let me fix it. There, look in the full-length mirror."

Emma walked over and looked at herself. She couldn't believe how fine she looked. "Is there anything else I'll need?"

"You have it, girl," Belle said, "and good manners."

"Can you wrap everything, ma'am?" Emma asked. "We now have to buy some evening attire for my husband."

They crossed the street and entered the men's store. A nice looking older gentleman asked, "May I help you ladies with something?"

"Yes, I need evening attire for my husband. I was thinking something in light brown."

"What about something in corduroy?"

"I'd like to see it."

"You wouldn't by chance know his measurements, would you?"

"I have them right here," and she handed him a slip of paper.

"I like the looks of that lighter brown corduroy. What do you think, Belle?"

"I could sooner see Rascal in something like that than a black suit."

"Emma, what about a light-weight vest? That would top it off."

"Okay, also a white shirt, shorts, tie and socks, tan, and a light weight suede jacket."

"I am going to have to make some alterations to the trousers."

"Can you do that while we go for lunch?" Emma asked.

"Yes."

"And could I leave this package here while we eat?"

"Certainly."

As they were eating Emma said, "This has been fun."

"Are you getting anxious about returning home?"

"Yes, both Rascal and I are. But I must say I have certainly enjoyed myself here and I have seen so much.

****

They were back in time for Rascal's therapy. "We're back early Betty, so I'll take over this afternoon."

Betty left.

"Well did you get everything?"

"I can't wait to show you, but not until tomorrow evening."

"Okay, Rascal, what did nurse Betty have you do this morning?" Belle asked.

"Walking around the room."

"Okay, walk, I want to see how you are doing."

"You still have a slight limp, but that'll disappear eventually. That's good, Rascal. Now we're going to do something different. I want to see how you do on stairs. Take this cane to steady yourself."

He took a couple of steps and said, "This is altogether different than walking on a flat surface."

"Does it hurt your leg any?" Belle asked.

"Not hurt exactly. It just feels so weak."

"Okay, Rascal just remember how long you were recovering from the last operation. You are two weeks ahead now, from that time."

Rascal made it to the top of six steps and went down and then back up. He did this three times and then sat down to rest his legs.

"Three more times, Rascal. Don't try to hurry."

"You know both legs are hurting some—but it's a good kind of hurt. I think my muscles are beginning to wake up."

Emma was smiling as he started three more repetitions. He kept doing this for an hour and then Belle said, "That's enough for today, Rascal. I'll see you in the morning. And, Emma, when you walk up the steps to the White House tomorrow evening you might want to hold his arm to steady him. If he should fall now we would have to start from the beginning again."

"I will, Belle."

"Can I walk back to our room?"

"Yes, but, Emma, take the wheelchair just in case."

****

As they lay in bed that night, Emma said, "Oh, Rascal, I'm so nervous."

"Why? You know President Cutlidge and Prime Minister Kingsley."

"I don't know, maybe just being invited to the White House for dinner. Aren't you a little bit nervous?"

"Not about the dinner or that we have been invited to the White House—but, I just hope I don't fall down."

Emma began laughing and then, too, Rascal laughed. "If you do, Rascal, I'll be there to pick you up."

Belle met them at breakfast the next morning. "I forgot to say something yesterday, but, Emma, you should get your hair done this morning. There's a beauty salon downstairs. And you need a haircut, Rascal, and a shave. We'll go to the therapy gym first, Rascal, and then to the barber.

"How were your legs, Rascal, when you got out of bed?"

"They felt like the muscles needed a little stretching."

"That's certainly understandable. Come over here and lay down on this table and I'll massage your muscles and see if we can loosen them." She worked on both legs until her back was getting tired.

"Okay, stand up now and see how they feel."

Rascal did. "They feel like new legs."

"Okay, walk around the floor for me. You still have a slight limp, which I said earlier will go away in time. My biggest worry is the steps going up to the White House. Make sure Emma is by your side and holding your arm before you even start.

"Now, Rascal, sometimes at these dinners there is music and maybe dancing. Do you think you can dance? If not, don't try."

"Let's see right now if I can."

Belle stepped over close to him and he put his arm around her and they started dancing. "I can as long as the music is slow and not too long." But they kept dancing.

"Remember when we danced in New York, Rascal?"

"Yes, it was great wasn't it."

They danced for a couple of more minutes before stopping. There was no shame or embarrassment. They only smiled at each other. Belle broke the silence when she said, "Wait until after your haircut before you shower or take a bath."

"Are you leaving?"

"No, I'm going to stay around to see you and Emma with your new clothes. And I want to speak to Mr. Butler."

After a haircut and shave and shower, Rascal was feeling like a new man. He turned and looked in the mirror at the incision.

It looked so much neater and cleaner than before.

When Emma came back from the beauty salon Rascal didn't recognize her at first. Then she smiled and there was no mistaking her smile. "Wow, Em, you look like a new person."

"So you like it?"

"Yes. I have never seen you with the ends curled up like this."

"How is your leg?"

"I think it'll be just fine." He wasn't about to tell her about dancing with Belle. He really liked Belle. She was one of those special people and whatever he felt towards her would have to remain his secret. He would not jeopardize losing or hurting Emma. He was that much in love with his wife.

"I need to take a bath." He watched as she removed her clothes. She stood facing him and grinning.

"You sure do look tantalizing, you do."

"You just wait until I get you home, Rascal."

****

An hour and a half before Mr. Butler was due to arrive they both started getting dressed. "I have never worn such fancy clothes, Em."

"Me neither."

When Rascal was fully dressed, Em said, "Turn around once, Rascal.

"You look like someone I don't know."

"Everything fits, even the shoes."

Emma was a bit longer getting dressed, but when she had finished it was well worth the wait. "Wow, Em, I can't believe how beautiful you are."

Just then the door opened and Belle entered the room. "Excuse me, I must have the wrong room." Then Rascal and Emma started smiling.

"Wow," she said, "I wouldn't have believed the change if I weren't standing here looking at you two."

"Isn't she beautiful, Belle?"

"You certainly are, Emma, and so are you, Rascal."

"Any last tips, Belle?" Emma asked.

"Look the only thing I can say is the president and prime minister liked you for what they saw of you at Whiskey Jack. Don't put on airs, just be yourselves—with good table manners.

"Okay, it's almost time. I'll walk out to the lobby with you."

"You look real distinguished, Rascal, with the cane. Don't forget to use it. Everybody is turning to look at you. I wish there was a photographer here that would take your photo."

Right at 6 o'clock the front door opened and Mr. Butler entered, "Hello, Emma, Rascal, are you ready?"

"Mr. Butler," Belle said, "I would ask that you drive as close to the steps as you can, and walk on one side of him, just in case. Emma will walk on the other side. Remember his operation."

"Yes, Lieutenant, I will. I will escort them to the dining room."

"Thank you." Belle hugged each one then and said, "Have a good time, I love the both of you."

No one else at Walter Reed knew what was happening, only that a government man had come for the two well-dressed prominent looking people, 'Who were those two people?' everyone was asking.

There was another secret service person who was driving. Mr. Butler opened the door for Emma and then Rascal and then he climbed in front and nodded his head and the driver left.

"When will you be returning to Whiskey Jack?" Mr. Butler asked.

"Hopefully soon. We are both getting homesick."

"Well you certainly do have a very comfortable home."

"Pull up close to the steps, Henri. I'll be staying outside of the dining room. So once we are clear you can park the car. I'll send someone out to tell you when you are needed again."

"Yes sir."

"We're here, Rascal."

Mr. Butler was out first and held the door for Rascal and Emma. "Okay, Henri."

"Now I'm getting nervous, Em."

"Me too."

"Ah folks think nothing of it. Just look at as if you're visiting two old friends."

Mr. Butler was to the right of Rascal and Emma on his left holding his arm. "Right, you ready?"

"Let's do it."

"Go at a comfortable pace, Rascal," Mr. Butler said.

They climbed the steps one at a time and when they reached the top they stopped a moment, and then continued. There was someone at the door to hold it open for them. Once inside another man asked to see their invitation. Emma took it out of her purse and handed it to him, and then he gave it back. "Go on in, folks, you are expected."

There was another man positioned at the dining room door. "Good evening, Mr. & Mrs. Ambrose. They can enter anytime, sir," and he opened the door for them.

"I must leave you here. I'll be here when you are ready to leave."

"Thank you, Mr. Butler," Rascal said.

As Rascal and Emma entered, "Everyone is looking at us," Emma whispered.

"I know."

The president and his wife Pearl and the prime minister and his wife Myrissa came over to greet them. "If I didn't know better I'd say you were two different people," President Cutlidge said. A maid took Rascal and Emma's coats and took them out into the hall closet. Introductions were made and the president said, "I am so glad you could come this evening." Then he shook Rascal's hand and hugged Emma and kissed her cheek. The prime minister did also.

"And how is your leg, Rascal?" the president asked.

"I think when the muscles and tendons fully recover, I'll be like new. Right now both legs are weak."

"How do you like Washington, Mr. Ambrose?" Pearl asked.

"I haven't seen much of anything besides the Walter Reed Hospital. But Em has been touring the city with Lieutenant Belle."

"I have really enjoyed the stay here and I'm so happy Rascal's operation was successful."

"I don't suppose you brought any of your biscuits with you?" Prime Minister Kingsley asked.

"Folks, folks, may I have your attention please," the president said. "We have a short matter of business to discuss before dinner is served, so if you would please find your place and be seated."

The president and his wife Pearl sat side by each at the head of the table and the prime minister and his wife Myrissa on one side and Rascal and Emma on the other side. And the vice president and his wife next to Rascal. Emma sat close to Pearl.

The president stood up and said, I'd like to introduce two very special people and friends, Mr. & Mrs. Ambrose from Whiskey Jack, Maine, just north by rail, from Beech Tree. Oh, and by the way they each would prefer to be called Rascal and Emma."

"Mr. Prime Minister and I met at the Whiskey Jack Lodge last November under the guise of two hunters to discuss the possibility of our two countries merging into one great country. Mr. Prime Minister you can take it from there," and President Cutlidge sat down.

"I want to thank you, Mr. & Mrs. President, for inviting my wife and I here for this auspicious occasion. Immediately on my return to Canada after our meeting in November, I contacted Canada's Ambassador Fredrika Dubois to Great Britain and advised him what President Cutlidge and I had been discussing.

Ambassador Dubois, tell us what you learned while in Great Britain."

The ambassador stood up and said, "I advised the British Parliament that Canada wanted complete autonomy. That Canadian citizens were tired of having to comply with British rule. I put it as simply as that and waited. At first there was complete silence and then everyone started talking with the person next to them. At this point I wasn't sure how this was going to be accepted, if at all.

"I interrupted their discussions amongst themselves and said that Canada feels very strongly about this and we would not consider anything less. And then I added that Canada was serious enough to declare our own independence if we had to and were prepared to fight for autonomy.

"I decided I had said everything that was necessary and left, so that they might have the opportunity to discuss this amongst themselves.

"Once I was back in my apartment, I didn't know but what I had been overly direct. But that's what Prime Minister Kingsley wanted. I wasn't scheduled to leave for three more days and by the end of the second I hadn't heard a word from Parliament, and I thought perhaps I had blown it. But during dinner that evening, I was approached by a messenger from England's prime minister that I was to join him in his study at once.

"I was greeted socially and after I was seated he became very angry and I was afraid it would never happen. I reminded him that Great Britain had just come out of a very costly war and I assured him that if England so chooses a war with Canada, it would be just as expensive. He calmed down a little and I told him what we wanted was complete autonomy and I also assured him that Canada would remain an ally, but under our own direction.

"We talked until 3 a.m. and the more we talked the more agreeable he was becoming. Before leaving his study, he asked if I would continue my stay over for another week.

"Right then I knew I had been able to talk some common sense into him. On the third day I was again summoned to his study. I didn't know but what he or Parliament might have some conditions attached to the autonomy.

"But I was wrong and completely taken off guard. He said that I had been correct that Great Britain could not afford another war and said Canada has Parliament's and his approval. He said, 'You know, Ambassador, you have us bent over a powder keg with a lit fuse. But I find your audacity quite refreshing over so much starch and gander. Papers are to be signed on June 1st this year in London.'"

Everyone in the room cheered and congratulated Ambassador Dubois on a fine job. Until this very moment no one knew the outcome except for Ambassador Dubois and Prime Minister Kingsley. President Cutlidge was happier than a little boy on Christmas morning.

President Cutlidge stood up and said, "Very well done, Mr. Prime Minister and Ambassador Dubois. But this is only the first step. We still must keep this idea of a merger secret until after June 1st. And now I believe it is time for,"—he paused there and looked at Rascal and Emma and said—"supper. This won't be as delicious as your beaver, deer, and moose meat and topped with frog legs and crab apples, but it should be good."

"And don't forget those delicious biscuits Emma made, Mr. President."

The ice had broken and both Rascal and Emma were very much at ease.

"This is such a beautiful evening gown, Emma. Where on earth did you find it?" Pearl asked.

"Thank you, ma'am. Our friend Lt. Belle took me to Vernon Square and a ladies shop."

"Well, it is exquisite."

Everyone complimented Emma on how nice she looked and after dinner everyone wanted to listen to Rascal tell stories of Whiskey Jack Lake.

Ambassador Dubois said, "If I understand you correctly, even though this game warden Jarvis Page had arrested each of you for different offenses, you remain friends with him and you invite him into your home. How outstanding. How simply wonderful. I'd like to sit down and listen to you two and this Jarvis Page tell your stories. I'm not sure if I could remain on friendly terms with the man who put me in jail and then of all things, my wife. Someday I would like to visit. This Whiskey Jack Lake and Beech Tree towns have produced some real genuine people. It's too bad there aren't more places like them."

Now after the discussion of the two countries merging, Rascal and Emma seemed to be at the center of everyone's interest.

"Right after President Cutlidge and I arrived at Whiskey Jack we went for a stroll out to the Hitchcock farm. Jarvis Page and Francois Dubois were along also. When the rest of us went upstairs to look at the farmhouse Rascal didn't come along. From one of the upstairs windows I could see this big bear coming towards Rascal." The president started laughing, trying not to and so was Emma. "I said something to the others and we all looked out the window and saw the same thing. We ran down stairs and then outside. Rascal raised his hand and made a noise like laughing and the bear did the same thing. Then the bear started running at Rascal. Rascal turned away from us toward the other side of the field and twice that bear tripped him. Rascal would get back up and start running and again the bear tripped him, and Rascal started running again and this time the bear head bunted him in the butt knocking him down. Then the bear ran on top of a small knoll at the edge of the field, stood up and raised his paw and I swear to God he started laughing."

At first everyone looked at President Cutlidge and he said, "It happened just as he said." Then everyone began laughing, even Rascal and Emma.

"Does that bear play with you, Emma?" Myrissa asked.

"No, and thank God. I was with Rascal once when he chased us out of the field at the farm."

"Folks," President Cutlidge said, "let's adjourn to the sitting room while the maids are cleaning up."

"This is more comfortable. That dining chair was beginning to hurt my butt," Rascal said.

"Mr. President," Emma asked, "once the prime minister has signed the autonomy declaration then what?"

"We both have been doing a lot of talking on the subject and I have a list of lobbyists that will go through the country telling people of the plan and how it will benefit everybody in both countries and Vice President Daves has already spoken to a team of writers who will submit similar articles in every newspaper and magazine in the county."

"I have also done the same in Canada," Prime Minister Kingsley said.

"What are the chances that the popular vote in both countries will be in favor of the merger?" Rascal asked.

"I believe that there'll be on both sides a few that will oppose the change, but I'm guessing seventy percent will be in favor in Canada."

"I'm looking at maybe sixty to seventy percent in favor. But it will be a tough sell in places. For now we'll just have to wait and see if England's word is any good."

"I must stress the fact that if England hears wind of any of this they probably will be very difficult to deal with," the president said.

Just before they were departing for the evening, "May I have your attention please. I have invited a well-known photographer here to photograph the group and I have been informed that he is now waiting in the other room."

Mr. Gilbert was shown in and asked to set up in the sitting room. As special guests Rascal and Emma were in front and behind them the president and prime minister with their wives and the ambassadors and their wives in the back row.

"When these are developed I will send you a framed print."

"Thank you, Mr. President. This has certainly been an evening to remember," Emma said.

"I would like to thank you, Mr. President, for your help and referral to Walter Reed Hospital and Doctor Rollin," Rascal said.

There were warm handshakes, hugs and kissed cheeks, as all were leaving. "Emma," the prime minister said, "say hello to Anita for me."

Back in their room at Walter Reed, Emma said, "I kind of hate to take these clothes off now. What an enjoyable evening. I was afraid, Rascal, they would look down on us because we live in the wilderness. But it wasn't like that at all."

"I know what you mean, Em. I was awful nervous when we arrived. If you had asked me to go back to the hospital, I would have."

They crawled into bed and Rascal said, "I'm tired."

"Yeah, me too."

Chapter 6

Lt. Belle joined them for breakfast the next morning. "How'd it go?"

"We both were so nervous when we arrived, but once we were inside and socializing we were more at ease. Like talking with old friends," Emma said.

"And your legs, Rascal?"

"I made it up and down the steps alright, but we sat in the dining room for a long time and my butt began to ache. From there we moved into a sitting room where it was more comfortable."

"I'm glad you had a nice time. And you still can't tell me what it is all about?"

"We were sworn to secrecy again last night," Rascal said.

"If you are through with breakfast, Dr. Rollin wants to see us in his office," Belle said.

Rascal had left his cane in the room and he was doing just fine without it.

"Come in please and sit down. Lieutenant Belle tells me that she has completed your therapy. That you can walk without assistance and that you can go up and down stairs just fine."

"Yes, Doctor Rollin. If I sit for any length of time in a hard chair my butt will ache. But there is less soreness now than before the operation."

"And with time that too will disappear, as soon as your muscle tissue and tendons have fully healed.

"I'm discharging you but until spring I want you to take it easy. I don't want you carrying anything heavy, trapping, snowshoeing or shoveling snow from your roofs, and I want you to walk often. As much as you want. Your leg will tell you when enough is enough." He looked at Emma and then continued, "I'm counting on you, Emma, to see that he follows my directions. If you don't, Rascal, you could be back where we started and there won't be another operation. So take my advice seriously."

"I will, Doctor Rollin."

"Good, then you're free to leave," he stood up and shook hands with them both.

They stood up and Rascal said, "Thank you, Doctor Rollin."

"You go back to your room and pack and I'll call the train station and see when there's a train out for Boston."

"Thank you, Belle."

As Emma was packing her evening gown she was saddened by the fact that you would probably never have another occasion to wear it. Or Rascal his suit.

Belle was back as they were finishing. "There is a train for Boston that leaves at twelve noon. That gives you about two and a half hours.

"I have another new case this afternoon. I also called for a taxicab to take you to Penn Station." Her eyes were beginning to water and she hugged Emma and said, "I really hate to see you leave." Then she hugged Rascal and kissed his cheek and whispered in his ear.

Emma saw this. She would let them have their goodbye. She understood there was a strong friendship bond between them and she would let Rascal have his secret.

She pulled back from Rascal and said, "Look at me carrying on. It's just I love the both of you like you were my own family."

"When Richard finishes his training you'll have to come back and visit us. And family doesn't charge family. Come anytime, Belle," Emma said and hugged her again.

Belle waited in the lobby with them until their taxi driver came inside. This time there were real tears and more hugs and kissing. "Say hello to Richard and give him our best, Belle," Emma said.

They pulled on their new coats and with luggage in hand they left Walter Reed Hospital. "I have directions to take you to Penn Station, folks."

There was a hubbub of people coming and going. "Rascal," Emma said excitedly, "There's Samson. Samson!" she hollered.

He turned about and saw two people coming towards him and he immediately recognized them. "Are you going up the line?"

"Yes, we're heading home."

"Follow me and I can get you aboard."

They followed Samson on board and to a private berth.

They were still tired from the night before and went to bed as soon as they had eaten supper. "I'll be glad to get home and eat your cooking again."

****

Each day as they traveled further north the air was getting colder and they could feel the change and had to wear warmer clothes. Sitting so much, Rascal could feel his muscles and tendons tightening, so about once every hour he would get up and walk the length of the five passenger cars and back again.

After four days of riding the rail, they boarded the B&M train and a day later the S&A train pulled to a stop at Whiskey Jack Lodge.

The wind had blown the lake free of snow and there was about three feet of snow. "We're home, Em. Just look at the wind blowing snow down the lake. Yup, we're home, listen to the lake making ice still."

"Yes, Rascal, we're home. Come on. I'm cold."

Herschel came out to see why the train had stopped and was surprised to see Rascal and Emma. "You two go inside out of this cold. I'll get your luggage."

When Anita saw them she let out a scream of joy and ran to hug them. "I thought you were going to telephone me before you left?" she said.

"We wanted to surprise you."

"Well, you surely did. My, that's a pretty coat, Emma."

"Thank you it's rabbit fur."

Herschel came in and set the bags down and then all four sat in the living room sipping coffee while Rascal and Emma told them all about their trip.

"But, Rascal, you are still limping," Anita said.

"Yes, the doctor said when the muscles and tendons finally heal I won't limp anymore."

"Oh, Anita, Prime Minister Kingsley said to say hello."

"He was in Washington also?"

"Yes, he and his wife Myrissa were visiting President Cutlidge and his wife Pearl. Our last night there we were invited to dinner at the White House," and Emma showed them the invitation.

She and Rascal both were careful not to mention anything that had been discussed at the dinner.

"The snow has been so dry and fluffy every time the wind blew it would clean off the roofs. I did have to shovel out the valleys on the farmhouse and the log cabin has been okay. Needing something to do sometimes, I'd go rabbit or partridge hunting and Anita would cook 'em."

"I was going to ask you to stay for two more weeks. The doctor said no snowshoeing, shoveling off the roofs and not to carry or lift more than twenty pounds. But it looks as if you have everything pretty much under control."

"I tell ya what I will do for you though. I'll bring up enough firewood to last you a good long time."

For an hour he carried wood up and piled it on both sides of the fireplace and the kitchen stove wood; he piled wood in the hall and under the eaves on the platform. "There that should last you through the rest of March."

Anita had already fixed a pot of fish chowder and biscuits. "We ate well in Washington, but nothing this good, Anita."

"It has been so quiet out here. Nothing like two hundred snoring men sleeping in one barracks. The only noise has been the train going through twice a day and lying awake at night listening to the lake making ice. The last hole I cut down by the dam I was on my knees before reaching water," Herschel said.

"How was the fishing this winter?"

"At first real good. Then as the ice froze thicker and thicker it wasn't as good. I haven't tried for three weeks now."

"There were a pack of wolves around here earlier, but we haven't heard anything from them for two or three weeks now," Anita said. "Their howling at night was creepy."

"I hope they don't move in permanently," Rascal said, "They'll drive all the fur animals and deer out of here."

"Are you excited, Herschel, about becoming a game warden in July?" Emma asked.

"I sure am. I can't wait. I'll have the same area that my dad had.

"If you don't need me to stay around, then maybe I should put out the red flag."

Rascal paid him the rest of his wages and then there was the train signal. "Herschel, I can't thank you enough."

"It was my pleasure," and he hugged Anita and said goodbye.

"I need to walk around some to stretch my legs."

"I'd rather you didn't go outside, Rascal, until the weather warms up some. We have been in a warm climate and it's going to take a few days to readjust." He walked around the lodge and made two trips upstairs and back without his leg hurting.

After supper they sat in the living room with a glass of brandy enjoying each other's company, the warmth of the fireplace and listening to the news on the radio.

"Okay, what's the news of Canada and the United States merging?" Anita asked.

"England has agreed to give Canada complete autonomy and official documents will be signed on June 1st. Then both leaders are going to start an aggressive campaign to convince people of the many benefits."

****

Rascal was good for two days. He'd walk back and forth inside the lodge and up and down the stairs. Sometimes he'd put on his heavy jacket and walk out to the platform for the newspaper. His muscles and tendons were healing. The following week the weather turned warm and he'd go for walks along the snowshoe trails Herschel had packed down. He was now going to the hen house each morning to feed the hens and gather eggs.

In the middle of the third week home the train stopped and delivered a package and a pouch full of mail.

Anita said, "Rascal, Emma, ahh—this package is from Washington, D.C. In particular, the White House."

Without saying a word Emma began to open it, while Rascal and Anita stood and watched. She was being painstakingly slow. Finally she had both ends open and began to pull the contents out. She screamed a little high pitch shrill. "It is our portrait, Rascal." Anita held the box while she pulled it clear.

"My, oh my, isn't that a beautiful photograph," Anita said. "Just think you two had dinner with all these important people. And in the White House no less. You two surely do take an awful nice photo. Emma this has to be you. Your hair is still fixed like that in the photograph, so this has to be you. But, Emma, I have never seen you look so beautiful."

"Doesn't she, Anita," Rascal said. "Everyone there thought so too. Even the other wives."

"Rascal, you sure are a nice looking man," Anita said.

"There's only one place to hang that, you know," Anita said.

"Right above our plaques."

"Now that you two were invited for dinner at the White

House, I hope your britches don't get so big you forget us lowly people."

"Anita," Rascal said as he put his arm around her shoulders, "you are just as much a friend to the president and prime minister as we are."

While Rascal hung the framed picture up Emma and Anita opened the many pieces of mail. "Most of these are for fishing reservations in May and June."

"There are twelve in all, Emma," Anita said.

"You know it'll seem good when we start having guests again," Rascal said. "And I'm looking forward this year to spring and dry weather."

****

After that week of warm sunny weather, winter came back with a last punch. The snow came down so heavy they couldn't see the lake or log cabin across the cove. The train didn't come through for two days. But with the temperature so cold the snow was dry and fluffy and blew off when the wind came down out of the north.

Jarvis called the first evening of the blizzard. "Just checking to see if you folks are all right there. If you need anyone to do any shoveling, Rascal, after the storm stops just let me or Herschel know."

Being the end of March, Rascal knew the snow wouldn't last very long. Since it was a fluffy dry snow, Emma did allow him to break out a trail with his snowshoes to the hen house.

"How is your leg after that work out?"

"I'm tired but I'm not hurting." And his limp now was barely noticeable.

During that wintery cold snap they used up most of the firewood Herschel had brought in and it was now up to Rascal. "Don't overdo it, you hear me, Rascal. You take small arm loads."

He knew when he was beat. "Yes, Em."

Anita smiled and walked away.

Requests for fishing were still coming in about four or five a week. May and June were pretty much booked up and when Emma received requests for July and August when it would be too hot for good fishing, she would recommend September.

April turned off unusually warm and the dry fluffy snow didn't last long. The ice in the lake was more than four feet thick and it wasn't until the middle of the first week in May when the lake was clear of ice.

"After breakfast, would you ladies like to go for a walk to the farm? I'd like to check out the buildings."

While Anita was changing her clothes Emma asked, "What about Bear, Rascal?"

"Well, he should be hungry and looking for food and we probably won't even see him. If we do, then we do. I'll give him a run for his money with this new leg."

"You just be careful, Rascal."

Anita had heard some talk about a bear but she had not paid too much attention. She had figured it was men talking about hunting.

"I missed the smell of the woods in Washington," Emma said. "I had a wonderful time and saw many things, but I am sure glad to be home."

They went through the house looking for spots where water might have leaked. And in the cellar also. The building where most of the crew slept, there was one window that had blown out. He found another window in the tool shed and replaced it. Everything was looking okay.

Rascal walked out into the field some to look down across to the lower edge. There were three deer at the very lower edge feeding on leafed weeds that were coming up through the grass. They paid no attention to him.

Anita and Emma came out to join him. "Anything?"

"Three deer feeding at the lower end," Rascal knew what she had meant. *Was there any sign of Bear?*

They started back and just before reaching the mouth

of the road, Bear came running out of the woods on the right towards them. Anita saw him coming and screeched, "Bear! Bear!"

"We'll be okay, Anita. He won't hurt us."

Bear slowed to a walk and stopped fifty feet away.

"Hello, Bear," Rascal said and held up his arm.

Bear sat down on his butt and raised a paw. "What's he doing?" Anita asked.

"You watch this, Anita."

Rascal took a few steps closer.

"What is he doing, Emma?"

"Watch."

"Anita, come here," Rascal said.

Anita froze in her tracks. Emma put her arm around her to encourage her to step forward. Anita took two steps back, "It's okay, Anita. Walk up to Rascal."

"Are you sure about this, Emma? I wish I had stayed home now."

"Go on, Anita."

Very slowly Anita stepped up beside Rascal. "Anita," Rascal said, "I'd like you to meet Bear. Bear this is our friend Anita."

Bear lifted his paw again and made the nose that sounded like 'arrahy'.

"Did he just say hi? You have a talking bear? Unbelievable."

Then Bear started running towards them. Anita screamed and ran back to Emma. "It's okay, Anita."

Rascal took off running and Bear right behind his heels. Rascal made two circles and then Bear reached out and tripped him and Rascal went down laughing. Anita thought the bear was going to maul him.

But Bear waited until Rascal was up and running again. This time Rascal ran a figure eight pattern and this confused Bear for a moment and Rascal was able to gain some distance on him and then Bear tripped him again, and then sat on his butt laughing.

"Is he laughing now, Emma?"

"We think so."

Rascal was up and running straight ahead for the road and Bear butt-bunted him and Rascal went on his face. And like before Bear ran out of the field and stopped on the top of a bank only a short distance away and began laughing again. Rascal raised his arm and made that same laughing noise.

Rascal turned to see both Emma and Anita laughing, "Okay, we can leave now."

"Is that the same bear that chased you and Elmo on the tracks?" Anita asked.

"Yes."

"I wish Silvio was here to see this. A bear that says hi, laughs and waves and plays with you. Does he play with you, Emma?"

"No, only Rascal. This is why we do not allow any bear hunting here."

"We must keep this amongst ourselves. We wouldn't want people coming here to see Bear."

"Certainly."

"How is your leg after playing with Bear?" Emma asked.

"It feels fine."

Back in the lodge Anita asked, "Why does he do it?"

"Jeters came up with the only reason any of us could think of, he's lonely and needs a playmate."

Anita shook her head and went to the kitchen.

During April the ground dried out fast. As much as Rascal wanted to plant the garden, he knew it was too early.

He knew that there would be a good chance of a frosty morning even as late as the end of May. But he did work on firewood before the blackflies and mosquitos were out. The only way Emma would let him go work on firewood, was if she went also to keep an eye on him, "So you don't overdo it, Rascal. You know as well as I what Dr. Rollin said about over taxing your leg so soon."

He knew what she was saying, and she was right. She even took one end of the two man crosscut saw and when it came to sawing the tree into fireplace and stove size, she would help with that. "I never knew how tiring, working on firewood could be. Right now I'd like a cool dip in the lake."

"Yeah, but you'd have to cut a hole through the ice first."

"I'm not that hot and sweaty, I guess."

She would only let him work up one wagon load of wood each day. "You know this ain't that bad with you helping."

****

One night it rained all night and the wind was strong coming down the lake. By morning the cove behind the dam was full of broken up ice, blown down the lake by the strong wind. "Well, that surprised me. Do we have any fisherman coming the first week?"

"Four from the Portland area."

"I was afraid the ice would still be in."

The four fisherman arrived and while they were out fishing Rascal cleaned the smoker and had material ready to start a fire. By the end of the day the four men had only landed two five pound togues, which they wanted baked. "If we catch more than we can eat we'll let you smoke those."

Their last day of fishing they came back to the lodge with two large brook trout apiece. "It's too late to smoke these but I'll put 'em on ice in the cold storage room and you shouldn't have any problem getting them home."

On the third week of May, Alfred and Beverly Cummings arrived and because of so many guests that week they chose the log cabin. Beverly wasn't all that interested with fishing, so while Al was fishing she would spend much of her time talking with Emma and Anita.

The picture of Rascal and Emma at the White House

certainly caught everyone's attention and then when they saw the plaques beneath the picture, everyone had questions. Earlier the three had agreed to say only that the fall before the president and prime minister had met at Whiskey Jack Lodge for a week of uninterrupted relaxation and a little hunting. That seemed to appease everyone's curiosity. Except for Al Cummings, Lt. Belle's father-in-law.

"Belle told us about you and Emma being invited to the White House for dinner. Usually that is reserved for dignitaries and high officials. And then there are those plaques in the dining room."

Rascal knew Al was fishing, but all he would say, "He and the prime minister had an enjoyable time here last fall and we became quite good friends. He had recommended me to his doctor at the Walter Reed Hospital and he knew we were in the city and he probably invited us to dinner as a courtesy and to inquire how the operation had gone. We left Washington the next day."

By Al's expression Rascal figured Al knew there was more to the story, but he was polite and didn't ask any more questions about the picture.

"Your business has certainly grown in the short time you have been running the lodge," Al said.

"It gets better with each year."

****

Eight days before June 1st on May 23rd, Prime Minister Kingsley, his wife Myrissa and Ambassador Fredika Dubois and his wife boarded the steamship passenger liner in Quebec City for London, England. The North Atlantic is rough even on a calm day and what the wives thought would be a pleasurable crossing was anything but. They all stayed pretty much in their rooms and ate very little.

Before leaving Ottawa the prime minister had given the Deputy Prime Minister Victor Arsenault a pre-written press release to be sent out to every major newspaper in Canada declaring their separation from Great Britain and the Commonwealth, on June 1st. At the same time President Cutlidge would have his staff release a similar statement to the media in the United States.

The prime minister and the ambassador had to steady their wives as they walked down the gangway.

****

On the morning of June 2nd Rascal went out to the platform to sit in the fresh air and wait for the train to go through and deliver that morning's newspaper and any mail. The whistle blew a half mile out and the train slowed as it went by the lodge and the conductor threw off the mail pouch and paper. "Read the paper first!" he hollered.

Rascal opened the paper and there in big bold letters on the front page was the story they had been waiting for. He went running into the lodge hollering, "Em! Em! Anita! They did it. Canada is its own sovereign country, completely autonomous from Great Britain!"

There were a few guests still in the dining room and wondered, "What in the devil are you talking about, Rascal?" one of them asked.

"Rascal, turn on the radio. Maybe there is something there," Emma said.

Every station he tuned into was carrying the same story. Anita, Emma and the five guests and Rascal sat silently in the living room listening. "They actually did it. Ambassador Dubois must be a real statesmen to pull something like this off."

One of the guests, Carl Amsbury, a college professor, stood up and walked over to the picture and reread what was on the plaques. Later when he was alone with Rascal he said, "I recognized Ambassador Dubois in that picture of all of you taken in the White House. The President of the United States and the Prime Minister of Canada meet here for a hunting vacation and now Canada obtains complete independence from the Commonwealth is too coincidental. There's more to the story isn't there, Rascal? And it would be my guess you are not able to talk about it."

Rascal didn't know what to say other than, "It's a nice day isn't it, Mr. Amsbury."

Amsbury cracked right up laughing. But he had his answer.

That night in bed, Emma said, "Well that much of their plan is done. I wonder when we'll hear about the merger?"

"You know I was surprised England gave up so easily. I really expected England to hang onto Canada as long as it could. From what was said at the dinner, I believe we'll hear something soon. Maybe not, though, until the prime minister is back in Ottawa."

Emma said, "I think we can expect a lot of good coming out of the merger." Then she rolled over and went to sleep. Rascal lay on his back a while longer thinking about the possible changes to come.

****

A week after the return of Prime Minister Kingsley, Rascal was sitting on the platform again and waiting for the train to drop off the newspaper and mail.

"Hum, they're late today. I wonder why?"

Twenty minutes later Rascal heard the half mile signal and he stood up and walked over to the edge of the platform to wait. The train came to a stop and Tom Whelling the conductor handed Rascal the mail pouch. "How come you're late today, Tom? Trouble?"

"No, read the paper. That's all people are talking about." The train started up and Tom waved goodbye.

Rascal took the pouch inside and first looked at the paper. "Hey, Em, Anita!" he yelled. "Here it is. Practically the whole paper is about Canada and the United States merging."

Emma turned the radio on and again every station was carrying the same story released by the White House.

That night at the supper table everyone was talking about the new idea. Everyone seemed to be in favor of the merger, but there was a couple of skeptics who didn't think it would work or pass a popular vote.

Every day after that first announcement the morning, noon and evening news broadcast was mostly about the two countries coming together. The newspaper had articles mostly supporting the move, and only a few with a negative outlook.

That last week in June it rained off and on for five days. The guests that ventured out had real success. And the favorite topic, of those who chose to stay in the lodge, was about the merger and by the end of the week they all decided that probably both countries would benefit. They also ate a lot of cookies, pies and drank enough coffee to sink a washtub.

When that week's guests left there was only a few booked in for the last week. That was okay with Rascal. He had firewood to finish working up for the winter, trout to catch and smoke, frog legs to can and in between all this he had to find time to work in the garden.

Almost every night wolves would start howling, then yapping and what sounded like fighting. Emma and Anita were so shaken they would not leave the clearing near the lodge, unless Rascal was with them. "Why do they sound like they are fighting, Rascal?" Emma asked.

"It may be a family pack of wolves and after the adults have made a kill the young ones will squabble and fight for their share of the meat."

"What do you suppose they are killing? Deer?"

"Probably a few, but it could be woodchucks, rabbits, partridges, almost anything. I think this trapping season I'll concentrate on wolves and not the other animals."

"Good, I don't like 'em around. They make me nervous."

"Well, maybe I'll try setting out some traps."

Rascal walked out along the farm road looking for tracks. About half way to the farm he found the remains of a spotted fawn. He crossed through the woods and to the other road. It had mostly grown in with grass and weeds and tracks were difficult to see. He did find one place where a wolf had scratched the ground to cover its urine spot. He wished there had been snow, then tracks would have been easy to see. He'd try one set on each road tomorrow.

At supper that night he told Emma and Anita what he had found. "Not much for sign for all of the yowling we have been hearing."

Rascal didn't sleep good that night. The yowling started about 10 p.m. and Emma woke him up with an elbow in his ribs. There was nothing to do but lay there and listen. The rest of the night he only cat-napped and tossed and turned. About an hour before first light he managed to drift off in a deep sleep, only to awaken on the dream side of life. He saw Emma and a wolf running at her from one direction and a bear running towards her from another. He awoke in a start and sat up in bed.

"What's the matter, Rascal?"

"Oh wow, just a bad dream." It was already beginning to fade from his memory.

He lay back down and said, "Have you ever noticed that the only time we hear the wolves is between sunset and about midnight? Never in the early morning hours."

"No, I have never thought of it, but you're right."

They laid in bed talking until the sun was up. "Do we have any guests coming this weekend?" he asked.

"Yes, I think a father and a son."

"You know, Em, this has made us a pretty good business and living. I'm sure glad we decided to do it."

"Come on, get out of bed, Rascal. What would you like for breakfast?"

"How about thick slices of bacon and flapjacks?"

"Sounds good to me."

"I'll be outside looking for tracks around the edge of the clearing. Give me a shout when breakfast is ready."

There were deer tracks everywhere. Even in his garden, but they had only walked through. He saw raccoon and skunk tracks, but no wolves.

Emma hollered at him to come in.

"This is sure good bacon," Anita said.

After eating while Emma and Anita were cleaning up the kitchen Rascal cleaned out the ashes from the woodstove in the kitchen and the ram-down upstairs and took them out to the garden to spread 'em.

"Em, I'm going up to the cabin and get my traps and gear. I may not be back before lunch."

"Okay, while Anita is baking I'm going to pick strawberries from the little field for strawberry shortcake."

Rascal strapped on his revolver, just in case he were to see a wolf. He picked up four traps, wire, axe, a jar of canned beaver meat that he had buried in the sawdust in the root cellar and took a dried beaver castor for lure.

It was a nice day and he stopped on the dam only long enough to look up the lake. There was a breeze coming down the lake, but not enough to make the water choppy.

Emma picked up a bowl and headed for the wild strawberries as Rascal headed up to the cabin. The berries were plentiful this year and good sized for wild strawberries. As she was picking, turning her fingertips read from the juice, she inhaled deeply to smell the sweet scent of the berries. It wasn't long before her bowl was half full. "These are going to be so good," she said out loud.

A female wolf during the night before had killed a rabbit and before her three pups could start fighting over it, a large male came in and tried to take it. The female growled, warning the bigger male. But he was hungry and was determined to have the rabbit. When he took another step closer the female attacked and this was the fight that was heard. The male took enough of a licking and limped off. The three pups then came in and started fighting for the rabbit. That was the only kill the female made that night and she and her pups were still hungry.

The wolf had smelled the bacon cooking and had wandered to the edge of the clearing and laid down. There had always been too much human activity around the clearing and the buildings, so she had kept away from it. But this morning, she and her pups were hungry and when she saw a woman walking in the clearing towards the edge, well this was an opportunity she just could not pass up. She flattened herself in the bushes watching. The woman was kneeling on the ground and inching closer to the wolf every minute.

The she wolf raised her body off the ground into an attack mode, training her eyes on the woman and seeing only the food, woman, directly in front. Now only about fifty feet away. In one quick leap the she wolf sprang towards Emma.

Emma had no idea she was being watched. Just as the wolf started her dash towards Emma, Rascal walked around the corner of the lodge and saw what was about to happen. With is pack basket on his back he started running toward the wolf. Just then he saw something moving on his left. Something big and black and also running towards Emma.

He stopped and shouted as loud as he could, "Emma! Wolf in front of you!"

She looked up just in time to see Bear run in and tackle the wolf. It wasn't much of a battle. Bear was so much bigger and heavier. It was no contest. Bear pinned the she wolf to the ground with his body. And when he did the wolf started ki-yi-ing. The wolf didn't have a chance. Bear grabbed it by the back of the neck and bit down. The wolf was instantly dead.

Bear kept mauling the wolf and tossing it up in the air like a rag doll and then pick it up in his jaws and shake it until there wasn't much left intact. Then he dropped it, and turned around to look at Emma, who was crying by now. Rascal was standing by her with his arm around her. They just stood there amazed and stunned.

Emma was still crying from the shock of everything then she said in a soft voice, "Thank you, Bear."

He acted happy. He tilted his head slightly to one side and opened his mouth and it sounded like he was saying "aarhh."

Emma took a few steps closer and looking at Bear. He was now looking in her eyes, she said again, "Thank you, Bear." And she raised her arm like she had seen Rascal do and then she tried to make that same noise.

Bear sat on his butt and raised a paw and made the same noise. Then he grabbed the wolf in his jaws and ran off into the trees.

Emma was still shaking from the experience. "That wolf would have killed me, Rascal, if not for Bear."

"I know. We have never seen him in the clearing and now he's here to protect you."

Emma picked up her bowl of strawberries and as they were walking back Rascal stopped and said, "Damn! Em, I saw this whole thing this morning when I was sleeping . Seeing this is what woke me in a start. I had forgotten all about it, until just now when I saw the same images in my head."

"Hum, that's strange."

Anita had heard Rascal when he yelled and she had looked out the window and was horrified when she saw the wolf coming for Emma. And even more so when she saw the bear running towards her also. And then the bear had tackled the wolf and killed it. She was overwhelmed with emotions. She came out running and met them in the clearing. "I saw the whole thing, Emma. Bear saved your life."

"He sure did." Then she turned around to see if Bear might still be there. But he was long gone.

"Let's go in and sit down," Emma said.

Anita had a few minutes earlier set a pot of coffee on to make and when she poured the first cup the liquid looked more like tar. "I'll make a fresh pot."

Both Rascal and Emma sat silently, thinking. Anita wasn't long bringing in another pot of coffee. They all sat down and now even Anita was silently thinking about what she had witnessed. And it was Anita who finally broke the silence. "Have you ever heard stories, Rascal, about a wild animal protecting a human being?"

"Can't say that I have. But then again, I have never heard of a wild animal, a bear, playing with a human being—that had not been domesticated."

Anita said, "Bear looks towards you, Rascal, as a playmate. And Emma—he has found it necessary to protect you. Maybe when that wolf started hunting closer to the lodge, Bear decided to follow it and keep track of what it was doing."

"Maybe you're right, Anita, but there is still the question of why. Why does Bear do it?

"Em, you're being awful quiet. What are you thinking about?"

Her eyes were red and watery. Rascal noticed this and got up and sat down beside her. "What is it, Em?"

"This is the month I wanted to get pregnant. That way the baby would be due in April. But that experience this morning with the wolf has me wondering if having a baby is a good idea or not."

"How do you mean, Em? I thought you were ready."

"I was, Rascal. But I just couldn't stand losing another child. We live in the wilderness with wild animals all around us. There was some security here when there was a village. The noise from the mill, the train coming through more than twice a day and the people kept the animals back. Most of the time. And when the village was here, we never had any problems with wolves. If it hadn't been for Bear this morning I'd more than likely be dead."

"I have an idea," Anita said.

They both looked at her and waited for her to continue. "You get a dog. A companion that'll go for walks with you and protect the lodge. The smell of a dog and the sound of it barking will keep all the animals back, and away from the clearing."

"You know that would be a good idea. What do you think, Em?"

"I would like a dog."

"I'll talk with Jarvis. And about having a baby, Em—well just think on it. If you don't want to, I'll be just as happy."

****

That afternoon Rascal telephoned Jarvis.

"Jarvis isn't here, Rascal," Rita said. "Herschel is a game warden now and the Chief Warden asked Jarvis to come out of retirement for the month of July to help him get started. I'm not sure if they're up your way, Kidney Pond or just where they are. Is there anything I can do to help you?"

Rascal told her about wanting a dog. A pup actually. "What kind, Rascal?"

"We've decided on a black lab. Do you know of anyone around Beech Tree that might have any pups?"

"Yes I do, by-gory. Are you familiar with the Lone Pine Road?"

"Yes, somewhat."

"Two miles out of town on the left is Blanchett's Farm. Nice people. I was talking with Mrs. Blanchett last week and she said they had seven lab puppies."

"That sounds ideal. Rita can you call her for me and tell her we would like a male pup and one of us will be out in the next couple of days."

"Sure, I'll do that, Rascal. If there's a problem I'll call you back. If you don't hear from me you'll know she'll have a pup for you."

"Thank you, Rita, and goodbye."

Chapter 7

Jarvis and Rita took the train to Augusta with Herschel the day he was to be sworn in and to pick up his gear. From the train station they took a taxi to Forest Avenue, directly behind the State House. Commissioner Arnold and Chief Warden John Pelletier—
"Long trip down, Jarvis?" Commissioner Arnold asked.

"It seems to get longer every time I come to the city."

"Commissioner, I'd like to introduce you to my son, Herschel."

"And this is my wife, Rita. Rita, Commissioner Arnold and Chief Warden John Pelletier."

After the introductions and niceties were made, Commissioner Arnold swore Herschel into service and then he had to leave for a meeting with the governor.

"Would you folks like some coffee?" John asked.

"Yes, that would be good."

The chief warden's secretary, Sandra, brought in a tray of coffee cups and then left. "You will have the same area that your father had, Herschel. There is a box out front full of things you'll need. There is ammunition, but for now you'll have to supply your own handgun. Tools of the trade more or less. There are two winter uniforms and two summer, boots, gloves, hats, a winter and summer jacket, a gray wool blanket and a pair of snowshoes, law books, summons and two pair of handcuffs and a flashlight. Have I left anything out, Jarvis?"

"Yes, topographical maps of the area."

"Oh, yes, they are in the box already.

"As of this moment, Herschel, you are a Maine Game Warden. You'll have a new inspector too, Dan Pelletier from up north. No relation. Since he will be new to the area also, Jarvis, this is why I asked and got approval for you to work a month with Herschel to show him the ropes. For the month you will be paid inspector's pay. And Herschel you'll start work at $160.00 a month, plus all the deer and moose meat you confiscate."

After everything was settled, they walked down off the hill to a small café three streets below. Pelletier offered to pay for lunch. While they were waiting for the daily special, beef stew and biscuits, Pelletier said, "Whenever a group of wardens get together there are always stories about you, Jarvis. I never knew a harder working warden in the agency.

"The short time you worked with Marcel Cyr really impressed him. He admitted to me that when he took the badge that he had no idea how much time he would have to spend in the woods alone and away from home. He said he would never be able to develop your abilities, Jarvis."

"Thank you, John. That means a lot coming from you," Jarvis said.

Rita smiled, she too was proud of her husband, in spite of the many long nights she was alone.

****

The three had to spend one night in the city and for supper Jarvis took his family to a fancy restaurant on Front Street, at a window table overlooking the Kennebec River. And of course this close to the ocean, they all had a variety of seafood.

Two days later, Wednesday, Jarvis and Herschel filled their backpacks with a loaf of bread each, fish line and hooks, a small piece of canvas and some canned venison and vegetables and one sharp axe and then they were ready to leave the house. "When will you be back, Jarvis?" Rita asked.

"Not sure really. It may be a few days."

"Where are you going?"

"We'll take the train to Kidney Pond and start from there. Probably swing north and come down to Whiskey Jack and home."

"You take care of your father, Herschel; he isn't as young as he thinks. And you be careful and look out for Herschel."

"Yes, dear."

He kissed her and left. They walked to the train station. "Where to this morning, Mr. Page?" the conductor Tom Whelling asked.

"Kidney Pond. I'm surprised to see you on this spur, Tom."

"I was transferred last month. More passengers here."

"Tom, this is my son, Herschel, the new game warden in this area."

"Congratulations, son, you have a big pair of boots to follow."

"Yeah, I know."

"I haven't been to Kidney Pond since Hitchcock moved their lumbering business there. Both brothers run a pretty tight operation. If either one of them suspects one of the men doing something he shouldn't they'll let you know. They don't want any trouble or problems."

"Tom, what mile is the village at?" Jarvis asked.

"Mile twelve, Jarvis."

"Would you let us off at eleven and a half?"

Tom began laughing and said, "Sure enough. Up to your old tricks I see."

"Why a half mile before the village?"

"I have always found it an advantage to come into the village when the residents have no idea how I got there or how long I have been in the area.

"This sure looks like it would be good trapping. There should be many deer in and around the fresh choppings too. Sometimes someone will get ahold of you about a moose or deer the train hit. I always found it a good idea to see that the village and railroad workers got most of the meat. You know I often times brought meat home with me, but I made sure to share it. People will form a bond with you."

"We're coming up to mile eleven and a half, Jarvis," Tom said.

The train only slowed enough so they could jump off. "Thanks, Tom."

"Have a good hike."

Jarvis checked his compass and then put it back in his pocket. Herschel did also. Herschel had learned long ago, traipsing after his father, you always had a compass and matches with you if you were going to be in the woods.

"I see why Hitchcock moved their operations here. This is some fine looking timber. And with so many large pine trees the soil must be sandy."

"Have you ever seen the village?" Herschel asked.

"No. I was only ever through here a few times on my way to the border. I used to keep an old canoe here. If it is still here there probably isn't much left to it."

For now they circled the mill and village and went to look over the choppings. Lumbering in the hot dry months of summer with a horse is hard work. There were crews cutting fir and spruce high grade close to the mill, and two other crews cutting and clearing twitch trails and roads for winter.

As they walked through the choppings they counted over fifty deer that they had jumped and realized there probably had been another fifty that they didn't see. "This would be a poacher's paradise if not for the Hitchcock brothers."

"Was there ever much poaching at Whiskey Jack, Dad?" Herschel asked.

"There was some, but nothing on a big scale except for the Canadians I arrested for using a set-gun. But with the hotel at Whiskey Jack there was always the sport hunter who would think that being that far back in the woods, they could do about what they pleased."

"What about Rascal? I know you arrested Mrs. Ambrose once for shooting a deer in the summer."

"I could never prove anything against Rascal for poaching

deer or moose. I'm not saying he didn't do it, but I never could prove it. He was lucky and perhaps a better description would be he was clever, a smart poacher. But I never held it against him."

They found a spring and sat down to make lunch. Warmed up canned venison and bread and coffee.

"Dad, you must have come up against some pretty tough poachers, outlaws. Did you ever have to shoot anyone?"

Jarvis didn't answer right away. There was a lot to tell his son and he wanted to be sure he would give him the right idea. "I never fired at anyone. There were a few times when I did draw it to make the arrest rather than get into a fight with three thugs in the woods. I used it to hit a few to bring 'em to their knees and take the fight out of them. You break someone's collarbone and he's done for. I have had to hit a couple of men, but never with a closed fist. If you use the palm of your hand and hit someone on the end of his chin in an upward motion or on the nose you can stop anyone, even if they are much bigger than you. There'll be times in your career when you'll find yourself between a rock and a hard spot. And instead of shooting the thug, if you can't use your mouth to get yourself out of that situation, then you don't deserve to wear the uniform. The first inspector I had, Charles Barren, gave met the same talk and I took it to heart.

"I have always found the best way to approach a poacher is to get as close as you can without being seen. And depending on what they're doing you can either just step out and surprise them or scare the living hell out of 'em. That usually takes the fight out of them."

The fire had burned out and their coffee gone. "Thanks for the advice, Dad."

"It was my pleasure. Okay, son, how do you want to enter the village? Your choice."

"Well, no one knows we came up on the train and no one has seen us out here. I'd say we walk the road to the village as big as billy-be-damned. No one will have any idea how we got here."

Jarvis nodded his head and said, "Let's go." Meaning he wanted his son to take the lead.

As they were walking, Jarvis said, "There's something I want to tell you. It won't be long before people in your area will soon believe you are living out here in the wilderness. Any hardcore poacher I ever caught was timid about being out alone, let alone sleeping out here by himself. They'll know you do and that you are not afraid of the wilderness, and even the worst of the thugs will respect you for that and be just a little intimidated by you. You'll need to learn to use that to your advantage."

They had a half mile to walk to the village and it wasn't what Jarvis had been expecting. The housing was like a government barracks, all ground level, and off to the left of the clearing the mill, and the log yard was set up to the right. There was a spur set of tracks that ran by the end of the mill; when the sawn lumbar came out, the crews could load directly onto the freight cars. A good improvement. There was a hotel and cafeteria and train station—terminal—between the mill yard and housing and of course set next to the tracks; the Hitchcock brothers both had an office here also.

The Douglas's operated the hotel and cafeteria and Mr. Winston was station master. It was like a remodeled version of Whiskey Jack.

"Let's get us a room tonight instead of sleeping on the ground."

They put their gear in their rooms and then they walked over to the offices. "Hello, Jarvis, did you come out of retirement or something?"

"Or something. This is my son, Herschel—Rudy Hitchcock, Herschel is the new warden here. He took Marcel Cyr's vacancy. The agency is paying me to work with him for a month."

"You'll be welcomed around here anytime, Herschel," Rudy said. "Where are you living and what is your telephone number?"

"I'm living with my folks for now and the number is Beech Tree 433."

"Thank you. How about a tour through the mill. We have things set up different than Whiskey Jack." As they walked by Earl's office, Rudy looked in, "Hum, he must be out laying this winter's harvest area.

"You're a famous man now, Jarvis. Personal body guard for President Kevin Cutlidge and guide. I hope this merge with the two countries will happen. It would make our business so much easier."

"I think that is their intention, Rudy," Jarvis said.

"I hear Rascal went to Washington and had his leg operated on. How is he?" Rudy asked.

"I stayed at the lodge with Anita while they were away. He still limped a little, but he said that will disappear in time," Herschel said.

"So you took care of the buildings while he was gone?"

"Yes."

"Then I owe you some money."

"No sir, Rascal paid me."

"How is their business, Jarvis?"

"Very good, and getting better each year."

They entered the mill then. "We did away with the circular saw and replaced it with a band saw. It is so much faster, smoother and less maintenance. That old mill at Whiskey Jack, well, sometime we'll have to dismantle it and sell it for salvage."

"This is quite an improvement over the old mill."

"This is a nice setup here. We have ten children and one of the wives is a teacher, and we have a first aid room, and all meals are eaten in the cafeteria. The meals are served in different intervals. My wife Althea now does Emma's job with one of the wives as an assistant, and Earl's wife, Martha, runs the cafeteria and there are three cooks now with a helper. The Douglas's run the hotel and have another general store."

"How long will you be here, Rudy?"

"Earl estimates that we have twenty years of harvesting hi-grade timber and then what was left will be ready to harvest again. We're here at least thirty years.

"We also have a bigger electrical generator so each unit can have more than one light. We tried to make this a more modern living and working village. Our intention is to keep people happy. That way we get good work from them.

"Feel free to look around; I must get back to work," Rudy shook hands with them both. "Hope to see you around here often, Herschel."

"Thank you."

At the supper table Jeters recognized Jarvis and sat down across form him. "Hello, Jarvis. What brings you to Kidney Pond?"

"This is my son, Herschel—this is Jeters. Herschel is the new game warden here and I'm working a month with him to show him around."

"What happened to Marcel?"

"He wasn't really cut out for the wilderness."

Jarvis recognized a few other faces, but there were many new people there.

****

The next morning after breakfast Jarvis and Herschel talked with Rudy about buying some food to take with them.

"Sure thing, anything you need; help yourself and you don't need to pay for it."

"Thank you, Rudy."

They went into the kitchen and asked, "Martha, Rudy said we could pick up some food here to take with us."

"Sure thing. What would you like?"

"Oh, five pounds of bacon, oh maybe two cans of mixed vegetables, two loaves of bread, and two cans of peaches."

"Is that all?"

"I think it'll have to be."

They filled their packs and waited on the platform for the morning train to Saint Renee.

"Well, it should be here—" He was interrupted by the train whistle. "Yep, she's coming in now."

"Mr. Winston, this is my son, Herschel; he is the new game warden in the area."

"Pleased to meet you. Sometime before cold weather, S&A would like you to remove some nuisance beaver at mile fourteen."

"Sure thing, Mr. Winston."

They boarded the train and Tom said, "Good morning, Jarvis and Herschel. Where would you like to get off this morning? Let me guess—a half mile before the border, right?"

"Yes, Tom, please. I thought you were on the other line, Tom."

"I have to fill in over here some," Tom answered.

"We'll see."

"How many miles to the border, Tom?"

"Let's see, this here is mile eleven and the border is nineteen. That'll be a long walk if you miss the train."

The engine on this spur was bigger than the Whiskey Jack spur, and it was pulling more freight cars and full tanker cars. It also hooked on to two freight cars at Kidney Pond with sawn lumber.

The terrain wasn't that much different than on the other spur line. "I doubt if people from the village ever come up here to hunt or fish."

"Jarvis, we are approaching the half mile marker."

"Thank you Tom." They shouldered their packs and were ready to jump off.

"Tell the engineer thank you, Tom."

"I'll do that."

After the train was back up to speed and they were still standing in the right of way, Herschel asked, "Why didn't we get off at the border? Shouldn't I get to know him?"

"Yes, but not until you have looked around his buildings and know a little about him. It took me two years before I trusted Alfons Dubois at the Lac St. Jean crossing and even then I was always cautious around him.

"We'll go up close to the buildings at the crossing, but stay back enough so we won't be seen. Then we'll head north along the border."

It was a warm day and they both were soon sweating. They stayed about two hundred feet back from the custom buildings and just as they were going to break off they found a trail leading away from the buildings. Jarvis pointed, indicating for Herschel to take the lead. They followed that trail for another two hundred feet and found an open dumping pit and laying on top of the refuse were deer remains; hide and bones. The head had already been carried off and some of the bones also.

"What do you think, son?"

"Well, it was a summer kill. The hair is too red for fall or winter. The hide doesn't appear to have a bullet hole. Could have been shot in the head though. There are no maggots on the hide yet, so this is a fairly recent kill."

"That's pretty good so far, but is it legal or illegal?"

"I suppose the train could have hit it and Mr. Rejean only salvaged the meat."

"Okay that's pretty good, but what are you going to do about it?"

"I'm not sure, Dad. I'd hate to go in and accuse an innocent man, arrest him and lose the case in court."

"You're beginning to think like a warden. What does your gut tell you?"

"That Mr. Rejean shot this not too long ago. But damn, it there isn't enough evidence to prove it—that is unless we could find the head and retrieve the bullet."

"Okay, let's look for the head. Chances are a bear has carried it off, but let's look."

They spent two hours circling and circling the dump pit and searching way behind it and didn't find a thing.

"Let's get out of here, Dad."

"I was wondering how much longer you were going to wait before you gave up."

They circled to the north and beyond sight of the custom buildings and started hiking along the cleared border. The afternoon westerly sun was baking them, so they pulled back into the trees for shade.

About a mile north of the custom building they found a bubbling spring and decided to make camp. "How far is it, Dad, to Lac St. Jean custom crossing?"

"From this one, about twenty miles. We should be able to do it in two days. That is unless we find something interesting."

They warmed up a jar of venison, one can of vegetables and bread. For dessert they split a can of peaches and washed it down with coffee.

"I don't think it'll rain tonight but there might be some dew. We probably should put up the canvas."

They sat up tending the fire long into the night talking. Herschel had decided he had always taken his father's abilities for granted. He was now beginning to understand there was much more to the man than what one saw on the outside.

"I would work the border for illegal Canadian hunters in the summer, but once their hunting season began I stayed away. The deer and moose, which are their prime targets, criss-cross back and forth across the border and no one knows if it is a Canadian or a Maine animal. But during the summer, well that's a good illegal hunting case in closed season.

"Once this merger between the two countries becomes final there won't be any across border hunting. But you'll surely be busy with summer hunters.

"The sooner you can establish yourself here, son, the fewer problems you'll have."

Herschel was wishing he had his father's knowledge of

being a game warden.

Eventually they became tired of talking and settled back on their wool blanket and slept. Right at daylight a wolf howled and he was not that far away. Herschel sat up in a start, while Jarvis, although he was awake lay on his back.

Herschel let his father rest while he started a fire and coffee. "You going to get up?"

Breakfast was fried strips of thick bacon, warmed up bread and coffee. "This sure is good bacon. It'll stick to your ribs. We have about ten miles to hike today."

They ate their fill of bacon and bread, put the fire out and packed up. They stayed out in the cleared swath where it was easier walking. Jarvis was looking at this country as a trapper would. He doubted if anyone had ever trapped here. "You know, son, I never spent too much time working the border for illegal trapping. I always had enough to do during the deer season. That might be something to think about if we find any well used trails."

When they came upon any muddy areas they would always stop and look at tracks. No deer or moose, but every mud flat had big cat tracks in it. They also saw wolverine and wolf tracks. "I'd like to take the time myself to come up here and trap," Jarvis said.

By mid-morning they came to a big beaver flowage and the border line went right through the center of it. They crossed down below the dam and continued on.

The sun was high in the sky when they came to a nice cold water brook. "Dad, let's stop here for a while and catch some trout for lunch. You fish and I'll start a fire."

Jarvis found several grubs in a rotten piece of maple wood and he put one on a hook and dropped it in a pool. He wasn't long catching one; it was difficult hand lining the trout without a fish pole, but he'd make do.

In ten minutes he had four nice trout and decided it was enough for lunch. They put the fish on a stick and held it over the fire and they soon had a delicious lunch of brook trout. Two each was all either one of them wanted.

"I'd like a camp in here somewhere. I really like this country," Herschel said. Jarvis smiled. He was happy to see his son taking so well to the wilderness.

They continued on and soon came to a heath and they could see two moose at the end and several deer at the other, probably does and lambs. As they continued on, Herschel couldn't help but think of his dad. Not once had he tired and needed to rest. He was sixty eight years old, but you would never know it. He decided that probably spending most of his life in the wilderness had kept him fit and healthy. He was seeing his dad differently now.

When they stopped for the day, Jarvis said, "We're getting close to the custom station. I figure we'll be there by mid-afternoon or sooner."

As they were eating more bacon and bread for breakfast the next morning, there was a faint small caliber shot a little ways north of them.

"That wasn't big enough for a deer or moose," Herschel said.

"No, you're right. It sounded like a .22 caliber to me."

"What do you think, Dad?"

"If he's a hunter he must be a sharp shooter to bring down a deer or moose with one .22 caliber shot. My guess would be a trapper."

They picked up as quick as they could and then started north at a slow pace. Then there was another shot but not from the same direction. "That one was a little further east. It's definitely a trapper and he is on his trap line. We'd better find his trail crossing the border."

They were still going slow, a few steps at a time and stopping to listen. They eventually came to the trail. It had been used so often in the past they had worn the trail below ground level and had trimmed the branches along the way. A blind man could have followed it. They checked the trail in both directions looking for man tracks while staying off the trail themselves. There was another shot and it was even further east. "We need to find tracks where they are coming back," Jarvis said.

Herschel went east and Jarvis west and across the border into Canada. The ground was too dry here and he returned. Herschel had come back also.

"I found to sets of returning tracks just up ahead," Herschel said.

"Okay, we need to find a good place to wait and then to jump 'em."

They had only gone a little beyond where Herschel had stopped and they found the first cubby set and a pack basket containing two fisher and a martin. Herschel saw where the ground had been disturbed behind the set and uncovered a big male lynx. "Dad look at this."

"Okay we have them solid now. They would not have left the pack basket and lynx here if they were not coming back. We need to find a good spot to wait where we can see them coming."

"Dad," and Herschel pointed up hill where years ago a tree had blown over and the rotted roots had left a depression in the ground. "Dad, you wait here and I'll go back on the trail so if they try to run."

"Good plan, son. Remember, trappers are more clever and harder to catch than a hunter. The trapper has to always outsmart his prey.

"When they go by me I'll step out and come in behind them. By then they both should have their pack baskets on."

Jarvis cleared some bushes out of the way and broke off a small fir tree and stuck it in the ground to lie behind and conceal his body and he took his own pack off and lay down. 'Oh boy, is this fun.'

Herschel was just as excited and he found a thick clump of fir and spruce trees to hide behind. Now all they had to do was wait, and he took his pack off.

There was another shot so far away this time they could just barely hear it. Jarvis wasn't concerned about the wait. He knew they would be back through. Herschel was new and he was becoming impatient.

The sun had risen overhead and about an hour later Jarvis could hear them coming. They were not even trying to be quiet. Probably figuring that so far removed in the wilderness that they would never be caught. And besides they both had heard that Jarvis Page had retired.

One of them uncovered the lynx and put it across his shoulders and pack basket. The other one shouldered the pack basket with the two fisher and martin. Both men were big, about six feet and weighing probably 220 or there about. Neither one had shaved in a week.

When they moved past Jarvis he stepped in behind them without making a sound and he followed about twenty feet back. He saw Herschel step out into the trail and the two trappers froze. They had not yet seen Jarvis and realizing this was just a young warden they both thought they could easily overpower him. And the one in front, Micheil Dufour, charged at Herschel. Herschel turned his body sideways and brought the palm of his hand up and under Micheil's chin. He heard the jaw break and Micheil fell to the ground screaming.

Now his friend Maurice charged at Herschel, he was a little bigger than Micheil. He saw what had happened to his friend and he was ready to block the thrust but Herschel took one step to the side and tripped him and he went sprawling on the ground and mad as all get out. He came to his feet and charged Herschel again. This time he hit him with the palm of his hand again in his chest sending him backwards. Maurice was as mad as hell now. Thinking someone so much smaller was licking him.

Herschel had had enough of this guy and when he charged again Herschel drew his revolver and brought it down hard on the bridge of Maurice's nose and it broke and blood was spurting all over himself. But he wasn't through yet. He reached out and grabbed Herschel and this time he brought his gun down on his collarbone. Maurice went down on his knees screaming.

Micheil wasn't done yet either. When he recovered and stood Jarvis started to step in, but he held back. This was important for Herschel to learn that he can take care of himself against someone who was much bigger than he was. So he waited to see what Herschel would do now. He was actually enjoying this.

Micheil came up behind Herschel and started to grab him in a bear hug. But Herschel sensing something wasn't right, turned in time to see Micheil coming at him. He hit him across the bridge of his nose with his gun. Micheil screamed some more and went down on his knees.

They both gave up and stayed down. Jarvis came walking up laughing. "Good job, son. I'm proud of you."

"Why didn't you help, Dad?"

"I wanted to see how you would handle the two. You needed to see for yourself also. Besides you didn't look like you needed any help.

"We'd better handcuff 'em now. In front, son."

Micheil looked at Jarvis and said, "You *Garde-chasse* Page?"

Jarvis understood he had asked if he was Game Warden Page. Jarvis shook his head no and pointed to Herschel and said, *"Garde-chasse* Herschel Page." Then he patted his chest and said, *"Fils"* (son).

Micheil looked disgusted and shook his head back and forth.

"Herschel, while I watch them you'd better search them. They each probably have a .22 caliber revolver and a knife."

Herschel removed a revolver from each of them, bullets and knives. He would not have thought of that if his father had not said something. That he would never let happen again.

They helped them right their packs and Jarvis led off. "This is going to be a longer trip than I had thought."

They were closer to the railroad than they had thought. They heard the half mile approach signal as the train approached customs from Whiskey Jack.

"They're late this morning. I wonder why?" Jarvis said.

They walked out to the tracks and crossed them to the custom house. "Hello, Alfons. Would it be alright if we wait here for the southbound?"

"Sure, only I ain't got enough food to feed you all."

"Well, we might be able to help you there. We have a little food left." He took Micheil's and Maurice's packs off.

Alfons looked at them and said, "Like old times, huh Jarvis?" And he laughed.

Herschel said, "Well boys, let's see what you have trapped out of season. In this pack you have two fisher cats and a pine martin, one lynx. Let's see what's in this other pack. A bobcat and two more martin. Not bad for one tend." He knew or guessed they couldn't understand what he had said, but he said it out loud for effect.

"Dad, I'm going to take some of these out back and skin 'em, will you watch these two?"

"Sure."

The fisher cats were more difficult to skin than the others. The skins peeled from the other pieces like a banana. When he had finished Alfons had lunch ready.

"Alfons, would you have a straw?"

"What for?"

"One of these gentleman has a broken jaw and probably can't chew too well."

"No straw, but I have a piece of small copper tubing, will that do?"

"Pour some of that broth in a cup and let's see."

He handed Micheil the cup of broth with a short piece of copper tubing. Micheil seemed to understand.

"You folks were kinda hard on these two, weren't ya?" Alfons asked.

Herschel answered, "They brought it on themselves when they attacked me."

"These two in particular finally got their comeuppance. They have been doing this sorta trapping for a long time now. Even before you got done, Jarvis."

"Why didn't you ever say something, Alfons?"

"And have them come after me for squealing? No siree. Sorry, Jarvis, but I'm out here all by my lonesome and too close to where these yahoos live. But I'm glad you caught 'em good."

"Herschel, write down your phone number and give it to Alfons. You have a telephone here, Alfons, use it."

"Yes sir."

Just as they were finishing their lunch they heard the half mile signal. "Boy, we timed that just right. Put out your red flag, Alfons, I hate to have to walk these two all the way to Beech Tree."

"Yes sir, right now."

The train stopped and they loaded their prisoners on board and Tom waved the engineer he was clear to leave.

Tom started laughing when he saw Micheil and Maurice, and said, "Up to your usual antics I see, Jarvis."

"Oh not me, Tom. My son was defending himself."

Tom began laughing again. "Son like father. He's a chip off the old block."

It seemed like a quick trip to Whiskey Jack.

****

At noon on July 4th the telephone rang at Whiskey Jack Lodge and while Emma and Anita were busy in the kitchen Rascal had to answer it, "Hello, Whiskey Jack Lodge."

"Rascal this is Greg Oliver in Beech Tree. I need you to stop the train there. There are emergency repairs at mile eight and a half and it is expected the track crew will have the tracks torn up for a day and a half. I couldn't catch the train before it left Lac St. Jean."

"Sure, Greg. I'll stop it."

"Thank you. I don't know how many passengers there will be, but I'm assuming you can put them up plus the train crew. Keep track of expenses and give the conductor, Tom Whelling, the bill. And thanks again, Rascal."

Rascal sat out on the platform waiting and when he heard the half mile whistle he walked off the platform and with the red flag waving over his head he stood in the middle of the tracks. The train stopped five feet away. And he walked up to speak with Fred Darling, the engineer.

"What's up, Rascal?"

"The station master called and asked me to stop you here. There is an emergency repair at mile eight and a half. I'm to put everyone up here until it is fixed."

"Okay, let me pull ahead so passengers can get off."

When the train had pulled ahead three passengers stepped off and then Jarvis, Herschel and their two banged up prisoners. Rascal looked at Jarvis and grinned and said, "Just like old times, huh, Jarvis."

"I didn't touch'em. They attacked Herschel."

"You'd better take them inside, they both need bandaging. You're going to be here for a while until the tracks are repaired between here and Beech Tree."

Emma showed the three passengers inside and upstairs to rooms. Tom Whelling sat in the cafeteria area and the engineer Fred Darling and the brakeman Ralph Smith were still securing the train. Mr. Smith also served as fireman when needed.

Just then a three month old back lab puppy came out to greet everyone. Herschel kneeled down to pat the pup. "Where and when did you get him?" Herschel asked.

"Actually he arrived by train this morning. I talked with your mother a few days ago and she said she knew where we could get one and she shipped him up this morning. Be sure and thank her for us, would you?" Rascal said.

"Sure thing."

"What's his name?" Jarvis asked.

"All three of us came up with the same name, Whiskey Jack."

"That's certainly fitting."

Emma washed the blood off of their faces and then Rascal applied a cloth bandage around Micheil's chin and head to hold the jaw in place and then he fixed him a sling to immobilize the broken collarbone. There was nothing he could do for their noses. He also put Maurice's arm in a sling and since they had been so inclined to fight, Jarvis handcuffed their good arm to their belts.

"There, that should take care of 'em until we can get 'em to a hospital," Jarvis said.

"What did you get them for, Jarvis?" Rascal asked.

"They were trapping south of the custom check point, way to the east of the border. And according to the custom officer these two have been doing this for years. They certainly had a well-used trail. Even a blind man could have followed it."

"How'd you get up there we didn't see you go through here? Or is that a secret like the Jarvis Trail?"

"We started at the Kidney Pond village, stayed there one night and took the train to the crossing and hiked up the border."

"That's quite a ways isn't it? How long were you?"

"Twenty miles and we had to stay out for two nights."

Jarvis and Herschel told them all about the adventure. "You sound like you really enjoyed yourself, Herschel," Emma said.

"I did, Emma. I never had so much fun in all my life. I learned a lot about my dad, too," and he looked at Jarvis and smiled.

Tom Whelling went back outside to help Fred and Ralph put the train to bed. The brakes had to be hand set and engine wheels blocked and reduce the fire in the boiler to only a few coals.

Emma said, "While the train crew is outside I think we

all should go into the kitchen. We have a story to tell you." Jarvis stood in the doorway so he could watch the prisoners.

"This has to be about Bear. He is the only reason I can think of why you three would be this secretive." Herschel looked at everyone. They all knew something he didn't and he was about to be taken into their confidence.

All three told them about Bear saving Emma from the wolf. Each one had a little bit to tell. And of course they had to tell Herschel about Bear. "You see, son, this cannot leave this room. I have never said anything about Bear to even your mother. If people found out about him they would want to come up and see this bear who talks, laughs, plays and saved Emma's life. I'm sure you can understand," Jarvis said.

"Yes I do. I won't say a word."

They moved back into the cafeteria and Jarvis walked over to look at the new picture hanging above the plaques. "Wow, holy gee! You two surely have friends in high places." Herschel walked over to look also and he began to wonder just who in heck Rascal and Emma were.

"That was the last night we were in D.C." Emma said.

"Rascal," Jarvis asked, "Who's this beautiful woman beside you?"

Emma blushed a deep pink color and the others laughed.

"Rascal, could I use your telephone? I'd like to call Rita."

"Certainly, help yourself."

Anita came in with a pot of coffee and cups and the train crew was through securing the train.

"Rascal," the engineer asked, "alright if I telephone the station?"

"Go right ahead."

The three passengers had come downstairs also and joined everyone. They were a French family, visiting family in Beech Tree. They immediately noticed Prime Minister William Kingsley and asked about him. "That picture was taken at the White House," Emma said anticipating their question.

And then they read the plaques and asked why. Emma told them all about their visit the year before and what had been discussed. The brother asked, "You think this is good? Canada and the United States as one country?"

"Oh yes, there will be many benefits for everyone and we will become stronger in the eyes of the world," Emma said.

The youngest sister nodded her head and said, "Maybe this would be a good thing to do."

Anita found a straw so Micheil could sip coffee without having to open his mouth. Both of their faces had swollen badly and they had to breathe through their mouth. They were not happy.

The train crew enjoyed listening to the conversations. The passengers also, but they seldom joined in.

Herschel said, "Rascal, your leg must be all healed now, I noticed you walk without limping."

"I feel like I did before I went overseas."

Jarvis told Rascal about the country he and his son had seen and the trapping possibilities. "Maybe someday, Rascal, you and I should plan a trip up and build us a little trapper's camp."

"I would like to, but I'd have to find someone to take my place here."

"It wouldn't surprise me none that in a month up there I could make more than all year in the fur business."

"Maybe you should talk Rita into going up with you."

"I bet she would go, Dad."

He chuckled and said, "I'll wait until sometime when she is in a good mood."

Anita had been baking beans served with smoked trout and biscuits. Emma also made a fish broth for Micheil. In a way she felt sorry for Micheil and Maurice. "They must be in pain all the time, Anita."

"Maybe, but they brought it on themselves when they attacked Herschel."

Micheil liked the fish broth and twice held out his bowl for more. Even though Maurice's jaw wasn't broken the swelling made it painful to chew.

"How much would you say the fur is worth that you confiscated, Jarvis?" Rascal asked.

"Oh, probably between four and five hundred dollars."

"If they trap all summer and fall too, they must have made a good living from it," Rascal said.

"I wish I could speak French so I could ask them some questions."

"Excuse me for interrupting sir, but my sister, brother and I speak French. I could translate for you," the older sister said.

"What is your name, ma'am?"

"Perline, Sir."

"Ask them where they live."

She did and replied, "He said they are from Saint Bellarmin and their wives are sisters and they have a summer cabin on Echo Lake, between Saint Bellarmin and the border. They also have a small trapper's cabin close to the border."

Maurice was saying something now and Perline translated. "He wants to know if you are the same garde-chasse who caught St. Pierre and Paquette?"

"Yes."

There was a long dialogue and then Perline said, "They had heard you had retired and were surprised to see an old man out there." Jarvis wasn't insulted. In fact he laughed heartily. "You explain to them that my son Herschel has the job now."

"He says your son fights like stories he had heard about his father."

There was more long dialogue and Perline said, "He wants to know why Prime Minister Kingsley was in that picture with the people who own this lodge and why the plaques?"

"Tell him the prime minister and the president met here a year ago to discuss the possibilities of our two countries becoming one."

"He says here, the prime minister came in?"

"Yes."

"He said his head is hurting too much to talk anymore."

"Tell him thank you." This seemed to surprise Micheil.

"Perline, are you doing anything Monday morning about 9 a.m.?"

"No, why?"

"Would you come to the courthouse and translate for these two so they'll understand what is going on?"

"Certainly, I'd be glad to."

This conversation seemed to relax Micheil some. He was not quite so nervous now.

Shortly after eating, the train crew had been up for fifteen hours and they all went to bed. The others stayed up for a while longer talking. Then the three passengers said goodnight. "Perline," Rascal said. "Would you give these two a message for me? Tell them they'll be sleeping right here on the two couches and one of us will be on guard all night. And tell 'em my wife is an excellent shot also."

She translated the message and said, "Maurice said they would not cause you any problem. They have had enough trouble."

"Thank you."

"Now that everyone has retired, except these two who don't understand English, tell us more about Bear killing a wolf," Jarvis said.

They started right from the beginning telling them about the spotted deer remains and the nightly howling and fighting and coming close to the lodge "When I went out to pick strawberries I had no idea any wolves were around and I didn't see Bear either," Emma said.

"It's all so strange," Jarvis said.

"What is?"

"I mean a four hundred pound bear looks at you, Rascal, as a playmate, and he protects Emma from being dinner for that wolf."

"How old do bear live?" Emma asked.

"Twenty-five, thirty years, if they're lucky."

"How old would you say Bear is?"

"Six maybe."

They were all quiet for a while then, and Herschel said, "You know, Dad, we still have to go back and pick up their traps."

"I was wondering when you'd say something. We'll be or might be home for the weekend and Tuesday morning northbound. There's more I want to show you on the border."

The puppy, Whiskey Jack, lay quietly on the rug in front of the fireplace.

****

At noon the next day as they all were eating lunch, the station master called and told Engineer Fred Darling that he could leave anytime.

"The tracks are opened and we'll be leaving as soon as we can get up a head of steam. It'll take about fifteen minutes, so finish your lunch and Ralph and I will start stoking the old girl."

By now Micheil and Maurice were pretty meek. They knew a jail cell awaited them at the end of the line. Plus they were hurting. "Rascal, would you stretch these for us? We'll be back this way probably late next week and we can pick 'em up then."

"Sure."

Emma gave a bill to Tom Whelling for food and lodging for ten people, for $75.00. It probably should have been more, but the S&A has used them pretty good in the past.

Jarvis and Herschel had to take their prisoners to the hospital first before leaving them at the jail.

"Hum," Doctor Haywood said, "seems to me that other game warden brought one of his prisoners in all bandaged up just like this one. I don't know who does it for you, Jarvis, but he's a damn good man."

The nose he reset and said, "Those will be sore for about a week. No need putting anything on them."

The collarbones were different. He had to make a cast around the shoulder and arm to immobilize it until the bone healed. "Somehow, Jarvis, you have to get it through to these two that those casts have to stay on for a month."

"I'll see to it, Doctor, and thanks."

It was only a short walk to the county jail and Sheriff Burlock was there. "They'll have to be held over the weekend, Sheriff. Herschel will pick them up Monday morning for court."

Herschel wrote out their names for Sheriff Burlock and what offense they were being charged with. "Micheil has a broken jaw and can only sip soup broth through a straw. No solid food for him.

****

Rita met them at the porch door, "Well did you boys have fun?"

Herschel started smiling and then Rita said, "Alright, you two, what did you get into?"

Herschel was two hours telling his mother all about the trip. "And we have to go back Tuesday as well to pick up the traps they left."

As they were eating a late supper, Herschel asked, "Dad, I have to ask you why you didn't step in and give me a hand with those two?"

"Oh, I wanted to, but you needed to know you could handle yourself in a rough situation. You did an excellent job too. I kinda felt sorry for Micheil and Maurice though. They never had a chance. You made me proud, son."

"Thanks, Dad."

"Now, tomorrow you have to write up a report for Chief Warden John Pelletier, and add that next week after court you have to go back after the traps and do some more exploring. This arrest will look good in your personnel file, when you come up for review."

The next day while Jarvis was working in the hide shop,

Herschel had a chance to talk with his mother.

"Mom, I never knew Dad while he was a game warden. I really didn't know anything about him. Where he went, what he did, nothing. Mom, everywhere we went everybody knew Jarvis Page and everyone spoke well of him. And seeing him in the woods, Mom, what he knows and how he handles himself—I wasn't just a tag along son or boy. He was teaching me what he knew. He's a legend, Mom, and I'm so proud of him."

Rita hugged her son and said, "Maybe you should tell him, son."

"I did, Mom. I wanted a chance to talk with you alone about Dad."

Monday morning Jarvis went straight to the courthouse and Herschel went after Micheil and Maurice and escorted them over. He had them sit in the front row. They both were looking pretty meek this morning. After all, spending a weekend in jail would make anyone subdued.

Perline and Jarvis were already there sitting in front opposite the aisle from Micheil and Maurice. Herschel joined them. "Good morning, ma'am. I surely appreciate you doing this."

Judge Hulcurt came in before she could reply and everyone stood and waited to sit until Hulcurt was seated. Hulcurt looked at the two bandaged prisoners and then at Jarvis and smiled. He took care of the minor cases first and then he turned his attention to Micheil Dufour and Maurice Cordon. "You will rise."

Jarvis stood up and said, "Your Honor, neither Dufour nor Cordon speak or understand English, and Perline Bowman has offered to translate."

"You came prepared. Then, you always did. I thought you were retired?"

Perline translated all this.

"I did, Your Honor."

"Well—this is obviously some of your handiwork. No one else ever brings prisoners to my court in casts and bandages."

Hulcurt had to laugh.

When Perline translated this Maurice and Micheil turned to look at Jarvis.

"Your Honor, I am retired. This is my son, Herschel, and I was asked by Chief Warden Pelletier if I would come out of retirement for a month and work with him. There is a new young inspector in the area that has no knowledge of this part of the state. That is why I am back to work for this month."

"So, Jarvis, what did these two do to deserve your handiwork?"

"Your Honor, I did not do this. I never laid a hand on them. Herschel, stand, you take it from here."

"You did this to those two young men? You must have had a good reason."

"Yes, Your Honor, I did. They both attacked me."

"But they are much bigger than you." Right then Hulcurt burst out laughing and said, "Son, like father," and he laughed some more.

"Did you hit them with a closed fist?"

"No, Your Honor."

"Let me see the back of your hands."

Herschel held them both up for Hulcurt to see. "No skun or bruised knuckles, so you must be telling the truth. Okay, Mr. Page, tell me what happened."

Herschel thought Hulcurt was speaking to his father when Hulcurt said Mr. Page.

"I didn't say sit down, Mr. Page. I want to hear the story"

"Where are the revolvers now?"

"I still have them, and the bullets and knives," Herschel said.

"What about the traps that they had reset," Hulcurt asked.

"We are going back tomorrow and pull everything and do some more exploring."

"What had they caught?"

"They had a lynx, bobcat, two fisher cats and four pine

martins. And Your Honor, it is very obvious that these two have been doing this for a few years, not just this one time."

"Where do they live?"

"Saint Bellarmin, Quebec. A little west of the border."

"And I understand they have been in jail since Friday, is that correct?"

"Yes, Your Honor."

"Well, I'll sentence them to three days in jail and time served. Jarvis, would you think $200.00 each would be enough for a fine for illegal trapping? I realized that is more than I would usually fine anyone but they did attack a game warden, which I doubt if they will ever do that again."

"I think that would be appropriate, Your Honor."

Micheil and Maurice had a lengthy dialogue with Perline. "Your Honor," she said, "they both understand but neither one of them have any money with them."

"You explain to them that they will remain in jail until the fine is paid. The sheriff or his deputy will help them make arrangements to have the money sent to Sheriff Burlock. When he has the money, then and only then will he release them."

She explained this and although they knew they would have to spend a few more days in jail while they waited for the money, there was nothing they could do about it. "They both understand, Your Honor."

"Okay, and thank you, Ms. Bowman, for your help. Court dismissed."

"Son, I'll take these two back to jail with the court's paperwork. Why don't you take Ms. Perline out to lunch, as a way to say thank you."

Perline was two or three years older than Herschel and country cute. "Maybe she could teach you some French. I never could get the hang of it, but it certainly would be good to know, especially when the two countries become one."

"Thanks, Dad." Herschel extended his arm to Perline and said, "Ms. Bowman, shall we?"

"We shall," and she linked her arm in with his.

Herschel learned that Perline, her younger sister Irene, and older brother Jacques were visiting an aunt, their mother's sister, in Beech Tree. "What brought them to Beech Tree?"

"My aunt's husband, Cameron Levesque, works for the S&A Railroad and he transferred to Beech Tree from Lac St. Jean two years ago."

"What does Cameron do for work?"

"He is an engineer. He switches rail cars around in the yard. We have a free pass because of him."

"How long will you be staying in Beech Tree?"

"Only three more days now."

"What does your father do for work?"

"He works in the woods in Lac St. Jean. His name is Armand and my mother is Priscilla."

"If I'm correct you and your father will be leaving for the border again tomorrow morning. How long will you be gone?"

"Probably for the rest of the week. I sure would like to see you again, Perline."

She gave him her address and telephone number. "We actually live in a small village beside the tracks before you get to Lac St. Jean, Chemin Station. By train from the customs it's only about a ten minute ride."

Herschel walked her back to her aunt's house and she insisted he come in and meet everyone.

He hated to leave but he said, "I really must be leaving now. We need to get ready for tomorrow."

"There's something I haven't told you about Micheil and Maurice. I only know about them. Their reputation. They are not good people, Herschel, and you need to be careful around them. There are many stories about them across the border. The police and garde-chasse are afraid of them."

"I will, I promise. Anytime you come to visit your aunt I'd like to see you."

Chapter 8

"Where to this morning, gentlemen?" Tom asked.
"We'll get off a half mile before customs."
"Going for another hike, I see."
On the way up to the border, Herschel asked, "I always assumed there would be a district attorney or someone to prosecute cases."
"They do the more serious crimes, but we prosecute our own cases most of the time. It has always worked quite well. I've only had a district attorney take over a case when someone dies from a hunting accident."
"So we are prosecutors as well as game wardens?"
"Yes."
"I liked Perline Bowman. I'd like to see her again."
"She seemed real nice."
The train only slowed enough at Whiskey Jack to throw the days newspaper onto the platform.
Jarvis pointed out Ledge Swamp to Herschel. "Rascal and Emma won't let any of their hunters hunt around here. Rascal seems to think this is Bear's territory. He won't even trap until beaver season and when Bear should be hibernating."
"What do you suppose ever got into Bear to look at Rascal as a playmate? I have never heard of anything so strange."
"Neither have I and that's why we must keep him a secret."
The engineer blew the half mile whistle and slowed just enough for them to jump off. They worked their way through the woods and came out to the cleared border below customs.

Without trailing along the prisoners, they soon found the well-used trappers trail. At the first set was another fisher cat and he was alive.

"Put your gloves on son," and Jarvis did also. "When I have a good hold on him you take the trap off and be quick about it."

This was a big male fisher and he was angry. Jarvis lured him closer to the end of the chain securing the trap and he waited until the fisher had his mouth wide open and screaming. Real quick like Jarvis reached for the fisher and grabbed his lower jaw to control his head. Then he wrapped his other arm around him and lay down on the fisher using his weight to pin the fisher to the ground. But that fisher was only caught during the previous night and he still had plenty of strength and energy. The fisher in his struggles had rolled Jarvis onto his back and growling that sent shivers up Herschel's back.

Finally after minutes of struggling Herschel was able to release the trap. "Okay, Dad, the trap is off." He was still on his back holding the fisher on his chest. "Roll me over, son, so I can let go of him."

Herschel did and the fisher was pointed in the right direction so Jarvis let go. The fisher only ran about ten feet and stopped and turned to look back. He hunched his back and began growling. By now Jarvis was on his feet and he spread his arms out wide and hollered at the fisher "Get!" and charged at him. The fisher turned and ran off, never looking back.

Herschel fell to the ground, he was laughing so hard. "You're crazy, Dad!" and then they both laughed some more.

"Just how many times have you done something like this?"

"Having to wrestle with a caught animal, not many, but I always try to release an animal caught illegally. He was nothing. I wouldn't advise you trying it if you're alone with a bobcat."

"And I take it you have, or at least tried."

"Yeah, just outside of Beech Tree one year I was checking some fields in the farm country and found this bobcat in a trap.

He looked like he had been in the trap for several days by how he had torn the ground up. He acted pretty tired so I decided to try. I grabbed his lower jaw okay and he came to life giving me an awful overhauling. A cat's best defense are their claws. He tore my pants to shreds and I had several deep scratches. I finally had to hit him with a stick to stun him and then I released the trap. When he came to he took off hell-bent-for-election. Your mother scolded me pretty good when I got home. You and your sister were still in school and your mother cleaned the scratches and put some merthiolate on the scratches—which hurt more than the scratches. Then she bandaged my leg."

"We never knew anything about that, Dad."

Jarvis didn't reply. They picked up the trap and put it in the pack and continued on. They had picked up four more empty traps and the next one had a dead martin in it and it had spoiled too much to salvage. The next trap had a live martin. "Okay, son, your turn. His teeth are like needles and if given a chance he'll twist around your arm. Do it just like I did with the fisher. Lure it out to the end of the chain."

Herschel lured the martin out all the while the martin was screaming a shrill high pitched scream. As soon as Herschel had clamped down on the martin's jaw, Jarvis released the trap. "Okay son, just throw him."

Herschel did and said, "I still think you're crazy, Dad. What if we had found a live lynx?"

"I hope we don't. We'd probably have to shoot it."

At the last trap at the end of the trail was a red wolf. "Oh boy, a wolf. You can't tell me we're going to release him are we?"

"No, but they are much easier than a fisher. Go ahead and shoot it in the head. Then we'll skin it."

"While I'm skinning, find some water. We might as well eat here," Jarvis said.

When he had finished skinning, he rolled the hide up and put it in the pack.

"Where were you the busiest, Dad?"

"Believe it or not, around Beech Tree. The outlying farms are the perfect place for deer and trappers.

"You will have to learn that the laws we enforce are not always black and white. There will be many gray areas. In hard times some people need food and will take the risk of getting caught to go out and get a deer or moose to feed their family. You will be faced with times like this and the choice of what to do will be up to you.

"But there is a clear difference between a poacher who will take an illegal deer to feed his family and one who takes one to sell. As I said the choice will be yours to decide what to do."

They picked up and walked back out to the border. "Dad, I sure would like to have a look at their trapper's camp."

"I was hoping you'd want to have a look. Let's leave our packs here."

Herschel let his father lead the way from the border. He was questioning the idea about crossing the border, but he was as curious as his father.

They had only hiked about a quarter of a mile when they found it. And it wasn't exactly what Herschel was expecting. It was only about eight feet long and maybe six feet wide. The four sides were small two and three inch softwood trees nailed to four big spruce trees, and the only window was a small pane of glass in the door, but then from the inside you could look out through to the outside through the many cracks between the logs. The roof was covered with metal sheets of old newspaper print. There were two bunk beds only about three feet wide and a mattress of laced rope. The stove was an empty five gallon can with a three inch stove pipe out through the wall. The floor was dirt.

"Not much is it, Dad."

"Actually it is quite nice compared to some I have found. This one has a dry roof. They're only here for one reason. To trap."

"There are no fur pelts or dead animals."

"They probably stay here only one night to a trip. They

tend their traps, stay here and return home the next day with the fur pelts. I was hoping to find a log book. But then neither of us can read French," Jarvis said.

"It wouldn't surprise me if they summer trap in Canada also," Herschel said.

"After this they may be shut down. At least in Maine."

They had seen all they wanted and headed back across the border.

The afternoon southbound blew the half mile warning and they circled around the custom building staying out of sight.

They hiked up to the heath where Jarvis and Marcel had caught Paquette and St. Pierre for illegal deer hunting. Marcel had come back later and burned their deer stand and there was nothing new here now. Jarvis told his son about the history with Paquette and St. Pierre and about other Canadian hunters he had arrested hunting this same heath. "It seems to be a natural place for deer and moose," Herschel said.

"I think this is a natural crossing through here, back and forth from the Canadian side, and I think the Canadian residents are aware of it.

"I never did much work along the border from here north. After a quarter mile the border follows the height of some very rugged terrain. While we're here we might as well hike up."

As Herschel was following his Dad, he couldn't help wonder about the man's stamina. He never seemed to tire. And he was also very much aware that his Dad was happy being out here in this wilderness. And probably some of his Dad's happiest moments were when he was out here.

After a few minutes Herschel said, "I can see why you didn't work up here. Nothing but a billy goat could live up here."

"Let's go back to the heath and make camp for the night."

As they were eating supper, Herschel asked, "Dad, after spending a month working with me and being a game warden again, are you going to be satisfied with the dull routine life of being a furrier?"

"To be honest with you, these have been fun days out here again. And spending time with you, which I didn't do much of when you were growing up. Your mother is a good woman, son. I couldn't have asked or expected another to be as good. She never fussed when I was gone for days at a time. I owe her a lot, son. In fact I owe her the rest of life.

"When you take a wife, son—well, find one with similar qualities as your mother."

They sat up talking for a long time after the sun had set and put more wood on the fire. Herschel lay awake long after his father began snoring, thinking about the last two weeks and how much fun he had had spending this time out here with his dad, learning what his father had been doing ever since he could remember. And now he could finally understand why his dad would come home after several days and that he was always happy and smiling.

****

The next morning instead of hiking back to customs and waiting for the afternoon train they went across country through the woods and hit Rascal's trap line behind the log cabin. They followed that out to the old log yard and then down the road to the dam and the lodge.

Rascal was outside working and his dog, Whiskey Jack, somehow the dog knew they were coming even before they reached the dam and he started barking. Rascal put his tools down and followed Whiskey Jack towards the dam when he saw Jarvis and Herschel. Their clothes were dirty and smelled of wood smoke with three days growth of whiskers. "Well, where have you two been this time?"

Jarvis let Herschel answer, "We had to pull the traps that those two had out and then Dad showed me some more of the border. Then today we hiked through the woods from the border here."

Rascal laughed and shook his head. "Come on in and

you can wash up. You missed the afternoon southbound."

"Could we stay the night?"

"Sure you can. Come on in and we'll have some coffee."

"That's quite a watch dog you have there. I thought we were being quiet, but he knew we were coming."

"You came cross country through the woods from the border huh? It seems to me, Herschel, you're discovering every square foot of this country. I hope you don't get tired of it after you have seen it all," Rascal said.

"No chance of that, Rascal. This is fun."

"You came downhill by the log cabin?"

"Yeah, Dad wanted to take a shortcut. Saw a lot of country, we did."

Emma and Anita brought in coffee and fresh donuts for all and then joined the men.

"You two must be tired after all of that hiking," Emma said.

"Hah!" Herschel exclaimed laughing, "That old man doesn't know the word tired. I've never seen the beat of it. Dad, you're sixty-eight years old, but these last two hours I had all I could do to keep up with you."

Jarvis never complained that he was tired, but he didn't move out of the soft living room chair until it was time for supper.

There were only two fishermen that week and they stopped early and came in and joined the men for coffee and good conversation. They seemed pleased to meet the famed warden and Herschel was not introduced as the new warden.

After supper and the kitchen cleaned, they all sat in the living room talking. The two fishermen had been up since daylight and were tired and went upstairs to their room early.

"Now that they are gone, Rascal, there is something I need to know. The not knowing has bothered me for years now." Rascal thought he was going to ask how he managed to get his wife caught for a deer in her garden. And he really didn't want to stir that up again.

"Ten years ago before you went into the army, you were fishing at the head of the lake. Do you remember?"

"Go on," everyone was staring at them both.

"I distinctly heard a rifle shot and I searched your canoe and you didn't have a rifle or handgun and you had not gone ashore. There were no tacks in the mud. But there was a freshly killed deer about fifty yards from shore. I sat on that deer for three nights and two days, hoping you would come back for it. But you didn't and I finally had to leave. Now I want to know the rest of the story."

There wasn't a word spoken and there was dead silence. Even the dog, Whiskey Jack, was waiting. "Rascal," Emma said, "I think you owe Jarvis an explanation. Tell him or I will."

Rascal started laughing and he was a few minutes before he could start telling his end of the story. "You were right, Jarvis. I did shoot that deer. I wanted to get the Antonys some meat. When I fired that .38-55 the report echoed back and forth and up and down the lake. I knew if you were around you would hear it and come up. I was getting real nervous and then I saw you canoeing up the lake and I began to panic. I shoved my rifle into the black muck as far as I could push it. And you were correct, I hadn't gone ashore yet, so my tracks were nowhere on that side of the lake.

"For two days I watched the terminal waiting for you to board the train and leave so I could canoe up and get my rifle.

"On the afternoon of the third day I canoed up and waded out to get it. I had to walk around in that smelly muck up to my knees for hours looking before I hit the stock with my toe. I had to go under a few times before I could get it and by then I was smelling as bad as the muck.

"I tried to wash the smell off before I headed back."

Emma was laughing now and then said, "He was still smelling so bad when I walked inside the cabin, I made him go back out and wash up with soap in the lake." By now everyone was laughing.

Whiskey Jack's Secret

"Dad, what is the statute of limitations on fish and game violations?"

"Three years," and they laughed some more.

"Well . . . ." Jarvis said. "What would you say to make up for that we get up early tomorrow and go fishing."

"I owe you that much. How about you, Herschel?"

"Yeah, I'd go for some trout fishing."

****

Later that night as Herschel was lying on his back in bed he was still thinking about his Dad and Rascal. Game warden and poacher stories of, "I almost got ya." Then he started laughing again. Thinking that this is what probably made him so liked and respected among even those he chased.

As proud as he was, a soft bed sure was comfortable.

The three men were up early the next morning, while the guests decided to sleep in. Without even a cup of coffee they paddled up to the head of the lake. The sun had not peaked over the treetops yet and the surface of the water looked more like a mirror. Brook trout were breaking the surface after a late hatch of mayflies and mosquitos.

"Herschel, Jarvis and I can paddle the canoe. Why don't you string out a line."

He tied on a warden's worry streamer and before he had all of the line that he wanted out a trout hit it and flew three feet into the air. They stopped paddling while he brought it in and Rascal netted it. "Wow, that is a beauty. About four pounds I'd say." It was a deep orange with a white streak running down the center of the belly and the back of the trout looked almost blue.

As they continued paddling, Herschel let his line out again and caught another, probably a male and a match to the first one. Rascal wasn't about to show them or anyone except Emma, where the big brook trout lay beneath the lily pads. He eased the canoe up within fly casting reach of the inlet.

Jarvis and Herschel were talking and moving around in

the canoe making too much noise. "Shh, be quiet and wait five minutes before you cast out," he whispered.

Jarvis understood and Herschel wasn't quite sure, but he did as asked. Rascal kept moving the canoe when it became necessary and then he sat there enjoying watching his friends enjoy fishing.

After an hour they each had four nice trout and the smallest weighing two pounds. "I'm hungry," Jarvis said, "how about you two?"

There was no trolling on their way back. They were hungry, "We'll clean your fish here on the wharf and then I'll put them on ice in the cold storage room. I think Emma and Anita are fixing scrambled eggs with smoked trout and fresh biscuits."

Emma made the three wash up outside, "I don't want that smelly fish smell in here."

The northbound train slowed and threw a mail pouch and newspaper and then regained speed, as they were eating. "Looks like you'll be home just in time for the weekend, son. But before you go anywhere, write up a report for the chief warden. Every time you finish a detail out."

While the others finished eating, Rascal went out for the mail and paper. Back inside he set the mail pouch on the table and opened the newspaper. The front page was all about Canada and the United States coming together. "It says here that there is very little opposition to the merger from either side of the border."

"That's going much smoother than I first thought it would," Jarvis said.

"Mr. Ambrose," one of the guests said, "we have decided to leave today instead of waiting for tomorrow."

"Okay, right after breakfast I'll check the smoker. Your fish should be ready to take out."

It was a warm sunny day and the two guests sat in the shade on the platform watching the lake and talking. Rascal had their smoked fish wrapped in paper and also sitting in the shade on the platform.

Back inside Herschel asked, "Rascal, I'd like to ask an awful big favor of you. If you say no, I'll understand."

"What is it?" Jarvis was curious also.

"Well, I have heard you and Emma talk so much about Bear, I was wondering if we could go out and see if he is around. I surely would like to see him play with you."

Emma said, "Go ahead, Rascal. Just make sure the two guests don't go along."

Rascal looked at Jarvis and he nodded his head. "Let's go. We'll walk out to the farm."

"If they ask where you are, I'll make up some excuse, so you three go play."

They all smiled and they left the lodge behind happily talking all the way to the farm. "Should we be quiet, Rascal?" Herschel asked.

"No."

"I'd love to live out here," Jarvis said.

"Mom wouldn't come, Dad."

"Yeah, I know. Look down at the bottom of the field, several deer," Jarvis said.

Then Bear stood up. He was in the middle of the field watching over a sow with two cubs. "There's Bear. Let him come to us," Rascal said.

Bear was in no particular hurry. He stood again and sniffed the air. He had scented his friend. He was coming straight towards them.

"Are you sure about this, Rascal?" Herschel asked.

Rascal didn't answer. Bear stopped about twenty feet away and sat down on his butt. "Boy, he's a big brute," Herschel said.

Rascal took a few steps closer and Herschel started to follow when Jarvis put out his arm to stop him.

Rascal stopped and extended his arm and said, "Hello, Bear."

Bear reached out with a paw. "I'll be damned," Herschel said.

"Bear, I'd like you to meet a new friend, Herschel."

Bear reached out with his paw again and made that sound that sounded like he was saying, "Hi." *Arrhy.*

"He speaks too! You never said you had a talking Bear."

Then Rascal took off running towards the edge of the field and Bear chasing after him. At first Herschel thought Rascal was going to be mauled. Rascal ran a circle around Bear before he was tripped then he got up and started running again, in a zigzag pattern and then he circled back behind Bear. Eventually Bear caught him and tripped him. Then Rascal got up again and started running for the trees. Bear bunted him and this time instead of running to the top of the bank he sat down in the field and started making that sound that sounded like—"He's laughing! I don't believe it!" Herschel said.

Rascal stood up and said, "Okay, Bear, that's enough." And he rejoined Jarvis and Herschel. Bear still sat there and Rascal said, "Goodbye, Bear." Bear walked back to the middle of the field to watch over the sow and cubs.

"I'm glad you brought us out here, Rascal. It's hard to believe."

"You see why, son, we must not talk about this to other people?"

"Yes I do understand. Has he ever played with someone else?"

"No, only me."

"He plays with you and protects Emma. I sure would like to understand his thinking."

When they were back at the lodge the two guests were still sitting on the platform with coffee and donuts. Emma met them at the door and said, "By the looks of you, Rascal, I'd say you and Bear were playing again."

Chapter 9

Jarvis and Herschel said their goodbyes and along with the two guests they boarded the southbound train.

For the rest of the summer there were a few fishermen each week and they were all repeats and didn't need a guide, so this gave Rascal time to work on firewood for the winter and catch enough frogs to can to last them until next year.

The station master had called and told Rascal about a beaver problem at mile nine. There was no morning southbound train now so he had to walk, and then hike back carrying four beaver hides and meat. "I'll have to go back tomorrow, I think I'll have a couple more beaver in the morning and then I'll have to pull the dam which is downstream of the tracks this year."

"Is your leg giving you any problems?" Emma asked.

"Not at all."

"Well, don't overdo it, Rascal."

While Rascal was at mile nine the next day Emma and Anita canned what beaver meat he had brought back the day before. He was surprised how well his leg was feeling now. It had been several weeks since he had limped at all. He was feeling like a new man.

There was only the two other beaver and he pulled the dam out and waited for the water to drop and then he dismantled the house. A family of mink had taken up residence in one corner. Apparently the two could get along living in a small space.

Life was good and especially for Rascal, Emma and Anita. One night in late August when there were no guests Emma announced, "Rascal, I'm pregnant."

Anita smiled and Rascal dropped his fork on the table. Then as the news began to sink in he started smiling and then a boyish grin. "Are you sure, Em?"

"Oh yeah, there's no doubt."

"When is he due?"

"Around the first of April or there about. What if it's a girl?"

"We'll send her back. No, only kidding, a girl would be nice also."

****

Every night they and any guests would listen to the evening news and without failure most of the hour was about the pros and cons of Canada and the United States coming together as one country. The pros or advantages were way more numerous than the cons. Even in Canada that's all people—or most of them—were talking about.

President Cutlidge and Prime Minister Kingsley met again and they both were so sure that in November, when both countries would vote on the idea, it would overwhelmingly pass, they decided to hire architects from both countries to start drawing plans for a new capitol building in Sault Ste. Marie They both wanted to be ahead of things with plans to start immediately.

Great Britain had yet to voice any opinion about the merger. They were still having enough problems recovering from what was now being called the Great War in Europe.

Most of the objections in the United States were coming from politicians and lobbyists, because no one knew what changes were coming and this worried them the most. But even they had to admit that the president and prime minister had done an excellent job orchestrating this.

The business communities on both sides of the border were jubilant, for they could see increased potential and expansion and more job opportunities. And those that lived close to the border could see greater freedoms when traveling to visit families or shop and work. Yes, it seemed everyone—or just about everyone—was wanting the changes to come soon. And President Cutlidge and Prime Minister Kingsley were happy with the acceptance by the people.

****

One Saturday evening after that week's guests had left, Rascal and Emma took a walk out to the farm. Whiskey Jack wanted to go also, so Emma hooked a leash to his collar. Neither Rascal nor Emma knew what to expect from Bear. Usually bears and dogs did not get along too well.

Whiskey Jack was now five months old and already a large dog.

When they reached the field, sure enough Bear was there. When he first saw Whiskey Jack he blew air through his nose to clear his sense of smells and then he was aware of a strange scent. One he had not smelled before.

"You stay here, Em, with Whiskey Jack." Rascal took a few steps towards Bear and raised his arm and made that peculiar greeting sound. And then Bear gave chase and tripped him. Rascal stood up and said, "Em, let Whiskey Jack go."

"Are you sure?"

"Yes."

She unhooked the leash and let him go. He walked slowly towards Rascal and Bear. Bear wasn't blowing or clicking his teeth which was a good sign and Whiskey Jack's hackles were not raised on his neck. They slowly walked towards each other and began smelling the other's nose. This really surprised both Emma and Rascal.

And then like Rascal had done, Whiskey Jack started running in a circle around Bear. He wasn't as easy to catch as Rascal. Eventually Bear tripped him and Whiskey Jack went rolling on the ground then he jumped to his feet and began chasing Bear. Rascal walked over to stand with Emma. They both were laughing at the antics. Whiskey Jack couldn't trip Bear of course but he ran between his legs and under his belly and that was the signal for Bear to chase him. "Will you look at that, Rascal. I would never have guessed. Looks like you have lost your playmate, Rascal."

Rascal whistled and called Whiskey Jack and he came running. "Goodbye, Bear," Emma said. And Bear waved his paw and happily bounded off for the woods.

"You know, Em, if'n I didn't know better, I'd say Bear is happy."

As they were walking home Emma said, "You know, it still bewilders me why Bear has befriended us."

"You're not alone there."

When they told Anita, she just couldn't believe that a wild bear and a dog would play together. "The next time we go out, Anita, you'll have to go with us."

****

September fishing was almost as good as May fishing and the first two weeks the lodge was full. In the evenings the guests would all gather either in the living room or outside on the platform and every night they would talk about the advantages of Canada and the United States merging. There was never any negative comments. As one businessman from Boston said, "The only thing I can't understand is why we didn't do it before now."

Some of the guests each of those two weeks saw what Rascal was doing, working up winter firewood and in the afternoons he would have help. By the end of the month he had all he could pile in the woodsheds and up against the cellar wall on the north side and even more piled up in the old sawmill.

Everybody that month wanted to take home some smoked fish plus it was now cool enough so the fish would not spoil on their way home.

They had not on purpose booked anyone in October until the deer season opened. So this gave Rascal two weeks to set traps, mainly for wolves. Although they had not heard any since Bear had killed the mother, Rascal was sure her pups could survive by eating grasshoppers, crickets and mice. And he didn't want a pack of wolves anywhere near the lodge.

By the opening day of the season he had managed to trap three yearling pups and one large adult male. "This should take care of the wolf problem for a while."

He also caught a few foxes, raccoons, fishers, martins and one skunk which he was able to release without being sprayed.

November 4th was election day for local politicians and the big question about the merger. One morning Emma telephoned the town office in Beech Tree and had three absentee ballots sent up.

A week before voting day on November 4th all of the radio stations were broadcasting the advantages of the merger and encouraging people to make every effort to go to the polls and vote. Emma found two Canadian stations that were broadcasting only information about the advantages. The whole world would be watching and people were buying feverishly into the stock markets: The New York Exchange, Ottawa, London, Paris and India exchanges. It seemed most of the world was anticipating the merger and the financial gain.

Emma made sure Anita and Rascal had filled out their absentee ballots correctly and sealed them, and the next day at noon she put up the red flag and left the mail pouch on the platform. All the guests that week had also already voted absentee.

On the day of the vote, November 4th, at sunset a guest hunter came into the lodge all nervous, "Mr. Ambrose, my friend Bill, I think, is lost. We met up on the tracks at noon for lunch and he was supposed to meet me back at the tracks at 3 o'clock. Figuring this would give us enough daylight to hike back here."

"Did you fire a signal shot before leaving the spot where you were supposed to meet Bill?"

"No, but I did a lot of hollering, but I didn't get an answer."

"That should have been the first thing you did, if you thought he was turned around. We can't get up there now before dark. Come into the kitchen and we'll get something to eat."

"How can you eat when my friend might be lost in the wilderness?"

"Well, you and I might be out there all night and I don't know about you, but I can hike a good deal longer on a full stomach."

They had soup and sandwiches and Rascal pulled on a pair of rubber boots. "Let's go." He gave a kerosene lantern to Tim and he strapped on his .45 and picked up another lantern.

"How far up the tracks were you?"

"We were supposed to meet at the mile eleven post."

"Which direction did Bill go from mile eleven?"

"He was going to circle to the north and come back on to the tracks."

"Where were you?"

"I went straight off the tracks and came back out to the same mile post."

Rascal was furious. He made a point of telling everyone the lodge rules on every Sunday night and not to hunt beyond mile eleven. Bill was the only hunter so far that had strayed into the forbidden area. He walked up the tracks as fast as he could hike, not paying too much attention to Tim or what he was saying.

Tim could guess why Rascal was upset. He had told everyone not to go beyond mile eleven. He understood—but he wished Rascal would say something.

They didn't stop until they reached the mile post and then Rascal fired a signal shot straight up into the night air. About fifteen seconds later they heard an answer and it sounded like it was north of them on the tracks.

"We'll wait here for Bill to come to us."

The moon was almost full and it had just risen above the treetops turning a black night into almost twilight. Enough so, so twenty minutes later they could see someone walking towards them between the rails about a quarter of a mile away.

Rascal still wasn't talking and Tim was feeling uncomfortable. He surely didn't want to trade places with his friend Bill.

As Bill came closer he said, "Boy, am I glad to see you fellas. That is some kind of a hell hole up there. I got turned around in a swamp. Boy am I glad to be out of there."

"Let me see your rifle, Bill." He handed it to Rascal and Rascal handed it to Tim. "How'd you end up in Ledge Swamp?"

"I circled too far to the north I guess, and I came to the back end of a swamp about sunset."

"What did I tell all of you Sunday evening about hunting beyond mile eleven?"

There was a long silence before Bill answered and then he said, "You said not to."

"We have a good reason why we do not allow any hunting beyond mile eleven. We treat the area as a wildlife sanctuary. I know I was very clear about no hunting up here. Bill, you are not welcomed here anymore and will board the afternoon southbound tomorrow."

It was quite a walk back to the lodge.

Anita gave Bill some leftovers from supper and then he went up to his room. "I told you not to go hunting at the swamp, Bill. When you leave tomorrow, I'm staying. I might have pushed the limit, but I never went beyond mile eleven."

"Emma, Anita," Rascal said, "Bill was hunting at the swamp and I told him he would have to leave on the southbound tomorrow."

The other guests were in the living room listening to the radio and the ballot returns on question 1 on the ballot about the two countries merging. So far it had been overwhelming in favor. "I'd like your attention for a minute, men. Sunday evening I explained to all of you about the lodge rules and one in particular. That no one was to hunt at Ledge Swamp or north of the mile eleven post. Bill violated that rule today and he will be leaving here on the afternoon train. We treat that area around Ledge Swamp as a wildlife sanctuary and we never hunt there nor allow any of our guests. That's all I wanted to say."

Rascal, Emma and Anita stayed up until midnight listening to the returns. So far there had been very little opposition to the merger.

Canada's returns were coming in slower, but as of midnight those in favor of the merger were far ahead of those opposed. Lower Canada's returns were in and those opposed were certainly a minority, which the prime minister had earlier thought the vote would have been in favor of those opposing the merger, but this was not the case.

"Well, this isn't going to be settled tonight. I'm going to bed," Emma said.

"Me too," Anita said.

"I'm going to stay up awhile longer."

A half hour later he was having difficulty staying awake, so he turned the radio and generator off and went to bed.

Both Rascal and Emma were up before anyone else. They couldn't wait for news about the merger. Rascal started the generator and started the fires and Emma turned the radio on and turned the volume up so she and Anita could hear it in the kitchen.

The radio announcer said returns were still coming in from the far reaches of both countries but it certainly looked as there would be a merger of the two countries. At 5 a.m., of all the ballots returned so far 76% of the people from both sides of the border were in favor and 85% of the returns were already in.

"Ladies and gentlemen of both the United States and Canada, it certainly looks as if there will be one country under the same democracy. Even if the last of the returns were to vote against the merger, there would not be enough to offset the merger. So ladies and gentlemen it looks as if we are now of one nation. The president and the prime minister will be making a statement to the people, in the near future."

By now everyone in the lodge was up and listening to the announcer. Even Bill who would be leaving on the southbound.

****

By the end of the week out of eleven hunters, six had shot a nice deer. Two were does, but they were novice hunters and just as happy. Everyone had seen deer and had had good food.

The next Monday morning on November 8th after the hunters were out in the woods President Cutlidge came on the air, at the exact moment that Prime Minister Kingsley did with the same talk.

"Prime Minister William Kingsley and I would like to express our gratitude to all of the people on both sides of the border. There was a lot of talking and planning that went into this idea. Things are not going to all change overnight. There will be an orderly procession. As the prime minister and I are now talking to you, officers at all border crossings are being notified that as of 9 o'clock this morning there will no longer be a border between us and that all facilities will be dismanned immediately. All tariffs have vanished and people are free to come and go at their pleasure, as well as companies and anyone looking for work.

"Last week I met with the U.S. Attorney General, the Speaker of the House and the Senate Majority Leader, and we discussed whether I would have the authority to make a unilateral decision when the safety and welfare of the people are in question. Ever since the implementation of the Volstead Act, it did not have the effect that voters thought it would have. Instead there are now organizations profiting from the illegal manufacturing and distribution of alcohol. Police officers as well as innocent bystanders have been murdered. It is time to stop this and as of this day I am terminating the Act. In the future, alcoholic beverages will be able to be manufactured and sold by licensed vendors and manufacturers. There will be a state and federal tax imposed to oversee the licensing and enforcement.

"The prime minister and I have employed a group of architects to draw up plans for a new capitol building which will be situated at Sault Ste. Marie. We plan to have this new capitol building completed in two years. There are now several committees, with people from the states as well as the provinces. They are all equally represented.

"We cannot complete everything in two years, but this gives us a point to start from. I can tell you this, there is a committee already working on two very important agendas that we believe everyone will be in favor for. The committee is researching a plan for the elders of our new country to retire. All of the issues have not been ironed out yet, but we are told they are very close. The other agenda is for everyone to have medical care when needed. This will require more hospitals, doctors and nurses.

"This is the big news for now and we will keep you informed as we progress. Oh, there is one more point of interest, while the prime minister and I were discussing the possibility of a merger at the Whiskey Jack Lodge in Maine, it was brought to our attention what would we call our new nation. There were seven people at the lodge during this time and we thought that since all of us are technically Americans why not call our new country simply North America.

"That's all for now my friends and thank you for your support."

"No more prohibition," Rascal said.

"Now we won't feel guilty when we bring back wine from Lac St. Jean," Emma said.

"I only hope not too many hunters and trappers come this way," Rascal said.

"Times are changing and Silvio would say, 'Too fast,'" Anita said.

Two days later Alfons Dubois had his bags and gear packed and set everything outside with his last cup of coffee to be had at the once custom cabin. He sat down to wait for the afternoon southbound. This had been a good job for him. After his wife had died he had decided to stay put, only going into Lac St. Jean on occasions when he needed food or something. He was too old to find a job in the woods or a sawmill, but maybe in Beech Tree there might be a security job. And he had liked what the president had said about having a retirement plan for the country's elder citizens. Yes siree, he liked the idea of that.

The engineer blew the half-mile warning steam whistle, probably for the last time, and Alfons set his empty cup on the porch railing and picked up his belongings and walked down to the edge of the tracks. He was truly sad to be leaving.

Chapter 10

Every Saturday evening at 6:30 p.m. the radio announcer would read a statement given to him by the president's chief of staff. And with each week the various committees were making great progress with writing a new format for the Bill of Rights and the many amendments and a new Constitution to include both countries.

The president said everything would be done in steps and by January 1st of 1933, he and the prime minister hoped everything would be in place.

After the incident with hunter Bill hunting around Ledge Swamp, the rest of the deer season went smooth. They had two weeks of twelve hunters and two weeks with fourteen. A man and wife chose the log cabin. John and Mabel, and she hunted everyday with her husband and even shot her own crotch horn on the last day.

Working by himself, Herschel had plenty of time to think about Perline Bowman, the woman who had translated for the two French hunters in court. He was quite taken with her and he wrote her a letter and asked her to meet him at the Whiskey Jack Lodge for Thanksgiving. Canada's Thanksgiving holiday was traditionally on the third Monday of October. And since the United States holiday was the last Thursday of November a compromise had to be reached for the new American nation. The date chosen was the date the vote was taken, the first Wednesday of November. This seemed to satisfy pretty much everyone.

Perline arrived on the morning southbound and since she had already been there when the train was held up in July, there were no introductions needed. When the Pages arrived on the afternoon on the day before Thanksgiving, it was like a family reunion and the first thing they did was drink a pot of coffee. And probably of the seven people there, Anita was without a doubt, the happiest.

They were sitting in the living room enjoying the comfort of the fireplace when Anita said, "Excuse me," as she wiped tears from her eyes. Everyone thought something must be wrong. "I have something to say to all of you. When my husband Silvio died, I thought my world had come to an end. Emma and Rascal, I love you both. You took me into your home and gave me a reason again to live and look forward to the next day. You two have given me such a nice life here. And Rita, Jarvis, Herschel and now Perline, I have known you for most of my years. Herschel, I can remember when you were born. Jarvis you were around the village so often everyone looked towards you as another resident and you always talked about your wife, Rita, so that we all came to know you. I loved Silvio, but I was never as happy as I am right now, I think of you all as my family."

Everyone was silent for a few moments and then Emma said, "I think I speak for all of us, that we feel the same about you. Rascal and I are so happy that you are with us."

By now everyone was a little teary eyed, even Perline.

"How was your season here this year?" Jarvis asked.

"We had a good season. Only one lost hunter. Actually he was turned around behind Ledge Swamp and managed to walk himself out to the tracks by the time I was up there."

"I thought you didn't allow any hunting there?" Herschel said.

"We don't, I told him to leave on the afternoon southbound. We didn't have any more problems afterwards."

"Have you seen Bear around this fall?" Jarvis asked.

"Not since the deer season started. He's probably busy cleaning up the numerous gut piles."

"What about you, Herschel? Are you tired of the job

yet?" Rascal asked.

"Heck no. It's a lot of fun. I spent most of my time working reports of gunshots around the outlying farming country. I caught two in August. I think because I was new and young they thought they could take advantage of that. And in September I caught three hunters with a moose down before the season opened."

"You have been busy."

While it was still twilight out Herschel, Perline and Whiskey Jack went outside to walk around. They went down to the dam looking up across the lake. There was a breeze blowing off the lake and Herschel asked, "Are you cold? We can go back inside."

"No, I'm alright."

****

The three men were up early and headed out Rascal's road in the long narrow valley. "Rascal, this year you sit on the rock and watch the crossing and Herschel and I will go up and hunt the valley back."

Rascal didn't argue, but it was somewhat boring sitting there. He knew they would be at least two hours. There were only scuffs of snow in the shady spots. It would be much easier to see deer with a white background.

There was a breeze blowing from the south which would be good for all three of them. An hour had passed and suddenly Rascal could smell the musky scent of deer in the air, being blown in the breeze. If they were coming this way, then something was wrong. Deer usually go into the wind. There must be something spooking the deer. Maybe only a larger buck driving a young one out of his territory. Two minutes later and three does, two young of the year and a huge buck ran across the road and headed up the valley towards Jarvis and Herschel.

Rascal was so interested with the deer, he never even pulled his rifle up to his shoulder. A minute later he saw why the deer were running north up the valley. Two wolves stepped into the road following the deer tracks and a larger lone wolf, probably the alpha male, was running on the road towards the first two. This is all he had to see. He instinctively pulled his rifle up and shot the big alpha male and one of the other two. The third one ran off up the road where the alpha male had come. He knew his chances of getting a deer now were next to none, with the scent of wolves and blood in the air.

He thought about walking down to look at the two wolves, but he stayed where he was. There just might be a chance, albeit a slight one, that those might come back across. But he doubted it.

Twenty minutes later he heard a rifle shot, only one which probably meant that one of them had shot one of that bunch. Ten minutes later there was another shot and not exactly from the same direction. Thinking they probably had two deer down he started up the valley to lend a hand.

By now they had both dressed their deer and had started dragging them to the road. Jarvis had the big buck Rascal had seen and Herschel had a smaller six point which he did not see cross the road.

"We heard you shoot, Rascal, did you get one?" Jarvis asked.

"Two actually," and he left it at that and watched as the expressions changed on their faces. And then he said, "There was a wolf pack chasing these deer and I shot the big alpha male and one other."

Jarvis and Herschel both breathed a sigh of relief. "I'd have shot wolves any day over a deer considering how close they came to attacking Em last summer."

"Did you trap for them this fall, Rascal?" Herschel asked.

"Yes and I only caught one. These probably have come into this area from somewhere else. This male is bigger than I have ever trapped before."

It was a tough drag back to the lodge on dry ground. They

had to stop often and Rascal would spell Jarvis some. After all he was sixty-eight years old and his deer a twelve point would go well over two hundred pounds.

Rascal helped them hang their deer on the game pole and the two wolves.

"Those wolves are going to be awfully tough eating, Rascal," Jarvis said jokingly.

"Maybe I'll go back out tomorrow morning. We don't have any deer meat this year. The hunters all wanted to take theirs back with them."

Perline had heard the men talking and she came out back to see the deer. "Oh, those will be good eating. Those wolves are beautiful. I have never seen a red wolf before."

****

Thanksgiving dinner was late and no one felt like eating any supper, except maybe a little smoked fish with a glass of wine. "That's the last of the wine," Emma said, "I guess we'll have to make another trip to Lac St. Jean."

For the most part of the evening Herschel regaled them about what he had been doing since the two summer trappers. When he ran out of stories, Jarvis entertained them for the rest of the evening. "I think the funniest case I ever had was two years before I retired. I was working the clover fields on the MacDonald farm. I had received a few complaints that year about shots around midnight. I worked those fields every night for a month before I figured out what they were doing.

"Two men would walk out through the fields between 10 p.m. and midnight, every night unless it rained. The only nights they would carry a rifle was on the week of the full moon. The other nights I decided they would walk out there so the deer would get used to their coming and going.

"On the night of the full moon I was watching the back field before sunset and I saw two men come walking in. It was light enough so I could identify them, Paul and Seth Morrison.

Brothers. I went to school with them. Seth had the only rifle. They had a ground blind set up on the opposite side on a point that jutted out into the field. From there they could see both sides. I knew I was too far away. So before it was completely dark I worked my way to the field staying just inside the shadows so they wouldn't see me. I found a place to wait where I had first seen them. Then I sat down to wait.

"The moon didn't come up until an hour after complete darkness. I understood then why they had come into the field so early. The field was thick with clover and in one of the corners they were watching someone had planted several apple trees years ago."

"Dad did you find that when you were in a situation like this and your adrenaline was high that you had to pee?"

Jarvis broke out laughing and then said, "Every time, son."

"Well, I had to, and just then Seth fired. My heart came right up into my throat. I couldn't sneak across the open field in the moonlight, so I had to wait. It wasn't long and I could see them coming towards me. But halfway across the field they turned left and were walking away from me. I still couldn't get to 'em without being seen, so I whistled and they stopped and in a low voice I called their names and said, "Come here." It was barely above a whisper, but they heard me and started towards me and then Paul asked, "Is that you, Dad?"

"I covered my mouth with my hand to hide my voice and said, "Yeah, now come here." Still barely above a whisper. But they kept coming. Twice I gave a quick low whistle to guide them. When they were about twenty feet away I turned my light on and said, "Paul and Seth, you are under arrest."

"They both were so shocked they froze in their tracks. I took their rifle and said, "You two drag that nice buck and follow me. I was surprised when they did."

Rascal could understand just how Paul and Seth must have felt.

"That was a good job, Dad. Whistling brought them right to you."

"Hulcurt fined them both a hundred dollars for hunting at night and in closed season. They didn't have the money and chose to stay in jail and work the fine off doing public work."

"I hate to brag, but, Dad, I understand now why you were always so dedicated. It's fun."

Dinner was finally ready and afterwards Perline helped to clean up.

****

That night it turned blistering cold and the wind blew. As everyone was going to bed no one said a word when Herschel went with Perline to her room.

Rascal and Emma woke up long before daylight and stayed awake listening to the lake making ice. "As sharp as those cracks, are the temperature must be below zero."

"Brrr, you make me cold, Rascal, listening to you."

"I think I'd better get out of bed and check the fires." Rascal dressed and lit the lantern in the upstairs hall. There were only a few coals left in the ram-down and he tossed in some dry kindling and two pieces of split beechnut. He had to start the fireplace from scratch and the kitchen stove also. The outside thermometer was reading -20°. "No wonder it is so cold in here." He checked the temperature in the living room and that was reading 52°.

But with the fireplace and two stoves going it wasn't long before the lodge had warmed up enough so you didn't have to wear a jacket. All of the windows had frost built up along the edges.

By the time everyone was up Rascal had the lodge toasty warm. "It was -20° at day break, and it's beginning to warm already."

Perline and Rita set the table while Anita and Emma made scrambled eggs with thick slices of bacon. Afterwards Perline went upstairs to pack. She had to take the morning northbound. Rascal went outside to put out the red flag.

Because of the cold the train was an hour late. Perline hugged and kissed Herschel and then hugged each of them and said, "Thank you so much for sharing your Thanksgiving with me."

The train didn't blow the half mile signal, it quietly stopped alongside the platform and Perline boarded.

****

The weather stayed cold and windy, day and night, for a week. And when the temperature rose to 20⁰ it began to snow for two days. And then the wind came back and cleaned the lake off and piled up much of the blown snow below the dam. Now Rascal had enough snow to bank the buildings.

By Christmas the ice on the lake was a foot thick, twice as thick as it generally was for this time of year. He had packed down snowshoe trails around the lodge and buildings and one to the farm. The snow was wind-packed which made snowshoeing much easier. Emma had to keep reminding him not to overdo it. "You don't have to have everything done in just one day, Rascal."

Perline had traveled to Beech Tree to spend Christmas with Herschel and his family, and after two days he went with her to her family's house. He could only spend the one night there, but in that short time he had been accepted into Perline's family and he liked all of them very much.

It had been decided that at Whiskey Jack Lodge they would only give one gift to each person. There was a tree and they enjoyed a pork roast dinner, a warm fire and good cheer.

A week following Christmas, the weather warmed slightly and one afternoon the train engine stopped at the Whiskey Jack Lodge platform and Rascal went out to see what was up. Fred Darling, the engineer hollered out the side window. "Rascal, I hit a moose at mile eleven. It should be dead; I hit it in the head."

"Thanks, Fred, I'll see what I can do."

He knew as cold as it had been his crawler wasn't about to start with the battery, and the crankcase oil would probably be so stiff he'd never be able to hand crank it, unless that is if he could warm it up first. So he started a small fire under the oil pan and engine block. He had to be careful not to get it too hot, so he stayed there to watch and once in a while trying the crank. After twenty minutes he could spin the hand crank quite easily and the engine started on the third crank. He let it idle while he went inside to put on warm clothes. "You aren't going up now are you?" Emma asked.

"If I wait until morning that moose will be frozen stiff." He took a lantern, knife and his handgun just in case it was still alive. He put his axe and a chain in the bucket and started up the lake. It would be so much easier than trying to navigate around the rocks and stumps in the railroad right of way.

The wind had stopped blowing and the heat from the engine was blowing back on him. He just hoped he didn't come across a spring hole somewhere.

He didn't have to go all the way up to the head of the lake to reach the eleven mile post. There was a grove of open hardwood and now that the leaves were gone, even in the illumination of his headlight, he could easily pick his way through the trees.

And he came right out to the moose. The engine had hit the bull in the left front shoulder and the head. Coming up the ice he had thought of a good idea about how to take care of this moose. The antlers had been torn off so he hooked the chain around the head and a short hitch onto the drawbar of the crawler. Once he was on the ice he lengthened the chain the full length to give as much distance between the moose and the crawler so not to have as much weight centered in the small area.

He was back out front of the lodge in an hour and a half after leaving the shed where he kept the crawler. He unhooked the chain and swung the crawler around so the headlight would shine on the moose. Then he began cutting off the hind legs and the one good forward shoulder. Then he went in after the heart and liver. He was getting too cold to try and salvage anymore. He loaded everything in the bucket and drove it up to the back door of the lodge and put everything for now in the woodshed except for the heart which he took inside and gave it to Anita. Then he went back out and put the crawler away.

The next day while Emma and Anita were taking care of the meat and making some moose mincemeat, Rascal cut a hole through the ice with his ice chisel big enough to slide the moose carcass part way into the hole so it would freeze in. He was going to use this for wolf bait to shoot from inside the lodge. If they were still in the area eventually they would come to it. They would not be able to ignore the smell.

****

Emma was really beginning to show her pregnant belly. Rascal would try to keep her from working so hard, but it was of no use.

A month had passed before Rascal noticed anything had been eating from the frozen carcass. He checked the snow for tracks and sure enough he could find three separate wolf tracks. He would sit up later after Emma and Anita had gone to bed and the gas generator shut off and all the lights were off. Then one night in the early morning hours he saw the three wolves at the carcass. He eased the window up only enough to stick the rifle out and he sighted in on the biggest wolf and pulled the trigger. The noise inside the lodge was deafening and Emma and Anita came running out. "You scared the devil out of us, Rascal. I hope you got one."

"I did, the other two ran off."

"Well, close that window and come to bed."

"Yes, dear."

****

Whiskey Jack could also smell the moose carcass and whenever he was outside they had to keep a close eye on him, so he wouldn't go near, and leave his scent which would keep the wolves away.

The wolves stayed away for six weeks before returning for something to eat. The snow was deep and fluffy and the wolves had a difficult time finding enough to eat, so when they were hungry enough they came back one night when there was a good moon. Their howling and fighting awoke everyone and Rascal knew exactly what was happening. Again he eased the window open and sighted in on the biggest one and fired. It went down and now three more ran off. He was beginning to wonder how big the pack was.

They were so hungry they returned in two days just as the sun was breaking daylight. There were three feeding on the carcass and this time Emma had her rifle at the same window. "You take the one on the left, Em, and I'll take the one on the right."

Rascal let Emma shoot first and he immediately fired. Two more wolves went down.

"That should leave only one more."

That wolf though got the hint and beat-footed it out of the area. That was the last of the wolf problem at Whiskey Jack Lake.

March came in like a roaring lion and by the 15th the weather changed drastically. Some days warmed to 60°, although the nights were still cold.

Rascal insisted that Emma have the baby in the hospital. "This is no place to give birth, Em. I want you at the hospital."

"I gave birth here with our first two babies, Rascal, and I guess I can do it again."

"There were more people here, Em, and the doctor would come up often, and now the train only leaves once a day for Beech Tree. No, you go to the hospital."

Anita agreed, and Emma said she would consider it.

Spring was here and Rascal had enough to do to keep himself busy. Whiskey Jack was by his side everywhere he went.

When the last wolf left, the eagles, ravens, bobcats and foxes cleaned up the rest of the moose carcass.

****

Both Prime Minister Kingsley and the president were happy with the speed the new changes were being set into place. President Cutlidge had insisted that the leader of North America be called the president. Whereas Prime Minister Kingsley insisted that instead of a congress he wanted a parliament and its members be called council members. This was approved by a special committee and this committee also called for two council members from each state and province and only one legislative level and not two. And that each council member could employ as many investigators as needed to investigate complaints. These changes were very agreeable to both men.

When the question arose would the states now be called provinces or vice versa, one committee member had a grand idea. That all provinces adopt as many states as necessary within each province. The provinces would remain the same, only they would now contain separate states within each province. And the states would be grouped into provinces like New England Province, the Mid-Atlantic Province, the West Coast Province and so forth. It was also decided that the maritime provinces, as individual states within the New England Province. No one objected to this.

The entire committee was in favor of this idea. That way everyone would be satisfied.

When the issue of currency arose, again President Cutlidge insisted they keep George Washington on the one dollar bill and that was agreed. The other denominations would have a different design incorporating historic figures from both sides.

Canada was now being referred to as Upper America and the states as Lower America. And again, nobody objected.

Companies were already doing business on the respective 'other' America without any problems. No one, not even those who supported the merger of the two countries, thought that the changes would move along so fast and with so few problems.

****

At the breakfast table one morning on the third week of March, Rascal said, "Em, I think you should go into Beech Tree now, so you'll be near the hospital when your time comes."

Anita spoke up, "I think you should also, Emma. I can go with you and we can stay at my sister's house until you need to go to the hospital."

Emma had also been doing a lot of thinking about this and taking to heart what both Rascal and Anita had said earlier. "I can be ready to leave this afternoon; how about you, Anita?"

Rascal and Anita both breathed a sigh of relief. "I thought you would put up a fight against going in now," Rascal said.

"Me too," Anita added.

As they waited for the train, Emma asked, "Will you be okay alone here?"

"Yes, Em, I'll be just fine. I'll tend the chickens, keep the fires going and if I get bored I'll find Bear and rouse him from hibernation."

"Have you thought of any names yet, Rascal?" Emma asked.

"I thought I would wait until he or she is born. A name will come to me then. How about you?"

"If it is a girl, I have and I won't tell you what unless I have a girl."

"I'm counting on you, Anita, to call me if something should go wrong."

"I will, Rascal. You can count on me."

"Thank you."

The train left and Rascal and Whiskey Jack suddenly found themselves alone.

As the days wore on, Rascal found it more difficult to be away from the lodge where he couldn't hear the telephone if Anita should call. Then one evening a week later, Emma called just to say hello and that everything was okay. "I just miss you, Rascal, and home. That's all I wanted to say."

Then three days later, as Rascal was starting the fire in the fireplace, the telephone rang. He jumped and ran to answer it and fell over a table chair. "Hello," he said, all out of breath.

"Rascal, this is Anita. You sound like you have been running."

"I fell over a table chair. Well?"

"Rascal, you have an April-fool baby. A whopping son, eight pounds and eight ounces."

"How is she, Anita? I mean Em? Is she okay?"

"Yes, but, Rascal, Doctor Thwistle wants Emma to stay in the hospital for a week to ten days."

There was silence on Rascal's end. "Rascal, are you there?"

"Yeah, I'm here, Anita. Why so long? You said she was fine."

"She is now, Rascal. Doctor Thwistle had to do a cesarean. The baby was breeched, Rascal, and this had to be done."

"But Em is okay isn't she, Anita? Now don't lie to me."

"She's fine, Rascal, and resting comfortably. She needs to heal, Rascal, that's all."

"Okay, Anita. You tell Em as soon as it is warm enough so the water in the lodge doesn't freeze, I'm coming to Beech Tree."

On April 5th, Rascal closed the doors to the lodge and he and Whiskey Jack boarded the train.

The nurse at the front desk almost had a fit when Rascal insisted Whiskey Jack was going to come in with him. Finally the nurse said, "Mr. Ambrose, I understand, but I cannot allow any dog beyond here. I'll keep him here with me if that'll be okay with you."

Rascal had to relent. He handed Whiskey Jack's leash over and said, "You stay here, fella. I'll be back soon."

He walked down to Emma's room. Anita was there also. When Emma saw him she started grinning and then crying with happiness.

"I think I'll let you two alone," Anita said. "I'll spend the night with my sister."

"Thank you, Anita," Rascal said and then asked. "I had to leave Whiskey Jack at the front desk. The nurse wouldn't let me bring him down. Could you take him home with you to your sister's and bring him back in the morning?"

"Sure, no problem."

"Thank you."

Emma moved the bed sheet so Rascal could see his son. "Well, have you thought of a name?" Emma asked.

"Yes, it came to me while I was on the train. Archer."

Emma rolled it around in her head for a bit and then she said, "I like it. Archer Bellamy Ambrose. I didn't know but what you might want to call him Rascal."

"No—no, I wouldn't do that to him."

"What do you mean? I always thought you liked being called Rascal."

"I do and I'm proud of it. But you wouldn't believe the amount of ribbing and laughter I have had to take. When I was in the army, the other guys always made fun of me, and I got into a few fights. No—I wouldn't do that to him."

He picked his son up and said, "Hello, Archer, I'm your father."

He began to cry. "He's hungry, I think," Emma said.

When Archer had finished feeding, Emma showed Rascal the cesarean scar on her belly. "Does it still hurt?"

"Not that much. Doctor Thwistle said it is healing real fast. It's my insides, Rascal."

Doctor Thwistle stepped in then. "Hello, Rascal. It has been a long time since I have seen you. I'm glad you're here. I need to tell you about Emma.

"Without getting into any great difficult-to-understand explanations, when the baby breeched, your wife's insides were put under terrible stress and before I could close the incision I had to repair the damage on her inside." Emma had been told all this before.

"I'm fine, Rascal. I'm okay."

"Yes, your wife is doing great. But she will never have another pregnancy."

"Will my wife be okay, Doc? That's all I want to know."

"Yes, and I will discharge her in five days."

"Okay, thank you, Doctor Thwistle."

****

Rascal stayed with his wife all night, sleeping in a chair by her bedside. He had forgotten that when a newborn isn't sleeping or feeding it is crying. He didn't sleep much that night and he had to leave in the morning. Anita was back early with Whiskey Jack and he thanked her and asked, "Do you mind staying with Em, Anita? I really should get back."

"Of course I'll stay. Now be off with you."

Rascal was glad to be home again but he worried for five days about Emma. Emma was doing well, although Doctor Thwistle still was restricting her to her bed.

On the fifth morning Anita helped Emma into a wheelchair and to a taxi that was waiting at the front entrance.

Rascal was waiting on the platform when the passenger car came to a stop. Once inside, Emma said, "I sure could use a cup of coffee."

"Emma," Anita said, "I think we should think about getting another woman to help out around here until you get back on your feet. Doctor Thwistle said absolutely you are not to do anything except tend to your baby, and I can't do everything by myself and we have a full booking of guests in May."

"Alright, you won't get any arguing from me. But who?"

Rascal spoke up, "What about Perline Bowman?"

"That would work."

"I'll take the train up tomorrow."

****

President Cutlidge, Vice President Daves and Prime Minister Kingsley met in New York for an unheard of executive decision. The president and vice president had already discussed this.

"Mr. Prime Minister, this year is usually the presidential election year. What Mr. Daves and I have discussed, and he agrees, I should remain as president and he will step aside and you become the vice president. You and I started this movement and we both believe you and I should see it through. We both have said we want everything to be in place by the 1st of January in 1933. I would like to remain president until January 15th of 1932, at which time I will step aside and you finish what we have started and then return to a four year term. Now, we can do this by making the move an executive decision for the protection of and execution of this merger. All we have to have is your approval."

"I agree with you, Mr. President and Mr. Vice President."

"This fall the first council members to parliament will be elected and sworn in immediately so they can get on board."

This news was broadcast on the usual Saturday evening radio hour and in all the media outlets and no one raised any argument.

****

Rascal took the train north and got off at the Bowman homestead. Mr. Bowman met him. "Hello, Monsieur, I am Rascal Ambrose. I'd like to talk with your daughter Perline, if I may?"

"Certainly, come in."

Perline was in the kitchen. "Hello, Rascal. I'm surprised to see you."

"Perline, my wife gave birth on April 1st and the doctor does not want her working for another two weeks. We are booked up full each week in May and could really use some help. Would you be available and would you be interested?"

"Yes, of course I'll help. When would you want me to start?"

"I had hoped you'd go back with me on this afternoon's train."

Perline looked at her father and he nodded his head. "Okay, I'll go pack. Sit down and have coffee with my father."

Armand and Rascal talked over cups of coffee until Priscilla shoed them outside so she and Perline could fix sandwiches and soup for lunch.

"I took train to Beech Tree and then to Kidney Pond and talked with Mr. Hitchcock, looking for work. He said wait 'til June this year and he would have work for me at Whiskey Jack."

"What did Mr. Hitchcock say you would be doing for work?"

"He didn't say. But I am a woodcutter." Rascal didn't ask any more on the subject but he would keep it on the back of his mind.

The train stopped and they boarded for Whiskey Jack. "Where are you getting off, Rascal?" Tom asked.

"We're both getting off at Whiskey Jack."

At the supper table that evening Rascal told them what Perline's father had said about coming to Whiskey Jack to work.

"Do you suppose Hitchcock is going to start the mill up again?" Emma asked.

"It must be that or why would he tell Armand there would be work in June."

"I wonder if doing away with the border has something to do with the mill reopening?"

After supper Anita took Perline aside and told her what

she would be doing. "In two days, on Sunday our first guests will be arriving."

That evening Perline wrote a letter to Herschel and told him all about her new job.

"What about the ice in the lake, Rascal? Can the guests get out on the lake to fish?" Emma asked.

"The wind has blown all of the ice down in this cove. The upper half is all open and there's a channel wide enough between shore and the ice so they'll be able to get through alright with canoes."

"I wish I was back on my feet so I could help out. I feel so useless."

"Two more weeks, Em. Dr. Thwistle made me promise to hold you to it."

Even though Rascal was busy all day, he looked forward to some quiet time after supper to spend with his son.

"Rascal, can you make me something that I can set Archer in and carry him around on my back?"

"Yes. It shouldn't be too difficult. I'll use one of the wolf pelts."

As they were lying in bed that night, Rascal asked, "In the hospital you said you had a name all picked out if the baby was a girl. What was it?"

"Belle," she let it hang there for a moment before continuing.

"I like Lt. Belle, Rascal. She is a nice person. And, Rascal, I understand there's a special bond between you two and I'm alright with that. You two had experienced some awful terrible times in the war. You saw your friends blown to pieces and Belle told me about some of the worse cases that she had helped with in the field hospital. I wasn't there, Rascal, when you needed someone, but Belle was and I think she was needing someone to lean on too. I couldn't be there for you, Rascal, and I'm glad Belle was. So you see, Rascal, I can understand this friendship that the two of you have."

"Hum, you're really something, you know that, Em."

Chapter 11

The fishermen were able to canoe up through the channel to the head of the lake, but the best fishing was out in the middle. By the following weekend all of the ice had melted. Sunday a new group of fishermen arrived. The Cummings didn't make it this year, and they wondered why.

That second Monday Earl Hitchcock and the S&A Railroad project engineer arrived on the train. "Have you room for two more, Rascal, for one night?"

"If you don't mind the log cabin. You can take your meals here in the lodge with the rest of us."

"Did you come up to inspect the mill and farm, Mr. Hitchcock?"

"We are going to start harvesting the prime hardwood sooner than we had planned, and the S&A Railroad is going to put a spur line into the farm."

"Are you going to restart the mill?"

"No. The equipment in that mill is too old now. We won't be doing any milling. Everything is going to Colong Lumber in Lac St. Jean. I'm going to show Mr. Howard where I want the spur line to go. Then in June after the ground has dried out we'll start. Crews will cut the right of way and Jeters will be coming up with the bulldozer. I don't suppose you'll have room in the lodge for our men would you?"

"How many are you talking?"

"Well, there'll be three, three-man crews cutting the right of way, a surveyor, Jeters, three men with dump trucks, a steam shovel operator. We'll have to open the farm. There'll be a crew to open the farm and get that ready next week. Then the cutting crew and a crew to build a temporary unloading ramp just above your lodge. Everything has to be ready for lumbering by November. We'll be busy.

"I have a man coming down from near Lac St. Jean to ramrod the cutting crews."

"Armand Bowman?"

"Yes, but how'd you know?"

"His daughter is helping out here while Em is off her feet."

"What's the matter with your wife?"

"She gave birth last month and the doctor doesn't want her working for a while."

"Congratulations, boy or girl?"

"Boy—Archer Bellamy Ambrose."

Hitchcock and Howard left the lodge and Rascal went over to tend the smoker. It was working every day and night now. Fishermen seemed to be a quieter crew and easier to please than hunters.

When Rascal had finished with the smoker he went back inside the lodge and told the womenfolk what Mr. Hitchcock had told him. "Your father will be ramrodding the cutting crew here, Perline."

"Oh, it'll seem so good to see the village back," Anita said.

"Well, the village won't be coming back. The mill is too old to restart and everything will be shipped by rail to Lac St. Jean. The crews will be staying at the farm with their own cook."

"Well, at least there will be the sound of men working and the train."

****

The next week a crew arrived with the work horses to build an off loading ramp right next to the railroad, just beyond the edge of the clearing beyond the hen house. It was built so close to the railroad that Jeters was able to turn the big bulldozer on the railcar and drive it off onto the ramp.

The cutting crews all arrived with their work horses and tools and a railcar of hay and grain and supplies for the men and two cooks. Armand Bowman arrived and the right of way had already been marked out and Bowman had the crews begin clearing. The trash wood was laid in gullies and buried with the bulldozer and the logs were cut out and there was plenty of semi-tree length firewood being piled up beside the right of way.

Most of the men chose to work all weekend, as long as they were going to be there anyhow.

One evening after the crews had stopped work for the day, Jeters walked out to the lodge to visit. There were guests in the living room so Jeters and friends stayed in the kitchen with Perline. "Is Bear still around?" Jeters asked.

"Yes, but I haven't seen him this spring. Maybe there has been too much activity for him."

"Why are you three smiling? You know something don't you."

First they had to explain about Bear to Perline. Then they told her and Jeters about Bear killing the wolf to protect Emma and how Bear now plays with their dog, Whiskey Jack.

"He sure is a strange bear."

"Yes, that he is. And Perline, what you have just heard about Bear you can't tell anyone else. The Pages know, but we would appreciate it if you didn't tell your family. We don't want it known about Bear."

"Of course not. I won't say a word."

As Jeters was leaving he stepped over to look at the new photos. He stood there in complete silence. Then he turned to look at Rascal and Emma. "Who the hell are you two?" He looked at the photo again and then at Emma. "Emma, I'm shocked. I never noticed before how beautiful you are. I just don't believe it. And you, ole buddy, this is a gentlemen in this photo, not a back-woodsman trapper. You two surely do have friends in high places."

"Come back in the kitchen and we'll try to explain." They were all seated around the kitchen table. "Go ahead, Em, you do a good job of explaining."

When she had finished, Jeters said, "I noticed you are not limping anymore. But to be invited to a formal dinner at the White House? Wow."

"It was Em's biscuits," they all laughed.

When Jeters left he was still shaking his head in disbelief. "Goodnight, friends."

"Goodnight, Jeters."

Emma had been walking now for a week and only helping out occasionally in the kitchen. Archer was taking up much of her time.

****

Greg Oliver, the station master called Rascal and said, "We have another beaver problem back at Ledge Swamp. Can you take care of this?"

"Certainly, I'll go up with the morning train."

Rascal put his pack basket with traps and axe on the loading platform. Then he and Whiskey Jack walked out along the marked right of way. The work was progressing fast. He watched Jeters operating the bulldozer ripping out tree stumps and pushing large rocks to the side and filling in gullies. Jeters had certainly found his niche in life.

He saw Armand Bowman and walked over to talk with him, "Good afternoon, Mr. Bowman."

"Hello, Rascal, how is my daughter working out? I haven't had much time to visit her."

"She's doing real well. She's a hard worker and happy all the time.

"What are you going to do with this small hardwood you have piled up in places?"

"It'll be good for nothing except to keep you warm in the

winter. If you want this wood, help yourself, Rascal. We already have plenty stacked up at the farm."

"I'll do that. Tomorrow I have to remove beaver for S&A, but I'll get it."

Rascal and Whiskey Jack boarded the train the next morning. "Where to this day, Rascal?" Tom asked.

"Mile twelve, Tom. I have to remove beaver and the dams."

"I was wondering why you were carrying that potato digger with you."

The train slowed just enough at Ledge Swamp so Rascal and Whiskey Jack could jump off. The beaver dams were exactly where they had them when Jeters came up with him. He set up the small coffer dam next to the left side of the tracks first and then he moved downstream.

The first house he came to was huge. There was probably as many beaver here as when Jeters had helped him. Before he had set the fourth trap on the first dam a huge beaver paying no attention to Rascal, probably because Whiskey Jack was barking on shore, was caught in the first set. He waited five minutes before pulling it in. He had caught bigger beaver, but not many.

Before he had it skun and the good meat cut off and rolled up in the hide another trap snapped closed and then another. As he was taking care of those two beaver, he cut off small pieces of meat and gave it to Whiskey Jack.

With three beaver gone from that flowage the remaining beaver were being cautious. He could see two on the house watching him. He picked up and moved down to the lowest dam close to Jack Brook. The house here wasn't quite as big.

After he had two more large beaver he decided to build a small fire and warm up some tea and roast beaver. The smell of the cooking meat was driving Whiskey Jack crazy. "Whiskey Jack, stop your barking." He barked once more as if challenging his master. "No! No more. Now lay down."

Whiskey Jack was a smart dog and he knew when not

to push it and he lay down and put his head on his front paws. When one piece of meat was cooked he tore off a piece and held it out for Whiskey Jack. "You old ham bone, you. You didn't even chew it to get the flavor. You simply swallowed it whole." Rascal chewed on his piece savoring every chew.

Before leaving there he had three more beaver and moved up to check on the middle dam. Two traps were pulled into the water.

The beaver activity had certainly quieted, so he walked down to the lower flowage and brought the carcasses up and then carried all of them up and across the tracks to the top of the bank. He was sure Bear would soon find them.

He checked his watch and decided the train would be through in a hour. He had just enough time to check the coffer dam, where he had two more. Only two-year-olds. After skinning those two and saving the meat he had a full pack basket and had to tie the last two on top of the basket. He lifted the pack basket and was glad the train would be through soon.

Whiskey Jack started barking and Rascal looked in the direction Whiskey Jack was facing. "Hello, Bear," and he raised his arm. Bear did also. Then he sauntered down to the tracks and stood between the rails. Rascal hoped Bear and Whiskey Jack would remember each other. He held onto his collar and took a few steps towards Bear. Whiskey Jack's tongue was wagging and his tail was switching back and forth like a whip. Whiskey Jack barked a hello. Rascal knew then they would be okay and he released him and he ran up to Bear and then ran circles around him and Bear gave chase. Rascal wasn't sure who was chasing who. Then Whiskey Jack ran up on the bank and Bear right behind him. Bear chased him around and back and forth for five minutes and then Whiskey Jack turned and now he was chasing Bear.

All of a sudden Bear stopped and looked up the tracks and then bounded to the top of the bank. The train was coming. Rascal couldn't see it yet but he could hear it. "You'd better go, Bear, the train is coming."

Right on cue, Bear walked off into the bushes. Fred Darling brought the train to a stop next to Rascal, "You want a ride back, Rascal?"

"Yes."

"I'll pull ahead a little."

"Thanks, Fred."

Tom knew why the train was stopping and he looked up ahead and saw Rascal. "Here, you'd better give me your pack, Rascal. Wow, this is heavy. Good thing we came along so you wouldn't have to carry this all the way back.

"Whiskey Jack is going to be a busy little place soon, ain't it, Rascal," Tom said.

"Yeah, but you know, Tom, I was more comfortable when it was just us and the lodge."

"Times is changing, Rascal."

Rascal nailed the eight hides to drying boards and ran his fingers through the hair. "Not bad for summer beaver." Then he took the castors to the woodshed and the meat to cold storage.

"Will you have to go back tomorrow?" Emma asked.

"Yes, I need to clean out all the beaver before I dismantle the dams. Bear was there and he and Whiskey Jack played and played. He never paid any attention to me as long as Whiskey Jack was there."

The next morning after breakfast Rascal had his pack basket ready to go and the red flag was up. "Whiskey Jack, you coming with me?" He came running with his tongue out.

"Remember, Rascal, you're up there to work and not just play with Bear," Emma said and laughed.

"Same place today, Rascal?"

"Yes, Tom, and I'll try to be done by the time you come back."

It was a hot day and the blackflies were terrible. There was one beaver in the coffer dam set and one at the next dam down and two beaver bringing brush down to fill in the troughs where the traps were. Rascal took that beaver back away from the flowage hoping the two would come to the traps if he wasn't there.

He was beginning to catch only small beaver now so he knew that he had already taken most of them. At the lower flowage he had another large beaver. He took care of that one and started roasting beaver meat. It was early, but he was hungry. He lay back waiting for the meat to cook and Whiskey Jack lay down beside him and put his head on Rascal's leg.

Rascal was almost asleep when he heard a trap snap closed and the beaver splashing in the water in the trough. Whiskey Jack heard this also and sprung to his feet and ran down to the dam. He could see the struggling beaver on the dam and the beaver was naturally something to hunt and maybe play with. Rascal wasn't far behind him, calling out, "Whiskey! Whiskey, no! Come here!"

But Whiskey Jack had other intentions. He saw the beaver as a target and he knew it was also food. He ran out on the dam after the beaver, but the beaver instead of swimming off, he stood his ground and started hissing at Whiskey Jack and snapping his jaws together.

Rascal knew the beaver could do real damage to a dog, especially if it took a leg in his powerful jaws. With one bite Whiskey Jack could lose a leg. Rascal was able to get to Whiskey Jack and pulled him back. The beaver then swam off but it soon drowned with the trap still on its leg.

Rascal scolded Whiskey Jack and told him to stay while he went to retrieve the trap and beaver. It was another two year old, but certainly full of piss and vinegar.

After he had taken care of that one he went back up to check the other large flowage and the coffer dam. There was only one small one there.

Figuring he had all the beaver he started at the lower dam pulling it apart with the potato rake. He had left the two traps on the coffer dam figuring if there were any beaver left they surely would head upstream when he started draining the water behind the dams.

When he had finished he brought up the beaver carcasses for Bear and checked the coffer dam. He had another small beaver. He was satisfied now that he had them all. He still had an hour to wait for the train. He took his pack basket off and set it down beside the rails.

Bear was sitting on the knoll where Rascal had just minutes ago left the new carcasses. But Bear wasn't interested in eating; he wanted to play. So Rascal let Whiskey Jack go. They took turns chasing each other. Whiskey Jack was smaller and quicker but Rascal was certainly surprised how agile Bear was. He laughed all while they were chasing each other. He wished Emma and Anita could be here to see this.

Both animals were panting from the heat and exhaustion. Bear sat on his haunches and watched as Whiskey Jack raced back and forth. Finally he too had had enough and he lay between the rails facing Bear.

All of a sudden Bear jumped up and ran off to the top of the knoll. Rascal then could hear the train approaching. Before it came to a stop, Bear had sauntered into the bushes and disappeared.

"How was your trapping today?" Tom asked.

"I finished up and removed all the dams."

"Them beaver, they sure is a mighty working little animal. How many for both days did ya catch, Rascal?"

"Twelve in all. Are they bothering at mile nine?"

"Not that I can see."

While Rascal was up the tracks, Anita and Perline canned the beaver. "Rascal should bring back a few more today, too," Emma said.

"Do you like beaver, Perline?" Anita asked.

"Yes, but my dad doesn't have much free time to go trapping."

"Well some night, Perline, you'll have to invite your dad to supper and we'll have beaver. Saturday evening would be the best time as we don't usually have any guests come in until

Sunday."

"Maybe I can get Rascal to walk with me out to the right of way someday, so I can ask him."

"Maybe today, Perline, if he gets back in time, which he should be coming in on the afternoon train."

Just then Fred Darling blew the half mile warning. "He's coming in now."

When Rascal and Whiskey Jack stepped off the train and onto the platform Whiskey Jack slowly walked over to a shady spot and lay down, still panting. "What is wrong with him?" Emma asked.

"He and Bear were playing again, steady for about an hour until they both were so tired they lay down between the rails facing each other. It was the darnedest thing to watch, Em."

Emma began laughing and said, "You sound a little disappointed, Rascal, that Bear has a new playmate. When you have a moment, Perline would like you to walk with her out to see her dad, and invite him for supper Saturday. I told her we would have beaver."

"Okay, let me put this meat and hides in cold storage and put away my tools. I'll do the hides later."

After supper and the kitchen was clean, Rascal and Perline were ready to start out. "Do you want to walk out with us, Em?"

"I would, but I don't think I should walk that far yet."

"Have you been feeling any pain?"

"No, I'm just thinking what Doctor Thwistle said. I should take it easy until the end of July. Then I can do anything that I feel like doing."

"Okay."

Rascal and Perline left with Whiskey Jack running out ahead of them. The crews were done for the day and they had to hike out to the farm. The men had done a lot work in only a month. The right of way was cleared almost to the farm. In another day they probably will have it finished. Jeters was coming up behind them with the big bulldozer. They found Perline's dad walking the right of way near the farm.

"You have come a long way, Armand, in a short time."

"Yes, we are ahead of schedule by a week. The weather has been good."

"Dad, would you like to come for supper tomorrow evening? Emma said we will have fresh beaver."

Armand's eyes and face lit up. "Qui, I like beaver, me. Yes, I come. What time?"

Perline looked at Rascal. "6 o'clock if you can get away by then."

"For the beaver, qui, I can get away."

One reason the crews were ahead of schedule, the men chose to work Sundays, since they were out there without anything else to occupy their time.

On their way back Perline asked, "Rascal, I've heard you, Emma and Anita talk often about a bear you call Bear and how he now plays with Whiskey Jack. Do you suppose I could see this sometime?"

"Until now, every time we come out to the farm, Bear would be here. Now with all this activity I think he'll stay away. We'll work on it, okay?"

All the guests left the next day on the afternoon southbound and they all were taking with them smoked fish, and who didn't have too far to travel were taking a couple of brookies or togue with them to have mounted.

Armand stopped work early that day so he would have time to wash up before going to the lodge for supper.

"Hum, the beaver, fried cabbage, fiddleheads and biscuits, this is food fit for a king," Armand said,

Afterwards they sat in the living room listening to the radio and the latest news about the changes North America was experiencing. The new currency had been printed and anyone could exchange the old bills for the new or they could continue to use it until the first of September at which time the old currency would no longer be redeemable. The foundation for the new capitol and parliament buildings had been completed and the work on the buildings themselves had started. Crews were working in shifts twenty-four hours a day, each day.

And the brightest news was that the economy of the new nation was stronger than ever before the merger, businesses were prospering and people in Upper and Lower America were investing their money in businesses.

And as of July 1st, alcoholic beverages could be purchased in special agency stores. There would be a local and federal tax imposed to fund the agency that was overseeing the distribution.

When the broadcast had ended, Armand said, "We should have done this merger many years ago."

Everyone agreed.

Chapter 12

After the spring fishermen, there were fewer guests each week. Some weeks there might only be two. This gave Rascal the time he needed to catch frogs and can the legs, smoke brook trout and togue and finish working up his winter firewood.

The train right-of-way was cleared and most of the track bed was in place. The switches between the lodge and where the spur line left the main line were in place and steel laid down. The track crews were now beginning to lay rails to the farm.

Armand's crews had finished their work with the new spur line and some were making repairs to the buildings and others were laying out and clearing twitch trails from the hardwood groves back to the farm. Once the rails and turn around were finished the men would build loading ramps close to the rails so they could roll the hardwood logs onto the cars. Jeters helped out with the bulldozer, filling in the ramps with gravel, trucked in from a horseback knoll behind the farm.

The S&A project engineer figured the rails, turn around and switches would be finished by August 1st, one week away and ahead of schedule.

Herschel would spend his days off at Whiskey Jack with Perline, and Emma gave them the log cabin to use whenever he could come. People around Beech Tree and the surrounding farms and unorganized territories had come to understand that Herschel was not someone they could push over or outwit. "He's worse than his ole man ever was," one disgruntled poacher said as the cell door was closed behind him. Sheriff Burlock only laughed.

Emma decided that taking care of a baby and trying to do her share of work at the lodge was too much. "Perline, I'm having a difficult time to do much work around and tend the baby at the same time, and we only have two to four guests a week. This fall we'll be full up. Would you consider staying on until the end of deer season?"

"Certainly, Emma, I'd love to. I really enjoy working here. Everyone is so nice and I even get a chance to see my father once in a while."

One Saturday evening while Armand and Herschel were both there for supper, Armand said, "My two best men are Fredk St. Pierre and Ralph Paquette."

"I know those names," Herschel said.

"You should, young man. Your father arrested the pair of them two times. The first time they tried to beat him up and your dad had to take them to the hospital before the jail. Next time he and the judge let them both go and your dad, he bought their rifle so they would have enough money for train tickets home. When I hired them I said no hunting, camp rule by Mr. Hitchcock. He wants men working, not hunting. No one in my crews has a rifle.

"Someday, young man, you make a trip through the woods to let crews see you, talk to them and there will not be no trouble. Ok?"

"I will do that tomorrow."

"Your dad, Herschel, he is legend even in Quebec along what once was border. And people now talking about his son, you. You be careful out there. I would not want your work."

The next day was Sunday but all the crews were working. There was nothing else to do. Herschel walked up along the newly cleared twitch trails and met a few of the men and talked amicably with them. When he found Paquette and St. Pierre, they acted like Herschel was their best friend. They had even learned a little English. "You see you dad, tell for us we no hold bad feelings. We like what he do for us. We no worry for you no more."

"Thank you, that means a lot and I will tell him."

Sunday morning Rudy Hitchcock stepped off the train. "Hello, Mr. Hitchcock," Rascal said.

"I've heard some awful rumors that you and Emma have special friends in Washington. I decided to come out and see for myself. You and Emma have certainly done well here for yourselves."

"Well, we have Anita Antony here, also, Mr. Hitchcock."

Rascal led the way to the photographs on the wall in the dining room. And then of course he had to explain how he and Emma had come to be invited for dinner at the White House. Rascal told him the story over coffee.

"How is your leg now?"

"It's fine. There are times if I try to overdo it there'll be a little discomfort in the hip, but nothing serious."

"I understand Armand Bowman, according to my brother, is doing an excellent job with the crews. And the spur line was finished ahead of schedule."

"Yes, we have heard the same. His daughter, Perline, is working here with us."

"Earl said that Armand was doing such a good job that he had decided to let him supervise the entire lumbering operations out here. And Earl would only come out on an occasional visit to check on things."

"How long do you intend to be out here, Mr. Hitchcock?"

"We are mainly interested in the large hardwood trees and an occasional spruce or pine if one is in the way or with a yellow or spiked top. I believe we can get the harvest done in two years."

"What about the old mill? Will you ever use that again?"

"Probably not. We have found that the band saw is working out so much better that it would be worth it for the company to purchase another band saw for here when we come back for softwood."

"Let's take a walk out to the farm," Rudy said.

Rudy was pleased how well Rascal had taken care of the property. He had patched holes in the mill and shed roofs and there were no bushes or weeds growing up around any of them.

Out at the farm Rudy was surprised how much space the new spur line, loading ramps and turn table had taken. "I guess it had to be. We found that at Kidney Pond it wasn't any more expensive to freight in horse feed and supplies than it was to try and produce our own. Times are changing fast. I still think we should keep the remaining field mowed, if only to keep the bushes from taking over."

Armand saw them and walked over to greet them. "Rascal, would you give us a minute alone. I'd like to talk business with Armand."

Rascal walked over to look at the ramps. There was a long ramp on both sides of the tracks so the rail cars could be loaded from both sides. Jeters was still filling in the last ramp and back dragging it.

"Armand, my brother and I have decided to let you supervise this operation. You'll be responsible not only for overseeing the cutting crews, but everything involved with the operations here. You make your own rules, you hire and fire as you see fit. I'll have the markets set up for you. All you have to do is make sure that they are filled. Either myself or Earl will come out occasionally, but only to look over the operation. You load the railcars and S&A will be responsible for getting the lumber to markets. Right now Colong Company has agreed to take everything that is harvested."

"I have one question, Mr. Hitchcock."

"Yes."

"My daughter is working at the lodge, my son has recently joined the new North American Navy. He wants to see the world. My wife is left alone at home. Could I hire her to help out with the cooking? She good cook, Priscilla."

"Yes, of course you can."

Armand began smiling and said, "Thank you so much,

Mr. Hitchcock. I afraid to leave Priscilla so long alone and I was afraid you'd say no."

"You hire and fire, right Armand?"

"Yes, sir."

Rascal saw Rudy was through talking and he waved goodbye to Jeters. "Maybe we can get back in time for the afternoon train," Rudy said.

They had to hurry to get back in time, but Rascal was able to put out the red flag as Fred was blowing the half mile signal.

* * * *

Rascal worked several days to bring in firewood from the piles of hardwood along the right of way. Even after he had the woodsheds full, he kept bringing in more.

One evening Jeters brought the big bulldozer down to the ramp by the main rail line. He'd have until about 2:20 p.m. the next day to visit with Rascal and Emma. "Have you had supper, Jeters?" Emma asked.

"No, I was hoping to get here sooner."

"Well, we have plenty of leftovers. Sit down and we'll heat some up for you."

* * * *

The next morning Rascal and Jeters left the lodge at sunrise and the sports waited until after breakfast to go fishing. This was their last day, and besides they had had plenty of fishing and were taking back to Rhode Island several pounds each of smoked brook trout and togue.

The water surface was like glass and a fog bank hung three feet above the water. It was actually kind of eerie, their heads were in the fog, but the canoe and water were clear. They canoed to the inlet without saying a word or banging the gunnels. A doe and two very small spotted lambs were feeding on shore near the rock fire pit where they had roasted so many trout in the past.

After five minutes of idle sitting, Jeters cast out just like he knew what he was doing and the line and red wolf fly softly laid on the water without slapping it. He must have landed the fly on a trout's nose as it immediately took the fly and jumped clear of the water. Rascal netted it when Jeters had brought it in close enough to the canoe. "Boy, look at that, Rascal. I bet it'll weigh four pounds."

Rascal caught one about the same size and then they each caught a few smaller ones.

Jeters began laughing then for no apparent reason. "What's so funny, Jeters?"

"I was thinking about the time soon after you were back from Europe, when we were fishing up here and drinking a little whiskey. We sure did have a good time that day."

Rascal had to laugh also, "It's a wonder we didn't tip the canoe over and drown."

"Those were good times, Rascal. I almost wish we could roll back time to the days when the village was here and everyone would get together for Thanksgiving and Christmas."

"You're making me homesick, Jeters."

"Yeah, I know what you mean. Let's head back; we have all the fish we need."

Rascal and Jeters had a late breakfast at 8 o'clock, of fish fried in salt pork, eggs, and biscuits.

"I'll make a fish chowder with those other fish," Anita said.

"Would you like to take some smoked fish with you, Jeters?" Emma asked.

"Maybe one; remember no one does any cooking at Kidney Pond, except in the main cook house."

Rascal and Jeters spent much of the morning sitting in the shade on the platform and talking. Rascal told him all about his last trip up to mile twelve and how Whiskey Jack and Bear played and chased each other until they had to lay down from exhaustion.

"Bear sure is a strange animal, ain't he, Rascal. Have you ever heard of a wild bear who plays with people and a dog? Not me. It sure will be a shame when he dies."

They walked around some more, "What will you be doing when you leave here, Jeters?"

"I'm not sure exactly, but this winter I'll be making new roads and loading ramps at Kidney Pond."

It was almost time for dinner so they started towards the lodge. "Right after we eat, I'll have to start the bulldozer to let it warm up before loading it."

Everybody sat down to eat. "This chowder is so good," Jeters said.

"And these biscuits—I've never eaten anything like it. They are so good." One of the guests said.

"I received a letter this morning from Herschel. He said he would be coming in on the morning train tomorrow," Perline said.

"Who's Herschel?" another guest asked.

Jeters spoke up first, "He's THE game warden around here. I hope you guys all have licenses," and he winked and grinned at Rascal.

After Jeters had eaten all that he could, plus a slice of strawberry rhubarb pie and a slice of sharp cheese, he excused himself and said, "Thank you for dinner, ladies, and now I have to tend to the bulldozer."

Rascal walked out with him. While walking over, Jeters started chuckling, "What's so funny?" Rascal asked.

"Please don't take offense. I wasn't laughing at you and Emma. Let me explain. First, you two are the best friends I have in the world and I would never make fun of either of you. But you and Emma, Rascal, two country bumpkins being invited to dinner at the White House. I bet Emma, before this, had never been much beyond Beech Tree. Who would ever have guessed,

Rascal. And I mean this in a good way. It's just unbelievable. By the way how is your leg since the operation?"

"Most of the time it is good, but if I try to overdo it then I begin to feel it some. But it is nothing like it was."

Jeters climbed up on the big machine and it started smoothly, then he climbed down. "How do you start this in the winter when it is so cold?"

"If it hasn't been running for a few days I have to build a fire under it to heat things up. If I'm going to use it again the next day, I let it idle all night."

The train blew the whistle and slowly pulled to a stop so the flatbed railcar was at the ramp. Jeters drove it on and Rascal helped him to secure it with the tie-down chains. "Thanks, Rascal."

* * * *

Herschel arrived Saturday morning. When he walked into the dining room the guests all turned to look at him. They were all older than the warden and didn't consider him a threat at all. After the breakfast dishes were cleaned, Emma gave Perline two days off. Perline ran into his arms and said, "Come on, the log cabin is ours."

After supper Herschel and Perline went fishing. "The best place to go when the water is warm is in front of no-name brook. Stay about a hundred feet out." He was not about to tell anyone about the trout under the lily pads. They managed to catch two, but their minds were really not on fishing.

Just before sunset they canoed back to the lodge and Herschel cleaned the two trout on the wharf and then went inside and the trout were put in cold storage. They all sat in the living room listening to the weekly broadcast about the new nation, North America.

The announcer began by saying, "For the first time since the start of this merger, a snag has arisen. Maybe not a snag actually, but the question has arisen about Lower America having more representation in parliament than Upper America. If there are to be only two parliament members per state and province.

"Since Alaska had only been a territory of the United States, it would be logistically better to include Alaska in the Northwest Territory Province. But then Vice President Kingsley reminded parliament that the states in Lower America would be grouped into larger provinces and therefore making representation in parliament on a more even keel.

"This has quieted any dissension any parliament members may have had."

"Other than that little problem the transition of the two countries merging to one seems to be progressing with unbelievable simplicity and the straight-forwardness of our government officials beginning to come together for a common cause. This in itself is rewarding."

Herschel commented first which surprised everyone, "I think this is going to be a good thing. If nothing else, it sounds as if our elected officials are working together."

"I'm not sure how it was in the United States," Perline said, "but when we were Canadians we never thought that we had much support or representation in parliament. That seems to be changing now."

The others' comments were pretty much the same. It was still a little light outside but Herschel and Perline said goodnight and walked up to the cabin.

No sports came the next day and it wasn't any wonder. The dog days of summer were hot, hazy and humid and the fishing would have been terrible. Perline took advantage of this week and spent days with her mother at the farm, or as it was being called now, the head of the spur line.

There were still enough odd jobs to keep the men working, but they had the weekends off now, and many of them would take the train home.

In September the weather turned off much cooler and the fishermen started coming back for the last hurrah before fall.

Whiskey Jack's Secret

The fishing was better now than at any time in the spring and many guests went home with trophy fish they wanted mounted.

One Sunday night after midnight, a mountain lion screamed up behind the cabin. There was a fight. There was a husband and wife from New York staying in the cabin and at daylight they both came running down to the lodge. Rascal was the only one up and he knew what the matter was. Everyone in the lodge had been awakened by the high pitched yowl and then the fighting. He knew this wasn't the same lions, as he had trapped two of them, but he thought it strange that the yowls would be in the same location behind the cabin.

Jean and Wilbur Smith ran across the dam to the lodge and slammed the door behind them out of breath. Rascal wanted to laugh but he wouldn't, as it would be making fun of them.

"That mountain lion must have sounded right outside your door last night."

"Yes! Why didn't you warn us about mountain lions here?" Wilbur asked.

"Well, it's been several years since we've had any lions here and I had no idea any were in the area."

"What was that fighting after that horrible screaming?"

"Well, last time a male lion tried to take a fresh deer kill away from a female with cubs and the female literally tore the hide off the male. I'm not sure yet what was the fighting last night. I'll go have a look-see after breakfast."

By now the rest of the guests and family were up and all asking the same question. "Are we safe here?" one of them wanted to know.

"Is it safe to go for a walk around here?"

"Look folks, I understand your concern. After breakfast I'll go see what I can find and then maybe I can answer some of your concerns. But you have nothing to fear from the lion, trust me."

A few guests went fishing after breakfast but many stayed inside or near the lodge waiting for Rascal to come back.

Wilbur Smith had asked to go with him against his wife's pleas not to go.

Rascal had strapped on his .45 and Wilbur asked, "What is that for?"

"Just in case, Mr. Smith."

They stopped and stood on the dam for a moment. Rascal was listening, while Smith was enjoying the scenery. The road was grass and weed covered making it almost impossible to see tracks. Then on top of the knoll in the middle of the road Rascal pointed to a pool of blood On his hands and knees now he searched through the grass and weeds. "What are you looking for?"

"Hair, so I can identify the animal. But there doesn't seem to be any. And there aren't any drag marks. Let's continue on."

Once in a while Rascal would see a little blood so he knew he was still on the injured animal's trail, but he still didn't know what the animal was.

As they were approaching the end of the road at the old log yard Rascal could see a patch of dark brown lying motionless in the grass. He put out his hand to stop Smith and then he withdrew his handgun and proceeded forward with caution. Smith wasn't about to walk any closer to a wounded animal and in all probability a wounded mountain lion.

Rascal didn't have to get close to see it was safe. "You can come up, Wilbur. This lion is dead."

Wilbur walked up and stood beside Rascal looking at the mangled carcass. The head had literally been torn off and was laying four feet from the body. There were deep wounds along the back and side, they could see the stomach had been ripped open and the heart, liver and some of the lungs had been eaten.

"What on earth did this Rascal? Another mountain lion?"

"I don't think a mountain lion would eat another lion. You stay right here, I'm going to look around for more signs."

Rascal made ever widening circles around the carcass and he couldn't find a clue. Finally he said, "I just don't know. I can't find any tracks in this grass and there's no trail through the bushes. Let's go back."

Rascal was deep in thought and didn't say a word until they were back in the lodge. Emma, Anita and Perline met them at the door. "Well?"

Everyone had gathered around Rascal and Wilbur Smith, "We found a dead male mountain lion, and I couldn't find a single clue what had killed it. The fight started on top of the knoll on the road that goes up and beyond the log cabin. We followed a blood trail from there to the end of the road, about a tenth of a mile." He stopped there.

"Tell them the rest, Rascal, everyone has a right to hear it," Smith said.

"The head of the lion had been torn off and lay about four feet from the body. Whatever had killed it ripped open the soft under belly and ate the heart, liver and some of the lungs."

Everyone was quiet then. And then Emma asked, "What do you think, Rascal?"

"I honestly don't know. A bigger lion could surely have killed it, but I doubt very much if it would eat its own. A wolf will feed from the carcass of another dead wolf. But I don't believe a wolf could have killed it, nor a pack of wolves. And the noise we all heard was not that of a wolf or wolves."

"What about a wolverine, Rascal? I hear they are furious fighters," Alex Jinkins asked.

"Yes indeed they are. The only wolverine I have ever known to be around here, I caught in a trap several years ago. Since then I have not seen any signs of one."

"What about a bear?"

Rascal and Emma looked at each other and in that moment they knew. "A big bear might be able to kill a mountain lion. But it has been my experience that the two keep away from the other's territory. Whatever it was I don't believe it will be back. Probably the two animals just stumbled into each other's path. I wouldn't worry."

"That maybe easy for you to say. You live here in the wilderness and the rest of us don't. I think my wife Jean and I will be leaving on the afternoon train." Two other guests had the same sentiment.

"Rascal, we'd appreciate it if you would walk up to the cabin with Jean and myself so we can pack."

"Certainly."

The Smiths were not long packing and they wanted to leave as soon as possible. The other two who were also leaving already had their things packed and sitting on the platform.

Even after the four left on the train, the remaining guests did not stray too far from the lodge and no one went fishing.

That night as Rascal and Emma lay in bed Emma said, "It was Bear, wasn't it?"

"That's the only thing I can think of. But it's also strange. I have never seen him on that side of the water shed."

"Maybe all the activity at the farm now had made him change his territory," Emma added, "He's watching over us, isn't he, Rascal?"

"I suspect he is. He saw that mountain lion as a threat."

"You know, Rascal, if I didn't know better, I'd say Bear must be lying back and watching the lodge and anything he sees as a threat to any of us he kills it," Emma said.

"I was thinking the same thing as I was walking back to the lodge. I just didn't want to say anything to the guests about Bear."

"It is still puzzling why he does it. It would be one thing if we had raised him from a cub, but he was a full grown bear when he first started playing with you," Emma said.

"Remember me telling you when Elmo and I reached Ledge Swamp on the railcar and there was another bear and Bear took off after it?"

"I remember."

"I wonder now if he was protecting us from the other bear."

"I never thought of it like that, but that could certainly be all he was doing," Emma said.

"He sure is an enigma."

"I hope he didn't get hurt fighting that mountain lion," Emma said.

"Me too."

* * * *

They didn't hear anymore mountain lion screams or fighting and slowly the guests went back to fishing and enjoying their stay at Whiskey Jack Lodge.

The last group of fishermen said their goodbyes the last Saturday of September. Now they had two weeks of rest before the deer hunting season. All of the rooms had to be thoroughly cleaned and a supply of food brought in from Lac St. Jean.

One morning after breakfast, Rascal went out back for the newspaper and sat at a table. On the front page was an article about Elinor Smith, a daring woman aviator. "Holy cow! Listen to this," and he read the article aloud:

> Seventeen-year-old Elinor Smith, also known as the Flying Flapper of Freeport, has pulled off another daring stunt underneath New York City's four East River Bridges. Many individuals had placed bets whether she would attempt to fly under the bridges or chicken out at the last moment. So newsreel teams were positioned on each of the four bridges to document that she had actually flown under them. But the bridges were not the only obstacles for the Flapper. There were several tall ships in the rivers that she had to maneuver around. At age sixteen, Elinor made her first solo flight and became the youngest U.S. licensed pilot.

Smith (right) with Helen Hicks around 1928-1930 in Farmingdale, New York

Anita said, "Why she's no more than a little girl. What is she doing taking risks like that? My word, what is next?"

"Well, if she became a licensed pilot at sixteen she must be awfully good. Maybe someone dared her to do it."

Anita began laughing then and she was awhile before she could speak. "I can hear Silvio now, 'Yessah, by God, give women the right to vote and look what they're doing now, flying airplanes under the bridges in New York City.'" Then they all had a good laugh.

When they had stopped laughing, Perline asked, "Who is Silvio?"

For an hour the three of them regaled her with stories of Silvio Antony. Anita enjoyed talking about Silvio and listening to Rascal and Emma telling stories about him, as much as Perline.

The quiet time between fishermen and hunters was a good reprieve. Anita and Perline went to Lac St. Jean shopping for last minute necessities. This would be the last trip now until after the deer hunting season.

Bowman was finding it difficult finding enough work for

the men to do, to keep 'em busy, so he had them start cutting the hardwood trees that were closest to the loading ramp, so the work horses wouldn't wear themselves out twitching logs over dry ground. It was slow work and after three days the two crews filled two railcars. The other crews were still busy preparing for winter. Armand telephoned the S&A and advised Greg Oliver the station master in Beech Tree that there were two cars ready to ship.

It was good to see loaded railcars leaving Whiskey Jack again. For Rascal, Emma and Anita it was a reminder of how things once were.

* * * *

On the 15th of October, a Sunday, all of that week's guests arrived. A few were repeats, but most of them were new hunters. After supper that evening, while they were all still sitting at the table, Rascal explained the lodge rules. "When I say there will be no hunting beyond mile eleven or at Ledge Swamp, I'm serious. Last year there were two hunters that didn't heed my warning and they were asked to leave the next day. We consider that area as a conservation area. And the last rule is there will be absolutely no bear hunting here. We want the reputation of a fishing and deer hunting lodge, not someplace you can go and kill anything you see. There are plenty of deer around here. You all may not get one, but there is no reason why all of you won't see deer.

"There are lumbering crews around the farm now and although this will be a choice place to see deer, I caution you about hunting too close to their operation. If you should accidentally shoot one of the lumbermen, I'm afraid you would not only be legally responsible, but other lumbermen might try to even the score with whomever were to shoot a friend of theirs. The men in wilderness lumbering settlings are a close-knit bunch of fellas. All I'm asking is to be careful."

The first morning out two first-time hunters went up the

tracks and found a nice spot about a half-mile from the lodge. Rascal was outside putting away all but one canoe for the winter when at 9 o'clock he heard a rifle shot not too far up the tracks. He waited and a few seconds later there was a second shot.

A half hour later Jody came walking back all smiles. "Mr. Ambrose, oh, Rascal, my friend and I have shot two deer. Neither one of us have ever cleaned a deer. Could you help us?"

"Certainly. I'll let Em know where I'm going." And he put the dog inside so it wouldn't be barking while he was up the tracks.

George was sitting on the bank happy to have shot a deer, but embarrassed that he and Jody didn't know how to field dress a deer.

Rascal worked like a butcher in a meat shop. "Who's the 6-point?"

"Mine," George said.

"This is a nice doe, Jody. They both should be good eating."

Rascal helped them drag the deer back and the two never stopped talking, they were so excited. Their first time deer hunting and the first hunters of the group to shoot deer.

For supper that night everyone had heart and liver fried in onions.

* * * *

There was eight inches of new snow on the ground by November 5th and it never melted. The temperature dropped into the 20's every night and the days were even cold. By the end of the fourth week of hunting everyone at the lodge was played out. It had been a busy season. There was still one week left and this week they traditionally set aside for themselves and Thanksgiving. Although the new date for Thanksgiving was November 4th they were still going to celebrate it on the traditional day for this year. Next year they might change.

Rascal checked the ice on the lake and there was six

inches everywhere he cut a hole. This was the earliest freeze up that he could remember.

Now that there was snow covering the ground, Armand's crews were putting out two railcars a day of high grade hardwood logs for the Colong Company in Lac St. Jean.

Wednesday morning Jarvis and Rita arrived on the morning train. "Where is Herschel? I thought he would be coming up with you?" Perline asked.

"He was and he was at the train station with us when Sheriff Burlock caught up with him before we left. There was a hunting accident this morning along the railroad tracks south of town. Apparently it was a fatal shooting and Herschel will be busy for a few days now. But he asked me to tell you, Perline, that he would come up just as soon as he can."

That afternoon Rascal and Jarvis went hunting behind the log cabin at the end of the old road. Jarvis followed Rascal to the cleared trap line while Rascal went off to the right. There were deer tracks running in both directions and there hadn't been any hunters out that way since the first snow. And there were no predator tracks. Rascal figured Bear had probably taken care of that.

Jarvis fired the first shot. He had come up on two large bucks that were fighting. They both had an open wound on their forward shoulder, but this didn't seem to be slowing them down any. Jarvis picked out the one he wanted and waited for a clear shot. But the deer were struggling so much he didn't know if he'd get a clear shot at either of them. So he whistled and they kept fighting. So he hollered, "Hey!" This did the trick, they both stopped and turned to look at him and when they did, he took careful aim at the closest one. It went down in a heap and the other one ran off towards Rascal.

Rascal had heard the whistle and was a little puzzled by it. But when he heard Jarvis holler, he knew what Jarvis was doing and he suspected he had come up on two bucks that were fighting. He backed off the deer trail about fifty feet and waited.

He could see well in both directions. He didn't have long to wait and a buck came running into view. Rascal whistled and the buck immediately stopped with his nose held high sniffing the air. Rascal shot him in the neck and he collapsed.

They had dragged them out to the old road at the same time. "I couldn't imagine at first what you were doing when I heard you whistle, then when you hollered I knew what you were doing. This buck was running too fast for a good shot, so I whistled and he stopped."

"This is pretty good hunting for only an hour or so. Two ten point bucks."

It was an easy drag on snow and downhill most of the way. They hung 'em up and Rascal said, "I'm going to skin mine now while it is still warm."

"Good idea. Maybe tomorrow we could make a box so I can quarter this up."

When they had finished they took the hearts and liver into the kitchen to wash them out. "Good," Emma said, "I was going to have some canned beaver tonight, but now we can have heart, liver and onions." Nobody objected.

They had soup and sandwiches for lunch and then they all sat in the living room talking and sipping coffee. Perline was even drinking more coffee now than tea. Whiskey Jack laid on the braided rug in front of the fireplace.

"Rascal?" Emma said in a questioning tone.

"What?"

"Aren't you going to tell Rita and Jarvis about Bear and the mountain lion."

"Why, of course. I was only waiting for the right time.

"Well, back in September we and all the guests were awakened one night by a screaming mountain lion and then the sounds of a terrible fight, coming from behind the log cabin. I went up the next morning and found a large pool of blood in the road not far from the cabin. A man and wife were staying there. I had taken the man, Wilbur Smith, with me. We followed the blood trail to the end of the road. Just beyond where we dragged the two deer out. There at the end was the mangled remains of a mountain lion. The head had been torn off and was laying four feet away and the heart and liver had been eaten.

"We figured it had to have been Bear, especially what he did to that wolf that was going to attack Em."

"What aren't you telling us?"

Emma looked at each of them before answering. "Bear had to have been already here the day he saved me from the wolf, or he had followed the wolf here. Rascal and I now believe his saving me was a deliberate act. He was protecting me, we now believe he watches over us, all of us, to see that no harm comes to us.

"I know how preposterous that must sound, but it's the only answer we have. I mean he even plays with Whiskey Jack. And bears and dogs are supposed to be sworn enemies."

* * * *

To everyone's surprise Herschel arrived the next morning. Perline ran out to greet him and jumped into his arms. "Come inside. It's too cold to talk out here." Herschel had the newspaper with him and handed it to Rascal once he was inside.

"It didn't take you long to wrap up that hunting accident. What happened, son?"

"Albert Norvak was shot by his fourteen year old nephew. The whole family were driving deer down towards the railroad tracks and when the nephew, Peter Norvak, heard Albert working his way through some alders, he shot at the movement and hit his uncle in the chest. The M.E. won't be doing the autopsy until next week. In all likelihood he'll be charged with assault while hunting, but I have to talk with the D.A. first."

"You know you have to be there, son."

"Yeah, that's what Sheriff Burlock said. You must have had to sit in on some, Dad."

"More than I'd like. If you can observe without thinking

it is a human body or someone you know, it will be better."

"Do you want to go hunting? Rascal and I both shot deer yesterday."

"After yesterday, I don't think so."

"I understand, son."

The four women were busy in the kitchen and father and son were busy talking about game wardening. Rascal looked at the headlines on the front page of the paper.

Ex-Corporal Adolf Hitler

Rascal read the article about Hitler while Jarvis and Herschel talked.

In 1923 Corporal Adolf Hitler, after being decorated with the Iron Cross, attempted to seize power in Munich and failed. He was imprisoned and then was released in 1924 and since then he has been an outspoken faction and gained support by attacking the terms of the Treaty of Versailles which ended the war in Europe. He convinced other supporters that this treaty was bankrupting Germany and he began preaching new ideas that he is calling Germany's New Order. In a time when much of Germany is starving and struggling to survive from one day to the next, the German people were very receptive of his New Order.

"Excuse me, Jarvis, have you been following the news about this Hitler guy in Germany?"

"I've read a couple of articles I guess, but I haven't paid much attention to him."

Rascal handed him the newspaper and said, "Read this and see what you think."

After a few minutes Jarvis said, "He sounds like a trouble-maker to me."

Rascal told Herschel about the mountain lion that had

been killed. "You really think it was Bear?"

"After what he did to the wolf that was about to attack Em—yes. It's the only conclusion we could come to."

"Hum, some people report angels protecting them and here you have Bear. You know if any of this leaked out of here you would be swarmed with news media and people wanting to see Bear."

"That's why we have tried to keep Bear a secret."

After Thanksgiving dinner and the kitchen was cleaned, they all went for a walk out to the farm. "Harvesting trees no harder than this will be good for the deer," Jarvis said. "They'll do well on the regeneration."

The southbound train was just backing in the two empty cars as they were walking up the road. According to President Cutlidge this was no longer a traditional holiday; it had been moved to November 4th to commemorate the merger of the two countries. So the crews were all at work and there would be two loaded cars for the northbound in the morning.

It was a smooth operation, the way the loading ramps had been designed and Armand Bowman's ability to work men.

* * * *

In February when the snow was deep, Bowman hired Rascal with his small bulldozer to open up twitch trails for the teams. After two weeks the horse teams could break open their own trails as the warm weather had moved in and the snow had settled.

Come April spring break up was early and Armand said they were done for the season and had slightly exceeded their contract. The men could all return home and they all signed on again for the fall start up. And he gave each man a bonus for filling their contract and one for promising to return in the fall.

Herschel and Perline were married in late April at Whiskey Jack Lodge and after their honeymoon she continued to work at the lodge. Herschel came to stay with his new wife when he had a day off, but continued living at his folks home. When he and Perline had saved enough money they would buy a place of their own. And they had agreed to wait until they had a home of their own before starting a family.

During that winter of '29 when Rascal wasn't bulldozing at the farm, he would pamper and coddle his son, Archer. Emma would watch him with Archer and her heart would ache with so much joy over Rascal's love for his son.

Archer was a year old now and sometimes he could be very fussy when a new tooth started to work through. And in these times Rascal would try to make him laugh. "Son, someday you'll be called the April Fool baby, and you can be well proud of it."

After their short honeymoon, Perline was back to work at Whiskey Jack Lodge. The lodge was full each week of May and June and only the occasional fisherman in July and August. Which was alright with Rascal. He used these dry months to work on winter firewood and getting enough frog legs to last them the winter. They had fifteen pounds of smoked trout and another fifteen pounds to smoke cure.

Since the lumbering crews had slightly exceeded their contract, Armand was slow this year to start cutting hardwood logs. Stores and supplies were brought by train and the barn was full of hay and grain for the horses. The cold storage room in the cellar was also full and without any doubt they would have to buy more to see them through the winter.

Before the fishermen started coming in September, in the evenings the four of them and Archer on Emma's back would venture out beyond the log cabin and sure enough Bear would be there and he and Whiskey Jack would play until they would collapse from exhaustion.

Once, before he turned Whiskey Jack loose, he ran around letting Bear chase him and trip him. Watching the two play was more entertaining than watching circus clowns. Once after Bear had tripped Rascal and he was sprawled out on the ground, Bear ran circles around him and Rascal reached out and actually tripped Bear. He rolled completely over and sprang back on his feet and began making that laughing noise. Rascal laughed also and raised his arm. "Okay, let Whiskey Jack go."

Perline did and Whiskey Jack ran barking around and around Bear, and then Bear suddenly started chasing Whiskey Jack. "He actually laughed, didn't he," Perline said.

It had seemed as Bear had changed his territory from the farm to behind the log cabin, and as Rascal had earlier suspected, because of all of the activity there now.

The economy and the labor force in the new nation, North America, was strong. The steel industries, building construction, and automobile industries were now stronger than ever before and it was mostly due to the fact of the merger of Canada and the United States. But in September the London exchange suddenly started to falter, and because of Upper North America's close ties with England, a bill was introduced into the new parliament to give aid to the London Exchange which prevented a total collapse.

And there were a few corrupt financial investor groups who were not satisfied with the millions they already had, and after the ripple in the London Exchange, they started manipulating some of the commercial bank investments and purchased large amounts of stocks, which would cause the value of that particular stock to rise. With a sudden sell off, the market value would drop extremely fast causing a run on the markets and lowering values. Then after the values had dropped low enough, these corrupt groups could make a killing by buying these low value markets and gaining control of industries.

With this new North American parliament there were fewer council members than the old two levels of Congress, and now there was less corruption and fewer special interests within the council body and real issues were being addressed more quickly. And since the two countries merged, the economy was the strongest of all. And parliament, with the help of the Attorney General's office, had put a quick stop to those groups that had tried to manipulate and control the New York Exchange.

On the evening of October 25th, the lodge was full of hunters and most were in the living room listening to the radio commentator.

"Ladies and gentlemen, this is new from President Cutlidge. Apparently a corrupt group of investors had tried to create an artificial run on banks and the New York Exchange on Thursday the 24th. These groups had been recently under close scrutiny by the Attorney General's office and were stopped before they could complete their plans of majority control of certain industries. If they had succeeded, it is now obvious that this would strategically affect our economy. The president says because of a stronger economy since the merger, what damage these groups did carry out will have little effect."

Everyone looked at each other and silence fell over the entire lodge. They all were probably thinking the same thoughts. *What would have happened if the two countries had not merged.*

* * * *

On the new Thanksgiving day, November 4th, everyone was so full of turkey and then pie they were all too full to even think about going hunting.

The last Thursday of the month the Pages all joined Rascal, Emma, Anita and Perline at the lodge for dinner. There was no snow on the ground yet and the number of deer taken for November was lower than usual, but no one was disappointed. The secret was to serve good food and plenty of it.

Snow finally arrived the first week of December. Only about six inches, but that made it good for twitching logs to the ramp. There were no big snowstorms that month, only a few inches at a time, which was ideal for lumbering. The crews were behind on their contract because of the dry going in October and November, but were now gladly working seven days a week. No one was grumbling.

For Christmas, Perline went out by train to stay with Herschel and his folks. But she was expected to be back at the farm in two days or the kitchen crew would be shorthanded.

All day the last day of December the radio commentator was saying there would be an important announcement at 7 o'clock that evening and to be sure to stay tuned.

Without any guests, Emma and Anita kept the radio on all day, so things would not be so quiet. "What do you suppose Emma? What could be so important?"

"I guess we won't know until this evening."

While the snow wasn't deep, Rascal decided to cut enough ice before it froze too deep.

"After we finish lunch let's go for a walk. It's a beautiful day and there is only a few inches of dry snow."

"I'll wrap Archer up good," Emma said.

"No," Anita said. "You two go on and enjoy yourselves. I'll take care of Archer."

"You don't mind, Anita?" Emma asked.

"Why would I mind? Archer is like the little boy I never had. How I wish I had had a couple of babies."

"Thank you, Anita."

They pulled on warm coats and hats and went out. "Where do you want to go?"

"Let's walk up the tracks. It'll be smooth walking now."

"Come on, Whiskey Jack, you need some exercise too."

The sun was bright on the white snow, the air was dry and even though the air temperature was 25°, it felt warmer. "I like days like this, Em. It's so quiet and peaceful here."

"The snow is like a white blanket covering the ground. I couldn't ever live in a city and give all this up."

"No, I couldn't either. But we did have a good time in D.C., didn't we, Em."

"Yes, it sure was. It was a dream of a lifetime come true. As much as I enjoyed seeing everything, Rascal, I was always missing this."

They walked hand in hand talking about almost anything. After a busy season they were glad now for the stillness of their wilderness. They saw deer up ahead and this soon after hunting season, they were still a little cautious of humans and they ran off.

Before they had realized it they had walked all the way to Ledge Swamp. "I wonder if bear is hibernating yet?" Emma asked.

"Oh, I'm sure he must be, or we would have seen his tracks."

They could hear the southbound coming and stepped off the tracks and waited. "Do you want to ride back, Em?"

"Yes, since the train is coming. Will it stop?"

"Oh, I think so."

Fred brought the engine to a stop where they were waiting. "Want a ride back?"

"Yes."

"Better climb up here then. The passenger car is cold. Tom had a problem this morning with the heater."

Fred reached down and took Emma's hand to help her to climb the steps. Rascal had to climb up on his own.

"It is warm in here."

Fred released the brakes and moved the throttle lever forward allowing stream to flow to the drive cylinders. It was a short ride back. But a warm one. Fred pulled up to the platform to let them step off. The switches had already been moved into position and Fred began backing the train in to the farm to leave two empty cars to be loaded tomorrow. Tomorrow morning he would hook onto the loaded cars and take them to Lac St. Jean.

Rascal, Emma and Anita waited anxiously all day, the last day of December, to hear what the big news was going to be. It was a cold day and no one had any reason to venture too far away, only to collect eggs and to feed the chickens. It was the day before New Year's and for dinner that day, Anita had roasted a pork loin.

They all ate so much that when it was time for supper Emma decided on opening a bottle of wine, and smoked fish warmed up with good sharp cheese. They sat in the living room listening to the radio and talking and watching Whiskey Jack and Archer play on the braided rug in front of the fireplace. The wine was enhancing the smoked fish and cheese, and soon Emma and Anita had to fix another platter and more wine.

There was suddenly a loud crack and grumble from the lake. It was so loud everyone jumped. Even Whiskey Jack came to all fours and he ran from window to window looking. "That was a loud one. It must be really cold out," Rascal said and got up to look at the thermometer. "Holy cow! Cold, I guess. No wonder the ice cracked. -25°." The good thing about it was there was no wind.

At 7:55 p.m. the radio commentator said, "Please stay tuned to this station. In five minutes President Cutlidge and Vice President Kingsley are going to address the nation."

"Ladies and gentlemen everywhere, President Cutlidge."

"Good evening my friends, and Americans wherever you are. I am happy to be able to talk with you tonight and tell you how things are progressing with the unification of North America. We are happy to announce this evening that all of the new government buildings have been finished and the capitol building and the White House are expected to be completed by March.

"And now, my friends, as of January 15th, I will be stepping down and Vice President William Kingsley will be sworn in to finish this term in 1932. This is an agreement he and I had made when we started this new direction of North America. Partly because we needed to show everyone that neither Upper or Lower America would have a biased position because of what area we hail from.

"Now, my friends, Vice President Kingsley has something very Important he wants to say to you."

"Good evening, my fellow friends. Thank you, Mr. President, for your introduction. First I would like to say for my vice president I have asked former governor of Minnesota Franklin Delbert, and he has graciously accepted. He shares similar views as President Cutlidge and myself.

"There is one more important topic I would like to talk about this evening. It is our judicial system. It has worked well for our early years, but it has never evolved and it is time that it moves into the twentieth century. Many complaints have come into the Attorney General's Office and President Cutlidge has authorized me to investigate the judicial system and the many complaints. I have formed a committee of myself, one parliament council member from both sections of North America, the Attorney General and two of his staff. For now I'll only tell you about one change we want to make. When someone, a defendant, is found innocent of the charge against them, they should be reimbursed for their expenses. There is no earthly reason if someone is found not guilty, why that person should have to pay for an attorney to prove their innocence. We believe that this will make the investigating officer, the prosecutor and the judges work more diligently and the courts to be more responsible and accountable. I feel very strongly about this.

"There is more to this, but as soon as the committee comes up with a final version to be drafted into a bill, then I will have it submitted to parliament.

"We have about used up our allotted time and

I'll finish by saying, no one has worked harder to bring this merger to a reality then President Cutlidge and I will continue to work in the same direction.

"Thank you all and Happy New Year."

They sat there in silence for five minutes before anyone spoke. "They were really serious when they said they were going to make changes," Anita said.

"Yeah, wow," Emma said.

"Boy I think this country is heading in the right direction now. And thanks to Cutlidge and Kingsley," Anita added.

Rascal was still silent as he was wondering where all of these changes would eventually take the country. The economy was obviously better and stronger. The failure of the financial group last fall of trying to manipulate the stock exchange was a good example of how strong the economy was since the merger. He hoped the new nation didn't have idea of taking over world domination.

* * * *

At least once a week there would be an article in the newspaper about this Hitler character in Germany who was preaching a lot of extremist ideology about how he considered the Aryan people to be superior to all others in every way. He was blaming the Jewish people for all of Europe's problems. And if he was emperor he would stop making reparations for the destruction caused in the earlier European war, which Germany lost. And if the other European countries didn't join Germany with his ideology, then he was prepared to use force to accomplish this.

What was worse than these articles about the raging of a mad man, Rascal never saw any articles where Europe was doing anything to stop this lunatic.

Chapter 13

Two years had passed and Armand and the wood cutting crews had a fourth winter to cut to finish out the larger high-grade hardwoods. An area was found with the best stand of rock maple and yellow birch trees that they had harvested so far. Cutting as they were, there was still a healthy forest left behind and much of the softwood could be harvested now, but Armand had recommended to the Hitchcock brothers to wait a few more years.

The S&A Railroad was also happy that operations at the farm had extended two years beyond their schedule.

Archer was four years old now and already Emma was beginning to teach him to read and write. Even at four he would go for walks with his dad in the woods and Rascal had made him a short version of a fly rod and he was doing quite well. He especially liked catching frogs.

He would watch Bear and Whiskey Jack, and sometimes his dad, play and he would beg to let him play also. Both Rascal and Emma had said, "No, you're too small. Maybe when you get bigger."

President Kingsley and Vice President Delbert were up for reelection in November and the whole country wondered why since the odds in their favor were so overwhelming throughout the country.

July that year, 1932, was extremely warm and the few guests who had booked a week of fishing had canceled because of the unusually warm weather.

On the morning of the 5th, Sheriff Burlock was not feeling well and decided to stay home. Deputy Kendall was left with the responsibility of escorting a prisoner to court. A Rudolph Meizer was charged with armed robbery. Two days earlier he had walked into the Beech Tree Bank and at gunpoint had stolen over $33,000.00.

But he had not gone far from the bank when he was caught. He was running on foot and had turned into the left-hand street and had literally run into Sheriff Burlock and Deputy Kendall, knocking all three to the pavement. Burlock had immediately seen the revolver Meizer was carrying and grabbed him around the neck with his right arm in a vice-like squeeze. Burlock was squeezing his neck so hard Meizer had no choice but to loosen his grip on the gun and Kendall immediately took possession of it.

"Okay, Sheriff, you can let him go. I have his gun, a snub-nose .38 special."

Burlock had to help Meizer to his feet. He had almost passed out from his chokehold. While Burlock held onto him Kendall handcuffed him. "Okay, you come with us."

It was only a short distance to the jailhouse. After he was fingerprinted and locked in the cell, Deputy Kendall counted the stolen money and then he returned it to the bank. Rudolph Meizer didn't have an address and with a very noticeable German accent, he said, "I wander town to town. No address. No mail."

With no address and with a German accent and what was happening in Germany, Sheriff Burlock telephoned the Bureau of Immigration and they notified the Federal Bureau of Investigation who telephoned Sheriff Burlock that evening.

Special Agent Covert was very interested with the capture of Meizer. "If this is him, we have been after him for months. How did you capture him?"

"He had just robbed at gunpoint the Beech Tree Bank. He literally ran into Deputy Kendall and myself."

"And where is he now, Sheriff?"

"He is locked up in a cell and will be arraigned tomorrow morning."

"Negative on the arraignment, Sheriff Burlock. Two agents from Boston will leave immediately and transport him to our headquarters."

"What is the FBI's interest in Meizer?"

"Rudolph Meizer is an alias he has been using since landing in New York two years ago. His real name is Hans Hessel. Believed to be an intelligence officer for Germany."

"Okay, we'll hold him for you."

The next morning Deputy Kendall went back to the cell to retrieve Hessel's food tray and spoon. He was too close to the cell bars when he turned his back. A rookie mistake. Hessel reached through the cell bars and got him in a choke hold like the Sheriff had done to him.

Hessel was able to remove the deputy's keys from his belt loop and he continued choking Kendall until he passed out.

After he had the cell door unlocked he dragged Kendall inside and locked the door. Before leaving the office he grabbed a double-barrelled shotgun from the gun rack, and then he went outside and started running.

Herschel was late getting to the train station and he missed the northbound. He decided to talk with Sheriff Burlock about the armed robbery arrest he and Kendall had made the previous day. But there was no one inside the office. "That's funny, it's too early to escort him over to the courthouse." Then he heard someone groaning, coming from the cells.

"Oh my God, what happened, Carl?"

"I came in to remove his food tray and I turned my back on him and was too close to the cell bars and he grabbed me. A rookie mistake."

"Are you okay now?"

"My neck hurts."

"You'd better lay down on one of the cots and I'll call Sheriff Burlock."

The phone rang and Mrs. Burlock answered, "Hello."

"Mrs. Burlock, this is Herschel. Is the Sheriff there?"

"Yes he is, Herschel, but he isn't feeling well."
"Mrs. Burlock, this is an emergency, please."
"What is it, Herschel?"
"The prisoner you had—"
"What do you mean had?!"
"He overpowered Kendall and escaped."
"I'll be right there."

Against his wife's wishes he had kept his uniform on. "Why? You're staying home."
"Just in case."

Burlock walked through the door ten minutes later. "Where's Kendall?"
"I told him to lie down, his neck was hurting."
"Kendall, are you okay?" Burlock asked.
"I think so, but my neck hurts."
"I'd better get you to the hospital. Herschel can you ask around and find out which direction Hessel went."
"Hessel, I thought his name was Meizer?"
"Long story. Better get moving. I'll be back as soon as I can."

Herschel did the only thing he could think to do, he hollered. "Has anyone seen a man running away from the jailhouse carrying a shotgun!"
"Yes," a woman answered, "and I thought it was strange."
"Which way did he go?"
"He was running north."
"Thank you," and Herschel began running. He knew if Hessel stayed on this street, it would take him to the north end of town.

Before he reached the end of the street where it made a sharp turn towards main street a man came running from a garage and hollered to Herschel, "Hey, Herschel! If you're chasing that fellow with the shotgun, he is heading towards the tracks."

"Thank you." He thought it would be best to return to the Sheriff's Office and wait for Burlock. He was already there.

"Sheriff, he ran to the north end of this street and from there towards the train tracks."

"Herschel, do you mind trying to pick up his tracks and follow him? I have some calls to make to the FBI."

"Sure thing. But first I think I should call Whiskey Jack Lodge and let Rascal know Hessel might be heading towards him."

"Good idea."

"Hello, Rascal. This is Herschel. There was an escape from the jail this morning and he was last seen heading for the train tracks. He may try to follow those north. He was arrested yesterday for armed robbery and he is also wanted by the FBI. His name is Hans Hessel but has been using the name Rudolph Meizer. He was wearing a light gray work shirt and he has a double-barreled shotgun. You need to be on alert."

"Okay, I'll alert the farm also. If he is coming this way he'll be a few hours, so I'll have time to go to the farm and back."

"You be careful, Rascal."

Rascal explained to Emma and Anita what was happening. "I need to go up to the farm and find Bowman and tell him. Keep the doors locked here and keep a rifle and handgun nearby, Em. I'll hook the dog outside for an alarm."

Rascal strapped on his handgun and hooked the dog and started the Model T tractor. That would be faster than walking. After he was on the road he shifted into third gear and he was moving along faster than he could run.

Armand was just coming out of the house when Rascal pulled up. "What's your hurry, Rascal?"

Rascal told him everything that he could.

"Do you want Perline to ride back with you to help keep watch?"

"That would be a good idea."

"Where do I ride, Rascal?"

"Well, it's going to be a fast trip and I don't want you

standing on back. If I move back in this seat I think you can fit here alright."

Once she was sitting between his legs and on the seat, "You be careful, Rascal."

"You too Armand. Keep a rifle handy and someone on watch."

They left then and the ground was so dry there was a cloud of dust blowing up behind them. After they were moving right along, Rascal said, "You steer, Perline. That way you can hang on. I'll hang on to the tractor."

"This is fun, Rascal. Bumpy, but fun."

They were only a few minutes getting back. Perline jumped off and Rascal put the tractor away. Once inside he told Perline more of what was happening. "I think Herschel is tracking him and if he is on the tracks, he'll be coming by here sometime if Herschel doesn't overtake him."

He made sure the rifle and shotgun were loaded, "Why does the FBI want this guy?" Emma asked.

"Herschel didn't say. Must be pretty bad though if the FBI wants him."

The three women stayed inside all day and made sure everything was locked up tight. Even the log cabin. When the southbound came in, Rascal flagged it down and told Fred the story. "If you see anyone on the tracks, Fred, that you don't know, don't stop. He has a double-barreled shotgun."

"Are you going to be okay here, Rascal?" Fred asked.

"Sure."

Fred left and Rascal went inside. "Rascal, Sheriff Burlock just called. Herschel is on his trail and Burlock and a posse are coming up behind him on both sides of the tracks. Deputy Kendall is spending the night in the hospital. If we see anything we are to call his office immediately. The state police are sending up help tomorrow morning."

"How long would it take him, Rascal, to get here from Beech Tree?" Emma asked.

"He will probably stay on the tracks, it's ten miles up here. He could make it in four or five hours."

"He's been on the run since 9 o'clock this morning. He's had six hours."

"Okay, if I were him I wouldn't try walking through here in the daylight. I'd wait for dark. So that said, I'm going back outside."

He had his binoculars with him as he sat on the platform where he could see where the tracks disappeared in the woods to the south and across to the cabin. Whiskey Jack was still hooked out back.

As he sat there he was thinking about how Hessel might get through. If he came through the woods on that side of the tracks and found the farm road that would take him in the wrong direction from what everyone was thinking he would go. But what if he came to the spur line and followed that to the farm thinking it was the main line?

He didn't think so. It would be his guess that Hessel had already seen the lodge and backed off and would cross Jack Brook and probably come out to the cabin. He knew he should be closer to the cabin, but he wasn't about to leave three women here alone. Besides the cabin was locked up tight and if he tried to break in he would be making a noise.

And then again Herschel couldn't be far behind him. He was guessing that Hessel would try to make his move as soon as it was dark.

* * * *

As Hessel ran up the street and then down through the trees to the railroad, nobody tried to stop him. Several people had seen him running carrying a shotgun. He was beginning to think that these people were all afraid of their own shadows. He had no idea what way the railroad would take him, but it was easy going and he was putting miles between him and Beech Tree.

He was hungry, though, and would probably get hungrier;

when he saw the dam at the outlet and the lake he knew he was close to something. On his hands and knees he crawled through the bushes. He could see an old weathered shed and behind that a large building. Across the lake up on a bank was a log cabin. He would have to wait until it was dark before he could do anything.

He was getting anxious. He knew the sheriff with or without a posse must be coming up behind him. And he didn't want to get caught between them and whatever was up ahead. In desperation he went back down the tracks for a distance and then crossed the brook to the other side. The rocks were covered with a slippery slime and he slipped and fell in the water and lost the shotgun. After struggling he managed to get across and then he started working his way up through the woods until he could see the log cabin.

He could see the log cabin clearly and the building across the lake. He still had no idea what it was or if anyone was around. But to be on the safe side he decided to wait for darkness to see if any lights would come on at either place. He didn't have long to wait.

Rascal stood up and walked back and forth on the platform. Hessel didn't see this at first. He only saw movement as Rascal was sitting back down. He still had no idea what was down there. And what was more confusing why was there a large building set beside the tracks out here in the wilderness.

The sun had set, but still too light for Hessel to move. A motor started running down by the tracks and lights came on inside. So someone was there.

Hessel was wet and was hoping to find dry clothes once he was inside the cabin, and something to eat, if only crackers or some canned vegetables. Anything to fill his stomach.

It had been almost an hour since he had seen the movement and it was dark now with no moonlight.

Bear had come in to the top of the knoll before the sun was gone. He sniffed the air and there was a definite smell of man and he knew it was not his playmate, Rascal. This one stunk. He lay down on the edge of the road and watched where this smell was coming from.

Hessel didn't want to wait any longer. He crawled through the bushes to the road and waited. There was still no movement from down below. Bear heard the bushes rattling and he stood up in time to see a hunched over man step into the road.

Bear started down the road towards this person who seemed to be stalking, noiselessly. Hessel had no idea he was not alone. Bear came up behind him and roughly pushed him off his feet and down the hill. Hessel screamed. Rascal stood up and with his flashlight in one hand and his .45 in the other, he started for the dam crossing.

Hessel came to his feet and started running towards the dam. Bear tripped him like he did Rascal. Only this was no game. Bear stepped around him and when Hessel regained his footing Bear was standing on his hind legs and he towered above Hessel, even though he was downhill from him. Hessel screamed again and Bear roared. He was so close to Hessel, spittle from Bear was blown into Hessel's face. Bear then swatted him with his paw with great force, breaking two ribs. Hessel was thrown into the bushes screaming. Bear grabbed his boot in his teeth and pulled him back to the road. He wasn't through with him yet. Bear stood again and straddled him and roared again.

By then Rascal was there and he said, "Bear! Bear, it's me, Rascal."

Bear turned his head to look at Rascal and he cried out with that laughing cry as he did whenever he and Rascal would meet. Rascal answered him.

By now Emma, Anita and Perline were standing on the platform. They had heard Hessel's screams and Bear roaring.

"It's okay now, Bear. I will take care of our friend." Bear turned and stepped over Hessel and dropped to all fours. "Good Bear, good boy."

"Have you had enough, mister, or do you want more of Bear's punishment?"

"I'll come peacefully. Just keep that bear away from me."

By now Herschel was crossing the dam and he hollered, "Hey, Rascal. Are you alright?"

"Come on up, Herschel." Then he turned to Bear and said, "It's only Herschel, Bear. You know him."

"I'm assuming this is the escaped prisoner Rudolph Meizer aka Hans Hessel."

"We'd better get him down to the lodge and I'll have to telephone Sheriff Burlock. Come on, you, stand up."

Hessel groaned and cried out in pain. "Come on, you. I don't know why you're crying in pain. That deputy you attacked is in the hospital." Herschel grabbed his arm and started him towards the dam and then the lodge.

"Take it easy, will you. That fucking bear broke my ribs."

Once inside they set him down in a chair in the kitchen and removed his ripped shirt. He had several scratches on his face where Bear had pushed him into the bushes and there was a large black and blue bruise on the left side of his ribs. Herschel handcuffed him with his hands behind him.

Anita and Perline started cleaning the blood from his face. And then they wrapped bandages around his ribs. "Are you hungry?" Anita asked.

"Yes, I am."

Herschel came back into the kitchen after calling Sheriff Burlock. "Guess what folks, Mr. Hessel here is wanted by the FBI. It seems as if we have ourselves a German spy. The sheriff said to watch him closely. A posse had set out earlier but were called back. I am to escort Herr Hessel back to Beech Tree on the afternoon train and he's to stay in jail until the FBI come after him. Oh, and by the way, Deputy Kendall will be alright. Just strained muscles in his neck."

"Are you hungry, Herschel?" Rascal asked.

"Yes."

"I'll make some sandwiches," Anita said. "Can you help me, Perline?"

"After we have had something to eat, maybe I should take Herr Hessel up to the cabin for the night. That way he wouldn't be any threat to the women."

"Nonsense," Rascal said. "I do think he should stay down here on the couch. I plan on staying down here tonight also. Besides Emma, Anita and Perline have a loaded gun in their rooms and they all are good shots."

"You'd better believe it, Herr Hessel," Anita said. "And I'm a light sleeper."

"I'm a crack shot," Emma said.

"So am I," Perline added.

"Okay, but you and I take turns staying awake."

Emma said, "If he does leave the inside of the lodge—well, Bear will have a playmate for the night."

"Just remember that, Hessel."

"No!" Hessel screamed. "Not over there!"

Both Herschel and Rascal knew why not.

"Okay, Hessel, but the first time you start to make any trouble at all, my friend here will take you over and tie you to a tree. Is that understood?"

Hessel nodded his head that he understood.

Emma made a pot of coffee while the sandwiches were being made. When the coffee and sandwiches were made, Rascal said, "Why don't we take him to the dining room where we can sit down."

"I'll handcuff you in front, Hessel, so you can eat. But remember what I said. Any trouble at all."

They each ate three sandwiches and two cups of coffee. When they had finished, Herschel asked, "What did you do with the shotgun you took from the Sheriff's office?"

"When I fell in the water the paper cartridges got wet, no good. I left the shotgun. No good to me with no cartridges."

"You know Herr Hessel, you are in a lot of trouble. I have no idea why the FBI wants you. But here you robbed a bank of $33,000.00 at gunpoint. You assaulted a deputy sheriff and you escaped from custody. Those charges alone will probably get you twenty years in prison. It might be worth your while to cooperate with the FBI when they arrive. Think about it."

"I think I should call my folks and let them know what's happened."

"Help yourself," Emma said.

In a few minutes Herschel came back and sat down. "Mom and Dad wanted to know who captured him and I told 'em Bear and they both broke out laughing."

"Perline, you should call the farm and tell your father we have Hessel and the threat is over."

"Watching you handle this, Herschel, is like watching your father. He never took any nonsense from anyone and I don't think you do either."

It was getting late and Emma said, "I think we should go to bed."

"Herschel, you're probably tired after that hike up from Beech Tree. Why don't you get some sleep and I'll watch him."

"I won't argue with you."

Emma had put Archer to bed after Hessel was caught. Rascal filled the upstairs ram-down and fireplace and left one lantern on in the upstairs hall and one in the living room. Emma gave Hessel a blanket.

Hessel tossed and turned all night with nightmares about a bear attacking him. After a while he was afraid to go to sleep, so he lay awake the rest of the night.

Herschel came down to relieve Rascal at about 2 a.m. "He hasn't slept much, Herschel. He's been tossing and turning most of the time."

Perline was the first one to get up and she started making a pot of coffee. Soon the inviting smell brought the others out.

While Emma was tending Archer, Anita and Perline fried up enough bacon and eggs for everyone with warmed up biscuits. Hessel was surprised when he was allowed to eat as much as he wanted. "I want you to know, I would not have hurt anyone. I was wet and looking for dry clothes and maybe something to eat. That's all. I am sorry I hurt young deputy, I was scared and that is why I robbed bank. I had no money. I hoped with money from bank I could go north far enough to disappear and your FBI would forget me.

"You have not asked me why I am here. Why?"

"I thought it would be better to let the FBI do that."

"I did not like what I was sent here to do. I did not want to go back. There are more here like me. I was afraid what they might do if I was discovered I was not doing what I was sent here to do. So you see I was running from my people also."

"If I were you, Hessel, it might be better if you cooperate with the FBI when I turn you over to them."

"This I will do."

Everyone was surprised with what Hessel had said and a few were feeling sorry for him.

"What is this place? You live here? What do you do?"

"This is a hunting and fishing lodge," Rascal said. "And this is my wife, Emma, our friend Anita, our son, Archer, and this is Perline, Herschel's wife."

"Growing up I would go fishing. I still like to fish."

"How do you feel today, Hans?" Emma asked.

"I can't take a deep breath or laugh. My side is sore."

"You probably have a broken rib or two."

"Thank you for asking.

Rascal excused himself and let Whiskey Jack off his run and then he collected eggs and fed the chickens. Whiskey Jack was eager to see what was happening inside and as soon as Rascal opened the door he rushed in and went directly to Hessel and smelled him all over. He could smell Bear.

The train went through and threw off the mail pouch. There were a few requests for the last week of deer hunting. And of course the newspaper.

"I doubt if I'll ever have an opportunity to fish again or to try hunting. But after last night I don't think I would ever feel comfortable in the forests again. But I probably will never see the outside of a prison."

"Don't be so discouraged, Hans. I don't know how much you know or what, and I'm not asking. But you have a huge bargaining chip to tell the FBI everything you know. It will be up to you to insist on a deal," Rascal said.

* * * *

Lunch was fish chowder and biscuits and coffee. Hessel was still handcuffed with his hands in front so he could eat. He seemed, to Herschel, that he was ready to accept his future; whatever that would be or take him. He had surrendered.

Rascal went out and put out the red flag. At 1:45 Fred blew the half-mile signal. "What was that?" Hessel asked.

"Half-mile warning. The train will be here soon. But if it stops at the platform here it'll have to unhook some cars and take the empty cars out to the farm. You still have a few minutes before you have to leave."

After Herschel and Hessel, left Emma said, "I feel sorry for him."

"But maybe some good will come from it," Anita said.

At the lodge they all went about their normal routine. In Beech Tree, Herschel and Hessel stepped off the train and had no choice but to walk to the sheriff's office. When Sheriff Burlock saw Hessel he assumed what anyone else would. "Did he try to resist, Herschel?"

"No, not at all."

"Then what happened to him?"

"He was mauled by a bear. He was across the dam from the lodge and when Rascal heard him screaming he ran over and the bear ran off. He should go the hospital Sheriff. I believe he has multiple broken ribs where the bear hit him."

Just then Deputy Kendall entered from the street. When he saw Hessel his expression instantly changed. "Deputy Kendall, I apologize for attacking you," Hessel said.

"Carl, will you stay here while I take Mr. Hessel to the hospital?"

"Walk with me, Herschel, to the hospital?"

"I need to get home, Sheriff. He won't give you any trouble. In fact he has much to tell the FBI." He looked at Hessel then and said, "Don't forget what I said, Hans, and good luck."

In the emergency room, Dr. Hausman asked, "What happened to you? Did you get into a fight?"

"I was attacked by a bear."

"Oh my word. It's a wonder you lived through it," Dr. Hausman said.

"Well I see someone taped your ribs so you probably have broken ribs. The lacerations on your face are not from claws, what happened?"

"The bear knocked me into some bushes when he hit me. My left foot hurts too. He grabbed my foot in his mouth and pulled me out of the bushes."

"As I said, you were lucky."

An hour later Hessel was rebandaged and wounds cleaned and on his way back to jail. "When will the FBI be arriving?"

"Early tomorrow morning."

"Why does the FBI want you?"

"I would rather not say anything until I can talk with them."

"So you want to talk with the FBI?"

"Yes, I only wish I had thought of that before robbing the bank."

"Hum. Then maybe you aren't as dangerous as I am led to believe."

Hessel was put back in the same cell and when the door closed he said, "I will not try to escape."

* * * *

At 6 a.m. the next morning Special Agents Harris and Billadoc stepped off the train in Beech Tree and before finding

Whiskey Jack's Secret

the sheriff's office they had breakfast in the terminal café.

When they had finished they asked the waitress for directions. Ten minutes later they entered the sheriff's office, "Good morning, Sheriff Burlock."

"Yes."

"I am Special Agent Harris and this is Billadoc. We are here for your prisoner, Hans Hessel."

"Yes, if you wait here I'll get him."

When they saw Hessel, Harris asked, "What happened? Did he resist?"

"No, he was attacked by a bear."

"Oh man, heaven forbid."

"Can you travel?" Billadoc asked.

"Yes."

"Good, the southbound for Boston leaves in two hours," Harris said.

"Sir, I will tell you everything I know, only if I am guaranteed immunity."

"I cannot give you immunity. That will have to come from higher up. We'd better wait and talk about this when we are back at our office in Boston."

"Most certainly," Hessel replied.

* * * *

Hessel remained in handcuffs all the way to Boston, although he was not mistreated. But it was apparent that his special agent escorts were not yet ready to hear what he had to say.

One advantage, he was no longer held in a jail cell with iron bars. Instead he was kept in a safe house where he was free to walk around, although he was not allowed to go outside.

Harris and Billadoc had tried several times to talk with Hessel, but he said, "Not until I have my immunity in writing."

A week later the regional supervisor Cliff Howard arrived and Hessel told him the same thing. "When I have my immunity I will tell you more than you can imagine."

"And I am supposed to take you at your word that once you have your immunity that you will tell us what we want?"

"I tell you what I will do, Agent Howard. You give me pen and paper and I will outline the information I have. But no specifics until I have my immunity."

He was given pen and paper and a half hour later he gave his outline to Supervisor Howard. Howard sat down and read over and over his outline. He was quiet for a long time and finally he said, "This is very interesting, but I cannot give you immunity. I will have to contact the director of the FBI."

"I wouldn't wait long, Agent Howard."

Howard went back to the headquarters there in Boston and telephoned Director Hoover in D.C. Howard told him everything he could and even read aloud Hessel's outline, "No specifics, Sir, until he has a written immunity."

"I will have to contact President Kingsley and I will get back to you as soon as I can."

President Kingsley was in a staff meeting in his office when his secretary interrupted. "Excuse me, Mr. President, you have a code 2 telephone call on line 3, Sir."

"Thank you."

His staff started to stand up, "Nonsense, sit down."

"Mr. President this is Director Hoover and I have an urgent request from Supervisor Howard in the Boston office." Hoover went on to describe everything that had been told to him.

"Who captured him, Director, and where was he captured?"

"He was captured at a place called Whiskey Jack Lodge and the owner Rascal Ambrose rescued him from a bear that had mauled him."

Kingsley started laughing and he was several minutes composing himself. "Sorry, Director, continue."

"Just as Rascal scared the bear off a game warden, Herschel Page, who had hiked ten miles up the tracks, took custody of Hessel and he was taken to the lodge where his wounds were treated."

"Any serious wounds director?"

"Two broken ribs, facial lacerations and the bear had bitten one foot. But he is okay."

"Yes, give him immunity, but get every piece of information from him that you can."

"Yes, Mr. President."

When Kingsley put the telephone down he began laughing again and remembering how Bear would play with Rascal.

The following day Supervisor Howard gave Hessel his written immunity and a stenographer joined Hessel and Howard and wrote down every word of Hessel's story. He was two days telling everything he knew about Hitler's plans for Europe once he was emperor; the names of six more operatives on the east coast of North America and their plans for recruiting members for a third reich in North America, to eventually attacking North America from within. And how Hitler had intentions of employing the help of the Japanese to attack the west coast of North America, hoping to engage North America in a Pacific battle, there by eliminating them from the European battle field.

Days later Supervisor Cliff Howard and FBI Director Hoover were summoned to the capitol in Sault Ste. Marie for a follow up debriefing.

All three men agreed how valuable this information was. And FBI Director Hoover was told to give Hessel a new identification and to find him a suitable place to live with a yearly stipend for five years, so that he may find suitable employment.

And President Kingsley wrote a personal letter of commendation for Warden Herschel Page and Whiskey Jack Lodge.

* * * *

The six other men Hessel had named were located but instead of arresting them now, they were put under constant surveillance. Some of the information the bureau already knew about and some had to be investigated further. But it had been agreed that Hessel had given them a jackpot.

It was the middle of August and at Whiskey Jack Lodge the mail pouch and newspaper was dropped off. Rascal waved to Fred to say thank you and he took the paper and mail inside. He gave the mail to Emma and he sat down with the paper.

All of a sudden Emma started hollering for Rascal, "Rascal! Rascal! Come here Rascal!"

He jumped up thinking there was something wrong. "Look at this, Rascal."

"What is it?"

"A personal letter of commendation from President Kingsley to all of us, for our help in the Hessel case. Even you Perline are named here."

"How does the president know about me?"

Anita laughed and said, "Dear, he is the president." That's all that had to be said.

Chapter 14

Five years has passed since the capture of Hans Hessel. The information he had given the FBI was all investigated and found to be a hundred percent accurate. The other six men that were trying to organize a Hitler movement in North America were kept under surveillance for months before being arrested and sentenced to life in prison for espionage.

Hans Hessel was given a new name with identification papers and had moved to Texas. He never again wanted to be in or near a forested wilderness where bear live. He still had nightmares of that night when Bear attacked him. And he could never understand when Rascal said, "That was enough, Bear." That bear seemed to understand and had let go of his booted foot and left. *Had that bear been a pet to those in the lodge?* That would bother him for the rest of his life, as would the nightmares.

President Kingsley and his cabinet staff had weekly meetings about Japan. It was decided that if Japan was going to attack the west coast of North America they would have to have a base of operations from which to launch an attack and the most probable site would be the Hawaiian Islands. A few Japanese spies had been arrested in Hawaii and special fortifications and preparedness were set in motion to stop the attack when it would come.

All of the government offices had by now been moved to Sault Ste. Marie, but all of the museums, memorials and libraries remained in D.C. or as it was now being called, the City of Washington.

Jarvis and Rita had sold their fur business and although

Jarvis would have liked to move into the log cabin that Rascal had offered them, he said, "If it was just me, Rascal, I would. Because I was away from home so much of the time when I was a game warden I owe the rest of my life to Rita. But you have no idea how much I appreciate the offer."

Herschel and Perline had a four-year-old girl named Emma and they had saved enough money to buy their own home in Beech Tree, not too far from Jarvis and Rita.

Archer Ambrose was now nine years old and he worshiped his dad. At age eight, Rascal taught him how to operate the bulldozer and help him mow the farm field with the old Model A tractor. And he also learned how to drive that.

Emma was homeschooling him and every May he had to go to school in Beech Tree and take a written exam to see if his studies were keeping up with the other children of his age. And each year he was doing the work of students two grades ahead of him. Emma was very strict about his education and she would not relax the standards that she had adopted.

When he turned eight years old, Rascal taught him how to trap. He started by letting Archer go with him when there was nuisance beaver along the railroad. Until he was a little older, Rascal would only let him set traps along the Jarvis Trail and the old road out to the narrow swamp that was always so good hunting. And wherever Archer roamed, Whiskey Jack was always there with him.

Anita Antony was no longer working but she remained at the lodge. When she suggested she go in town to live with her sister, Emma said, "Nonsense, Anita. You have always been a part of our family and you still are." This made Anita so happy she cried. She would do what she could, but she tired easily and there was no more going up and downstairs. For extra help, Perline suggested a younger cousin of hers who actually lived in Lac St. Jean, Paulette Bowman. She was nineteen and had graduated from high school now and didn't know yet what she wanted out of life. This made for an excellent job for her.

Whiskey Jack's Secret

The wood harvesting at the farm had stopped four years earlier. Armand Bowman said there was plenty of spruce and pine that could be harvested, but if Hitchcock was to wait a few more years they could probably double their profit. So Armand and his wife were asked to move to Kidney Pond and take over for Earl Hitchcock who was retiring. He was much older than his brother Rudy, and he had had enough. Armand Bowman had proved himself to be as good a woods boss and company supervisor as Earl.

The lodge was still doing a great business and they had to increase their prices some as cost of living increased. Rascal and Emma had been in business now for twelve years and had managed to save a little over $40,000.00. That's more money than either of them had ever dreamed of having.

It had been seventeen years since Bear had made an appearance at Whiskey Jack Lake. He was still there and always wanting to play with either Rascal or Whiskey Jack. Archer was too small to play with Bear and Rascal and Emma had made it clear to him, "Not until you are bigger, Archer."

At nearly 600 pounds now, Bear was the king. They never saw another lone bear, only a yearly sow with cubs at the farm. There were never any wolf signs or screaming mountain lions. Bear had made it quite clear they were not wanted at Whiskey Jack Lake.

When Armand moved to Kidney Pond some of the workers went with him. The new spur line and ramps were left intact for when they would come back and start up again for the spruce and pine.

In 1933, on January 30th, President Paul Von Hindenburg appointed Hitler as chancellor and not long after that the republic turned into a single party dictatorship: Nazi Germany. He put the German people back to work building machines of war that violated the Versailles Treaty agreement. He had no intention of bringing all the European countries into one glorious republic peacefully. He was determined to use military force to do so.

And all the while, neighboring countries knew what was slowly happening but they were so tired of fighting and war that not one tried to stop him.

* * * *

It was another hot beginning to July and at supper one evening, Rascal said, "I have me an idea. Now I want to know how you feel about it."

"Well, what is it?"

"Our gasoline generator has a lot of running time on it and before it stops working, I was thinking about replacing it with a new one."

"Okay, that's easy enough to understand. What else have you on your mind?"

"A diesel generator, and one big enough to run everything we have plus an electric water heater."

"Go on, I know there's more," Emma said.

"That way our guests wouldn't have to wait to take a bath. And we wouldn't have to depend on the heater built into the wood cook stove. The kitchen would not be so hot in the summer without the woodstove burning all day. And we could still use the stove heater when it was cold."

"I'll go along with that. How about you, Anita?"

"Oh yes, that kitchen is so hot in the summer."

"Anything else on your mind?"

"Yes, one more idea."

"Well, let's hear it. So far you're doing pretty good," Emma said with a chuckle.

"An oil furnace, to help heat the lodge. It would have a thermostat and the furnace would ignite whenever the temperature dropped to whatever the setting we had it at. Of course we'd have to have service people install these."

"How about some fans?" Anita asked.

"Yes we could have one in each bedroom, the living room, and the dining room and kitchen. We certainly can afford it. So why not? We and our guests would be more comfortable.

"I can go into town tomorrow afternoon."

"Good, and you can take the money from the safe to the bank.

"Anita, would you like to go in with Rascal and visit with your sister for a couple of days?" Emma asked.

"Why yes, I would."

"Archer and I will stay here." That was okay with Archer, as he didn't know very many people in town.

Emma would really have liked to go to town with Rascal. She had always looked forward to those trips with him. But it would also be nice to let Anita have a couple of days to visit her sister.

Anita had her bag packed and sitting on the floor in the dining room before noon the next day. She also enjoyed these trips out to town and visiting with her sister.

Rascal made sure that Anita made it safely to her sister's, and then there was just enough time to go to the bank. Then he got a hotel room and had supper. Afterwards he walked over to visit with Jarvis and Rita for a few minutes.

* * * *

In the morning after eating he walked over to the Beech Tree Plumbing and Heating Company. "Hello, Rascal, what can I do for you?"

"Do you have diesel generators?"

"Yes we do. What are you looking to run with it?"

"Well, an electric hot heater, an oil furnace and lights and cooling fans."

"I have just what you need." They went outside to the warehouse. "This little beauty will do all you want, Rascal. Are you planning to install it yourself?"

"No, I'll need your service people to do that.

"What about an electric hot water heater?"

"We don't have much call for electric. Most of the heaters

we sell are gas. But here is a fifty gallon heater. Should be plenty big enough for your lodge."

"Okay, now the big question. What about an oil furnace?"

"Hot air or water?"

"I read something about a floor furnace."

"Yes, that would be a good choice. It mounts right under your floor with a grate on top to let the hot air up and so people can walk over it."

"Do you have one I can look at?"

"Surely."

Rascal looked the unit over and over. "Do you think this would heat the lodge?"

"Oh, most certainly. How about fuel tanks? I would recommend two, two-hundred-and-fifty-gallon tanks. That should last you a year or at least through the winter."

"Before I can commit myself I must talk with Greg Oliver at the train station to see if there is any way S&A can fill the tanks. I know they carry diesel back and forth."

"You can use the telephone in my office if you want to call him."

After talking with Mr. Oliver, Rascal was told that S&A took a tanker of heating fuel north every month starting in September through April, and S&A would be glad for his business. Eight cents a gallon. "Will everything be installed by the fifteenth of September, Rascal?"

"Yes."

"Then I'll make a delivery notice now. When you need more just call me. But remember we ship one tanker in the middle of the month."

"Thank you, Greg. I'll have everything installed for September delivery."

"Everything is all set with S&A, Mr. Luce. So I'll take the furnace and the two tanks. And we want some electric fans—let's see, do you have twenty?"

"Not on hand, Rascal, but I can have them here probably

before we ship everything up. Three servicemen will come at the same time to install everything. They'll also bring ten gallons of fuel oil so they can test the furnace.

"Anything else?"

"Yes, a fifty gallon drum and pump, full of diesel fuel."

"Yes, of course."

"Do you want me to add in the service charge now along with the total for everything?"

"Might as well."

"It probably will take the men two maybe three days to install everything. Can they stay at the lodge?"

"As long as they come before September."

"I'll try to have them there before the end of July."

"That sounds good. How much?"

Mr. Luce was several minutes totaling everything. "That all comes to $485.00."

"I presume you'll take a check."

"Yes, of course."

He had spent most of the day talking with Mr. Luce and he was excited about the even furnace heat, hot water tank and the new generator. Before going back to the hotel he bought Emma some of her favorite wine. Anita had told him she was planning to spend three days with her sister.

He was excited to get home and tell his wife and son about everything. Tom gave him his newspaper so he would not have to throw it onto the platform. They were waiting for him on the platform.

"Have you eaten breakfast, Rascal?"

"No."

"Come in and I'll start frying ham and eggs." Archer was now responsible for the chickens and gathering eggs, so he left and went to work. Whiskey Jack followed him down to the hen house and he knew he wasn't allowed inside the pen, so he sat watching the chickens run around and scratch the ground for food.

Rascal sat at the table and opened the newspaper. In big headlines on the front page: JAPAN INVADES CHINA

Emma came running out from the kitchen. "What is it Rascal?"

"Japan. Japan invaded China near Peiping in northern China and Hitler is threatening all of Europe. I'm just glad Archer isn't old enough to fight." With that she went back in the kitchen to finish breakfast.

* * * *

Anita took two extra days to visit with her sister and she came up on the train the same day the furnace and the rest, along with the three servicemen. Rascal had his small bulldozer ready to unload the car. "We need to hook up the new generator first."

Years ago Rascal had built a separate shed to house the gasoline generator and it was large enough for the new diesel unit. He moved the gas unit to the old mill for now. There really wasn't much to do to install the new generator.

The startup procedure was different than the gas unit and Rascal would have to read the owner's manual.

While Pete was installing the generator, Richard and Bob carried the two oil tanks into the cellar and set them up. Then they carried the hot water heater down and while they were setting that up Pete ran an electrical cable from the circuit box to the heater.

While this was going on, Archer helped his mother open all the boxes with fans. "I can't wait to use one of these in the kitchen," Anita said.

Pete, Richard and Bob were there three days before everything was installed and operating properly. "We have to leave this afternoon, folks. We really hate to go. All of you are such nice people and your cooking is better even than my wife's or mother's," Pete said.

"This is so nice not having to work in a hot kitchen every day and cooling fans. What could be better?" Anita said.

The floor furnace had been installed between the dining room and the kitchen, a sort of small hallway.

The electric fans were a God-send. They all, guests included, were falling to sleep much faster with a breeze blowing over them.

What was happening in Europe and now in the Far East was beginning to affect the number of guests. No one knew what was going to happen and many young men were being drafted into military service. As President Kingsley had said, "It would be senseless to wait to prepare our military until they are needed. Then it would be too late."

During September over the last few years, they had seen an almost full house with fishermen. Now there would be between six and ten each week. And that deer season it was the same. No any week was full completely of hunters. As far as their gross income was concerned, though it was off some, they were still making a good living.

This Hitler guy who had proclaimed himself chancellor, began picking up Jews off the streets and breaking into their homes and hauling them off to concentration camps. Where he tried to justify the cleansing by telling them they would be better off.

But everyday Hitler was trumpeting hatred and proclaiming the Aryan race superior and how he was going to bring all of Europe together. Italy had already formed an alliance with Nazi Germany, the Rome-Berlin axis. As well as Germany and Japan agreeing to an anti-comintern pact.

And on March 12, 1938, Hitler took Austria, now as part of Germany. "Why don't these countries fight back, Rascal?" Emma asked.

"I'm not sure, unless it has something to do with their economy. When the London and Paris stock exchanges had a run and the value dropped they were worse off, I think, than we were. Our economy was stronger, I believe, because Canada and The United States merged making our economy stronger.

Maybe all of Europe is still struggling from the last war and can't financially afford a strong military. Where as Hitler is taking everything away from his own people to finance his glory of ruling all of Europe."

But what the folks at Whiskey Jack Lodge and the public in general didn't know is that ever since the information obtained from Hans Hessel, and the rest of the same spy ring was rounded up, is that President Kingsley had had several meetings with his staff, and North America had been secretly increasing their armaments, with ships ready to be loaded and deployed in a minutes notice. All this had to remain classified and much of the operations were accomplished at night.

The Joint Chiefs of Staff had also agreed to take Japan's move into China seriously and the same preparedness was occurring on the west coast; the ports of Vancouver, Seattle, San Francisco and San Diego were all put on alert and munitions were leaving daily via submarines to Pearl Harbor, Hawaii. And on overcast days, fighter aircraft and bombers were flown to Hawaii.

President Kingsley and his Joint Chiefs knew Japan had intentions of attacking Pearl Harbor. They just didn't know when. Japan needed Hawaii for a staging base for attacking the west coast of North America.

All this information was carefully classified and many people were beginning to wonder what President Kingsley, the Commander in Chief, was waiting for.

* * * *

That fall of 1937, Rascal decided he had better spend more time trapping. He was suspicious of what the next year would bring. That fall for the deer season, all of their guests were influential people. Mostly older men of business. He gave the Jarvis Trail to Archer and while the lake was still opened, he canoed up to the head of the lake and set traps along Jack Brook. It had been several years since he had trapped this area and his return was unbelievable. After that he trapped up behind the log cabin along his old trap line. He did well here also. Archer didn't do quite so well on the Jarvis Trail, although he did well enough that he was excited. So one day Rascal went with him and after checking the sets they hiked all the way down to the tracks and set up along the brook.

Rascal stopped setting traps at mile nine and said, "I don't want you going any farther down the brook, son. You can see the railroad from here so you won't get lost. We'll follow the tracks back and set another fox trap before we get back to the lodge."

Emma was concerned at first about Archer going out on his own and so far away. "He'll be okay, Em. I have given him physical boundaries that he is not allowed to cross. Out to the Jarvis Trail, down to the railroad and along the brook only as far as mile nine. The railroad is in sight all the way and then back up the tracks to home."

"I know you wouldn't let him go alone, Rascal, unless you were sure, but he's only nine years old."

By the end of trapping season Archer had five foxes, four martin, two raccoons and one fisher. He was so proud that he had done so well for a nine year old and by himself. Rascal had done well also, but no mountain lions or wolves. He had found two new beaver colonies on Jack Brook above the lake and if he didn't take 'em now then next summer they would be a problem for the S&A Railroad.

Fur prices had almost doubled in the last eight years, due mostly because of the strong national economy. Rascal took his money to the bank and Archer decided he wanted a savings account of his own. He put his entire earnings in the bank. He earned an allowance each week for helping around the lodge and that he figured was his spending money.

While they were in town they visited Jarvis and Rita. There wouldn't be a northbound train until the next morning anyhow. Archer told them all about his trap line on the Jarvis Trail.

Jarvis and Rita both were in their seventies, but no one would know it by their physical appearance. They each had slowed down some, but there was no doubt in Rascal's mind that Jarvis could still walk the pants off anyone else.

There were fewer poaching complaints around Beech Tree and the surrounding farmlands now. Herschel had developed a reputation comparable to his father's and even the older men in town were accepting him as one of their own. When he and Jarvis would get together for a Sunday dinner they would sit on the porch for hours telling stories about chasing poachers and exploring the wilderness. During these times, Rita and Perline would smile, and the closeness of father and son made them love their husbands even more.

* * * *

Every evening when they would listen to the radio for the news and weather broadcast, invariably either what was happening in China with Japanese trying to subject her or what Nazi Germany was doing. And as with Rascal, Emma and Anita, most people were real concerned about what would happen. Would North America be drawn into this war in Europe like the last war or being drawn all the way across the Pacific to the Far East.

Everyone was worried and wondering what would happen eventually in Europe and the Far East. Whenever they had to go to Beech Tree or Lac St. Jean, Emma noticed that there was a subdued attitude among most people. And she was very much aware of it at Whiskey Jack Lodge. She and Rascal would talk privately at night before going to sleep.

"Rascal, what do you think is the future for our lodge with all that's happening in the world?"

"If worse was to come to worst, we don't owe anybody anything. We have enough in our savings to see us through rough years. Besides what Archer and I can make trapping. There will always be people who'll want to go fishing or hunting and to get away from their normal routine of life."

"This is scarier than when we first took over the hotel," Emma said.

"We made it through that time, didn't we?"

"Yes, but I remember, Rascal, how I felt when you left and how empty and awful I felt when Rebecca and Jasper died and you weren't here. I blamed you so much for how I was feeling then. Because you were not here. I hate to think of some other mother having to experience that.

"And then there is Archer. I know you will not be called up to serve again and I realize he is only nine, almost ten, but these troubled times could go on for years."

"I know things in Europe have affected me also, but I try not to dwell on it. Even if worse comes to worst, we'll be okay here."

With that they both went to sleep.

Chapter 15

During the winter of 1938 they all tried not to talk too much about what was happening in Europe, and Japan seemed too far removed to be of any threat. In March of that year, spring would be showing its arrival soon. The snow was already melting away from the buildings and on shore around the lake. And they all were looking forward to spring and warm weather. But all of their fears and worries started to come to light again, as one evening on the evening news the commentator announced that on March 12th Hitler had annexed Austria. "Wasn't he from Austria?" Anita asked.

"Yes," Emma answered.

"These sure are unsettled times," Rascal said.

In April the snow was gone and the ice on the lake was black. "The ice is going out early this year," Rascal said.

Not having to be shut up inside the lodge now for day after day they all began to think ahead of the fishing season and less about what was going on in Europe or the Far East. And slowly they started to feel better. During the winter, because of what was happening in Europe, prices on almost everything jumped by five percent. Big business was fearing that North America would be pulled into yet another European war. Let alone what was happening in the Far East.

In spite of everybody's fears they still had a good spring fishing season. There were only a few less guests that spring and many said they would be back in the fall.

Business during the spring and summer was better than what they had feared and they all began to relax. During the slow months of July and August, Rascal and Emma, Archer and Whiskey Jack, would walk out to the farm in the evenings and invariably Bear would sense their coming and he would greet them and he and Whiskey Jack would run around and chase each other until they tired and lay down facing each other. Sometimes Rascal would join in and play with them and Bear seemed to actually enjoy it when Rascal would chase him.

"Dad, how long have you and Bear been playing?" Archer asked.

"Seventeen years now."

"And he had never hurt you?"

"Not even a scratch."

"It just all seems so strange," Archer added.

"Your mother and I have been saying that for seventeen years."

* * * *

Another year passed and that winter of 1939 it was so cold the ice on the lake froze four feet thick. And the wind blew so strong at times that it kept the lake swept clean of snow. There was a four foot pressure ridge that went across the middle of the lake. "This is the highest pressure ridge that I have ever seen out here," Rascal said one day.

When the wind was the worst, they had to use the new furnace plus the fireplace and woodstoves to keep warm inside the lodge.

Archer would turn eleven years old in April and one night while lying in bed, Emma said, "I think it is time, Rascal, that Archer goes to school. This has been a good life, growing up here, but he has no friends and he only socializes with our friends. He needs more, and I want him to have a good education."

"What do you have in mind, Em?"

"In September we send him to Beech Tree Academy School. I've looked into it and it is a very good school and he would stay there in the dormitory with other boys. Girls stay in another dormitory of course. And we can certainly afford it."

"That might be a good idea."

In the morning they talked with Archer about going to the Academy and much to their surprise he was excited about the idea.

In April, before spring fishing, Emma, Archer and Anita took the train to Beech Tree. Anita's sister had not been feeling well all winter and her doctor told Anita that he couldn't find anything wrong except her age. And he didn't expect her to live much longer. Anita took her home and decided to stay with her until the end.

Principal Jackson at the academy was concerned about Archer's homeschooling and would he qualify scholastically. "He will have to take an examination today. Are you ready young man?"

"Yes, sir."

Archer had finished the test much sooner than the time he was allowed, which surprised Mr. Jackson.

"Can you come back after lunch? It will take me a little time to correct this and then we can talk further."

When they returned after lunch Mr. Jackson asked them to sit down and he closed his office door. "You said earlier I believe that you have been teaching your son, Mrs. Ambrose. Is that correct?"

"Yes, Mr. Jackson."

"Well, I must say you have done a remarkable job. Young man you certainly qualify. In fact your test scores are so good I'm going to advance you a grade and into the 8th grade."

Emma signed the admission papers and wrote out a check for Mr. Jackson for the first year at the academy starting September 4th.

"Archer should be here on the 2nd of September, Mrs. Ambrose."

"He'll be here, Mr. Jackson, and thank you."

The next morning they took the train back to Whiskey

Jack. "You surprise me, Archer."

"How do you mean Mom?"

"I didn't think you would be this excited about leaving home to attend school at the academy. I've always thought you were so much like your father and nothing could pull you away."

"I do love home, Mom, and I will miss it. And you and Dad and Anita. But, Mom, I like learning and reading books."

* * * *

Two days before Archer was scheduled to start classes at the academy he and his dad boarded the train. Rascal knew, as did Emma, that this was best for their son. He needed a well-rounded education and he needed to know how to socialize with people. But Rascal was quiet all the way to the terminal. He felt like he was losing his best friend.

On September 4, 1939, as Archer was starting classes, Rascal read in the paper that one and a half million German soldiers invaded Poland. Poland's military and its generals were too antiquated to oppose a much stronger force. There was little resistance.

On September 3rd, France and Great Britain officially declared war against Germany. As soon as President Kingsley received word of the invasion, he summoned all council members to parliament. It was a short session. Much of Upper North America still had strong ties with both France and England. The decision to join the Allied Forces in Europe wasn't an overwhelming vote, but the majority was in favor and immediately the troops and supplies that had earlier been stockpiled in strategic locations, were deployed to France, Belgium, Holland and Great Britain.

This move by the newly formed nation of North America caught Hitler and his war department by surprise. They had thought that if North America entered the war in support of the Allies it would have been much later in his campaign to conquer Europe.

Hitler was furious and even more so when he learned of huge convoys of ships carrying troops, equipment and supplies were now halfway across the Atlantic. Escorted by fleets of American naval ships and submarines.

Bombers, B-14s, B-17 and B-24s and fighter aircraft were taking off by the hundreds every day from Portland and Bangor, Maine, and from Moncton and New Brunswick, Halifax, Nova Scotia, and St. John's, Newfoundland. Refueling in Iceland.

It was only but a couple of days, and Antwerp, Belgium, Rotterdam, Netherlands, were full of North American aircraft. Great Britain and France were to launch a simultaneous strike on the German front along France's border.

Two days after landing the Allied Air Force began their bombing runs against the advancing German line. The Allies did not have sufficient troops on the ground yet to push the German lines back, but their bombing raids, day and night, kept them from advancing.

Hitler was furious. His plans for a unified Europe under Germany's control looked as if he was going to be stopped before he had gained much. He began blaming his generals and replacing them.

* * * *

At supper four days later Rascal said, "I hate to say this, but this is actually good news."

"How on earth can you believe that, Rascal?" Emma wanted to know.

"Well, I believe the last war wouldn't have lasted anywhere near as long as it did if the United States had joined the Allied Forces much sooner. I don't like war, nobody does, but with our presence now in Europe I can't see this lasting very long."

"Oh I hope you are right, Rascal."

* * * *

The intelligence coming back to Sault Ste. Marie from the Far East was that North America's sudden move to join forces with Allied Forces in Europe had seriously upset Hitler's plans.

Emperor Hirohito still wanted to attack Pearl Harbor, but he was urged by his staff to wait. Hirohito became so angry he admonished his staff. So what was to happen simultaneously in December 1941, the attacks on Pearl Harbor, as well as Thailand, Malaya, Singapore, Hong Kong, Guam and the Philippines, now would be concentrated only on Pearl Harbor. But the South Pacific fleets would remain where they were. Vice Admiral Chuich Nagamo convinced Hirohito that his fleet could easily destroy Pearl Harbor and sink her battleships in the harbor's shallow waters, tying up their removal, preventing the North American Hawaii fleet from retaliating.

Admiral Nagamo had planned to attack Pearl Harbor with six carrier groups. But there were not six groups now ready to advance. There were only three. Admiral Nagamo assured the Emperor that three carriers would be all that was needed, since Hawaii seemed to be asleep and all the naval vessels should be in the harbor.

The emperor wanted to act now while the North American's task force was busy in Europe. Hirohito demanded that Nagamo attack Pearl Harbor on October 1st.

Nagamo had six days to fully finish equipping his fleet.

* * * *

President Kingsley, his staff and the director of the intelligence department met and the intelligence from the Pacific and Japan was that Admiral Nagamo was preparing three carrier fleets to set sail in time to attack Pearl Harbor at dawn on October 1st.

They knew there had been spies on Hawaii and President Kingsley ordered them to be arrested immediately. Daily flights were also ordered looking for Japanese reconnoiter planes, with the order to shoot them down.

This was all a move to protect a North American Territory and President Kingsley was the Commander in Chief and didn't need a declaration of war from parliament. That would come later if it was to be needed.

At midnight on October 1st, four North American carrier groups left Hawaii. The information they had was the Japanese carrier groups were going to launch their bombers and fighters two hundred miles out for a surprise attack. It was now planned to let the carrier groups use up as much fuel as possible. The Japanese had no idea they were sailing into a much larger force than their own.

At first light the Japanese planes started to take off. Only about a third of them had launched when the North American fighters flew in to attack first the aircraft carriers, to put their planes out of commission or to damage the carriers so heavily that they could not launch. All the while four battle ships were closing the distance. Six submarines were already there, and had taken out two Japanese submarines not long after the battle had started.

The battle lasted for twenty hours before the last Japanese battleship surrendered. It was so heavily damaged it could no longer fire its massive guns or the antiaircraft guns. Two of the three carriers were sunken and the third was listing heavily to port. It was really a one sided battle, although many North American planes had been shot down. But they had not lost a single ship. Although they were heavily damaged, but still afloat.

Two days later parliament officially declared war against Japan.

* * * *

Rascal read of the full report about the Pacific battle in the newspaper and told Emma and Anita about it. "Looks like we're fighting in Europe and the Far East now," Emma said. "Whatever happened to the good ole days?"

Because of what was happening around the world, there were only six hunters the first week of deer hunting season. In the evening as they sat in the living room enjoying the warmth of the fireplace the topic of discussion was of course about this new war, now being called World War Two. There was some discussion about, why had parliament entered the war so soon. And then there was conversation about entering now, before either Germany or Japan had managed to extend their conquests, the fighting probably would not last as long. The first World War should have been proof of that.

For many of their guests it was agreed that the fighting in the Far East would probably last longer than in Europe. The Allies pretty much had Hitler's forces cornered and he was fighting desperately.

The fighting was day and night, but the Axis troops were so undermanned compared to the Allies. Hitler had wanted to go into Russia from Poland, but he was now afraid if he split his forces the Allies would have an open door right to Berlin.

His vision of his conquest for all of Europe was quickly disappearing. Hitler was so afraid of being defeated he issued an immediate order to stop the imprisonment and killing of Jews. Some of his advisors and generals had already left Germany. Hitler ordered a battalion to protect Berlin and a company of troops to protect the Nazi headquarters. With each breath he took he was cursing North America for joining forces with the Allies.

German forces were being forced back towards Berlin a little with each day. At the start, the German troops were tough fighters, but slowly they began to question what it was they were fighting for. And soon they began to lose their spirit to fight. Hundreds of German troops were surrendering daily. They were calling the Allied front that was pushing them back the Fleish Reiben (meat grinder).

The Allies had also lost thousands of troops, aircraft and heavy artillery, but not to the extent of the Germans.

* * * *

By spring of 1940, Germany had had enough and companies and battalions were now surrendering and the German people were calling for a cease fire. By May, the fighting stopped but Hitler was nowhere to be found. It was rumored that he had fled Europe two months earlier.

There was a North American company left in Berlin to reestablish authority, but most of the Allied forces were now heading for the Far East.

During the winter of 1940 the North American troops had experienced a lot of tough, dug-in fighting. But they were like a slow-moving mowing machine. The British and French troops were just as busy in Thailand, Burma and Malaya.

With every battle the Allies were now winning, the Japanese were losing another base of operation and fueling depots for their aircraft and their war machines.

The battle to liberate the Philippines was costly for both sides. But once the Japanese supply line had been stopped, they had no other choice but to surrender. But this didn't happen overnight. There were many groups that were well dug in with supplies. But when those were gone, they too had to surrender.

In Lower North America a new type of bomb was being built that the engineers said would bring a quick end to the Japanese aggression with total surrender. The Manhattan Project, an atomic bomb, was being developed in Alamogordo, New Mexico. The project engineers had originally wanted to use it against Germany. But they had already surrendered, so they now were looking towards Japan to try out this new bomb.

But the Japanese were also surrendering faster than the final development of the bomb. The battles on Iwo Jima and Okinawa were long and bloody, for both sides. But once they fell to the North American troops, many in Tokyo wanted to surrender. It had been obvious they, too, were fighting a losing battle with no future. But Emperor Hirohito said no. To surrender would bring disgrace to all Japanese people.

President Kingsley had a meeting with his staff and recommended that the entire Pacific fleet advance on Japan. "Blockade Tokyo Bay; if fired upon, return fire. Shoot down any enemy planes that approach. I want the entire fleet in position before daylight on June 1st. Admiral, you send that ultimatum at 0800 and you tell Hirohito if you do not have his complete surrender by 1000 hours, that you will open up with everything you have available and you also tell Hirohito that there are one hundred B-29s on their way to Tokyo. If you do not have his unconditional surrender, Tokyo will be leveled.

"Gentlemen I do not want to use this new atomic bomb. The Japanese are so beaten now I do not believe it is prudent or necessary to use it.

"Admiral, can you do this? You have five days to get your ships into position."

"Yes, Mr. President, it will be done."

"General, can you have one hundred B-29s fueled and loaded and ready to launch so that you can be over Tokyo at 1000 hours'?"

"Yes, sir, I will make it happen."

"Okay, once you have Hirohito's surrender you are to proceed up Tokyo Bay and the marine and army troops will secure the city.

"Thank you gentlemen. These have been trying times and maybe this will put an end to it."

* * * *

It had taken Archer a month to feel comfortable at the academy. He was shy among so many people his own age. But once he was over that shyness, he became happy and did very well with his studies. He was two years younger than any other student in his class and because of his lifestyle he was stronger and more mature.

He was allowed to return home one weekend a month, and

since his grades were so good, he was allowed to leave on Friday mornings, as long as he was back at the academy by 7 a.m. on Monday mornings.

The school in 1941, last day, was May 29th. He would have the entire summer to enjoy being at home.

Because the war was still being fought in the Pacific, there still were not as many fishermen as there usually had been for spring fishing. But they still had enough to make the lodge profitable, just not as much.

Rascal had turned on the radio Sunday to listen for the news as they ate breakfast. That week's guests had left the day before on Saturday and today there were six more scheduled to arrive soon.

Just as the four of them sat down to eat, the radio commentator came on the air:

"Ladies and gentlemen!" he hollered over the air. "The war is over. The war is over, folks! Emperor Hirohito agreed to a surrender yesterday just before noon their time."

He went on to explain what had happened on Saturday, June 1st, to make the Emperor decide to change his mind and surrender unconditionally.

When the train arrived the radio was still broadcasting the previous day's events and this was all new to the arriving guests. All day practically everybody stayed inside the lodge talking about how fast the fighting had been brought to such a quick ending. And it was unanimously agreed that it was because the new nation, North America, had joined the Allies at the onset of the war. And that this never would have happened if Canada and the United States had not merged into one nation.

This was truly a great day for the new nation and President Cutlidge and President Kingsley were responsible for this great event to occur from the beginning.

Anita spoke up so all could hear and said, "And here at Whiskey Jack Lodge is the birthplace of the idea of the two countries merging. And folks, for those of you who are here for your first time, look at the plaques on the wall."

Archer hadn't been born yet, but he was now certainly feeling a lot of pride for his Mom and Dad and Anita. He wished he had been here then.

The next day Jarvis, Rita, Herschel, Perline and their little girl Emma arrived to help celebrate. "We just as soon stay in the log cabin if that's available?"

"Certainly, I'll go up and open it up and air it out."

"I'll walk up with you, Rascal," Jarvis said.

Herschel went outside with Archer and Whiskey Jack and Rita and Perline helped Emma and Anita.

Little Emma wanted to tag along with her daddy.

As Rascal and Jarvis walked up to the cabin, Rascal couldn't help but notice that Jarvis had no trouble keeping up with him and he wasn't even breathing heavy. "How old are you now, Jarvis?"

"I'll be 80 next month."

"Hum, you sure don't look or act like it." His hair, as was Rita's, was now gray, but their skin was tight and no wrinkles.

After they had the cabin opened they sat out on the porch talking of long ago years and times. "You know, Rascal, outside my family, I was always the happiest when I was up here in Whiskey Jack. I still dream of chasing poachers and instead of having supper with my family I dream of cooking fish or beaver meat over an open fire and sleeping under a spruce tree somewhere. God, how I loved those times.

"You know, Rascal, many of the people I had to arrest were good people. Even some of those that I had to rough up. When I surprised them, it would scare them and they responded the only way they knew how."

"What was the most serious case you ever had, Jarvis?"

"Without a doubt, those two Frenchmen that were working at the farm and were using a set gun to shoot deer. While I was waiting for them to come and check it, I started thinking what if I hadn't seen the gun when I did and hit the trip line to the trigger, that shotgun with double ought buck would have cut me in half."

They sat there in the sun just quietly enjoying the fresh air and the view up the lake. Then Jarvis said, "There is something, Rascal, that I hesitate to bring up, but it has bothered me for years now not knowing how you managed to pull it off. I just gotta know."

"Okay, what do you want to know?"

"The day Emma shot that doe deer and you and I were, by chance, standing on the dam. I know you set it up when you said, 'You would take me to jail if it were me.' You wanted me to take her to jail. But how did you do it? You had no idea I would be in Whiskey Jack that morning. I know you did it, but I would like to know how."

Rascal started laughing then, almost hysterically. When he could compose himself he began to explain.

"It all started not long after I returned home after WWI. Em had paid Jeters to take me fishing and get me drunk, so she could berate me and make me go to church. And she wouldn't cook for me and I had to sleep on the porch." He started laughing again.

"But we had one hell of a good time fishing. The best of it all, we only caught one small fish." Then he told Jarvis the whole story about he and Jeters fishing while drunk.

"And then there was the time when Jeters, Silvio and I were making brandy. I know it was Em that told Sheriff Burlock. When I came home I had to sleep again on the porch and cook my own meal.

"I was determined to teach her a lesson, so I started grooming a doe deer with a fawn, to the garden. I knew it would only be a matter of time when she would start eating Em's lettuce. To make it look as if I was going to shoot it, I left my rifle loaded leaning up against a door jamb. When you arrived that morning it was a real surprise. I knew Em was home and just maybe that doe would do her part. She did and you just happened to be here.

"When she returned from jail I made her fix her own meal and sleep on the porch like she had made me. Come morning all was forgiven and she stopped treating me so hatefully, just like we were right after we were married. It's been like that ever since."

"So it was all happenstance? You had no way of knowing I would be here that morning, no more than you did the doe was going to eat Emma's lettuce that morning," Jarvis broke out laughing and then Rascal.

"Do me a big favor Jarvis, don't mention any of this to Em. Please, we don't talk about it. Never have."

They continued talking, telling stories and laughing until almost noon, when Herschel stepped on the platform and hollered for them to come down for lunch.

* * * *

Once the announcement had been made that the war in the Pacific was now over also, life everywhere returned to normal, and requests for a week for deer hunting started coming in and they were soon booked fully for each week. Except that, is, for the last week. Although the Thanksgiving holiday had been moved to November 4th, the family all agreed to wait until the last week for more convenient. The family, consisting of Anita, the Ambroses and all of the Page family. It was a happy day and more stories were told.

Anita spoke up and said, "You know there is one member missing," and everyone assumed she was talking about Silvio, "Bear." Everyone laughed.

Chapter 16

Four more years had passed. Rascal and Emma were both forty-seven. Anita was ninety, and Jarvis and Rita were both eighty four. Jarvis didn't look a day over sixty, and he could still walk the legs off of many men much younger than he. He and Rita would walk five miles every day along a forested trail he had cleared out of the woods.

And Bear— Bear was still making his appearance whenever they walked out to the farm. Rudy had been in that April of 1945 and said, "We are going to set up again here. Not here, but at the farm. We are building a new sawmill with a band saw, like the one at Kidney Pond and we'll be building additional living quarters too. And Armand and his wife Priscilla have asked to come back here.

"Armand is a good man and he'll also be doing my job when the old mill was operating, and he'll have a forester working for him this time.

"I have already contacted the S&A Railroad and once we start sawing there will once again be a morning and afternoon train leaving Whiskey Jack, like the old days.

"The equipment in the old building will be dismantled and put aboard the train for salvage. If you want the building Rascal, we'll leave that.

"May I make a suggestion and this concerns both of you?"

"We're listening," Emma said.

"Once we're up and running with more train service coming and going there will be people, business people and the railroad coming and going, and they'll need a place to stay. I'd like to encourage you to expand your lodge to take care of this flow of people.

Rascal and Emma looked at each other before answering, "I think we can do that."

"Good. Now here is how I can help you. You draw up the plans of what you want. Do it soon. I have a crew of four very good carpenters who could put it together for you in short order. I presume you would want to have the addition log, to match the rest of the building. My men will cut the spruce they'll need. You have shipped in everything else you'll need. You pay the men's wages and room and board for however long it'll take.

"Would this be agreeable with you two?"

They looked at each other and without a word between them they both said, "Yes, Mr. Hitchcock."

"Good, I'll have my men here June 1st. It might also speed things along some if between now and then you could cut the spruce trees needed and twitch 'em here with your crawler."

"Consider it done and we'll have the logs peeled."

After Rudy left, Rascal said, "You know I was thinking about building an addition on for more guests. I just didn't want to tell Rudy."

"I had been thinking the same thing. And you know with business so good, we're going to need more help in the kitchen. I hope Perline's cousin Paulette will come back."

"Maybe to entice her you could say it would be a full time position year round, with time off, of course," Rascal suggested.

Anita had really slowed down in the last four years and she wasn't doing much more than sitting by the stove and stirring soup or checking the oven. That was fine with both Emma and Rascal. After all, she had through the years become more family than friend.

Emma telephoned Paulette that evening and "Yes, I would love to come back. When?"

"Anytime you can come."

"I'll be there in two days."

* * * *

By the end of April, Rascal had all the spruce trees cut and peeled that he had figured they would need, and piled up off the ground on racks to dry. He also ordered flooring boards for the addition, windows, doors and roofing.

They had decided to build on an -L- on the living room end of the main lodge. A hallway down the center of it with three additional bedrooms on both sides. This would accommodate twelve more guests. There would be a communal bathroom and showers in the end of the hall.

On Saturday evening May 5th, Emma answered the telephone. "Hello."

"Hello, Emma?"

"Yes, what can I do for you?"

"Emma, this is David Elliot."

Emma screamed and said, "Rascal! Rascal!"

"What?"

"Rascal. It's President Cutlidge. Yes, Mr. Elliot what can I do for you?" and she giggled. Rascal was now standing beside her.

"Emma, by any chance would your lodge be empty or full the first week of July?"

"We have no guests at all scheduled for that week, Mr. Elliot."

"Good. I would like to reserve your full compliment for that week, starting on July 1. Myself and my wife Pearl and Secret Service Agent Raymond Butler will be arriving Sunday morning on the southbound train from Lac St. Jean. Also arriving will be President William Kingsley, his wife Myrissa and his Secret Service Agent Fredrika Dubois for a week of visiting friends, fishing and relaxation. And also, if possible, Jarvis and Rita Page for the week."

"Yes, sir, we will be looking forward to your arrival."

Emma hung up the telephone, turned around and just stood there looking at Rascal, Anita and Paulette who had joined her. "I get to meet two Presidents?" Paulette said all excited.

Anita stood there smiling.

"It would be nice to have some frog legs, beaver and moose meat, Rascal."

"I hear ya. I'll see what I can do."

* * * *

The day before Memorial weekend Archer graduated from Beech Tree Academy at age seventeen. He was happy, but not as much as his Mom and Dad. They caught the northbound train the next morning. Anita had come out with them and like Emma, Anita was in tears. She was just as happy.

When Emma told Archer the news about the two Presidents coming for a week, he couldn't believe it. "Well, I'll be. I never thought I'd ever get to meet either one."

Emma had also telephoned Rita and of course they could come.

The building crew arrived that weekend and they didn't waste any time. The foreman Bruce Henry took one look at Rascal's sketch and set his men to work. "Sure was nice of you, Rascal, to have the trees all cut and peeled for us. That'll make the job go so much faster."

"I'd like to help too, Mr. Henry," Archer said.

After the second day they had the foundation, the bottom logs and subfloor all done. Archer was enjoying the physical work. He had sat behind a desk studying for too long.

By the end of the third week the new addition was finished, including an interior oak flooring. Later, Rascal would have to get an electrician and a plumber up to finish.

On the morning of July 1, everybody was scrubbed clean and wearing nice casual clothes. Jarvis and Rita had arrived the day before. The morning northbound had switched to the farm spur line to let the southbound through. When the train stopped so the passengers could step off, Raymond Butler and Fredrika Dubois stepped off first and surveyed the area and then stepped aside for Presidents Kingsley and Cutlidge and their wives to step off. Tom then signaled all clear to the engineer and the southbound left.

There were hugs and kisses all around and Archer and Paulette were a little shy until Kingsley noticed them staying back. Then he walked over and introduced himself and then his wife, Myrissa. Then Cutlidge and his wife did the same.

"Come inside, folks, where it is cooler. Anita has a fresh pot of coffee on."

"Archer, will you help Paulette take the luggage upstairs, please?"

As they were drinking coffee, Jarvis said, "Rascal, Rita would like to see Bear."

"Is he still around?" President Cutlidge asked. "I've told Pearl all about him and she would like to see him too."

"So would I," Myrissa said.

"Before we walkout to the farm there are two stories I'd like to tell you, first."

Rascal told them about protecting the lodge from the marauding mountain lion and how scared some of the guests had been. Then Emma told them about the time Bear saved her from the wolf.

And of course they all wanted to hear the story of Bear capturing Herr Hans Hessel. "After hearing the two stories about the mountain lion and the wolf, I can understand better now why Bear attacked Hessel. He must have seen him as a threat," President Kingsley said.

"A remarkable animal," President Cutlidge added.

"That is so extraordinary."

"Rascal, I notice you don't limp anymore, so I'm assuming the operation went well?"

"Yes, sir. There are times when it begins to ache some, but then I stop whatever I was doing.

"If everybody is ready it is a little more than a mile out to the farm. On second thought, with the crews working on a new building, Bear probably won't be there. He might be out behind the log cabin."

"Anita, how about you?" Emma asked.

"Go on without me. I'll sit out on the platform and wait for you."

Archer hooked Whiskey Jack on a leash and held on to it.

"This is such a beautiful spot," Myrissa said.

"Whose log cabin is this?" Pearl asked.

"This is where Rascal and I lived before we took over the hotel and transformed it into a lodge. Back then, there was an outhouse, gravity fed water, one light bulb that went out when the mill cut the power at 9 o'clock in the evening, and we heated and cooked with wood."

"My, such primitive conditions," Pearl said.

"Yes, they were, but we had a good life here."

"This is where President Kingsley and I worked out the agreement to merge the two countries."

"It would be better not to talk so much from here," Rascal said.

On top of the knoll was a fresh pile of bear scat. "He's here," Rascal whispered and pointed.

Bear was waiting for them at the end of the road. "He is so much bigger than when we were here before."

"Yeah, he'll go over six hundred pounds now. Archer you hold on to Whiskey Jack."

Rascal took a couple of steps forward and raised his arm and made that greeting sound that he always did. "He talks to the bear?" Paulette whispered.

"Watch what happens next, Paulette," Archer said.

"Bear, these are my friends. Some you know and some are new to you."

Bear outstretched his paw and said, "Aarrry."

"He talks!" Myrissa said.

Bear started running towards Rascal then, and Pearl, Myrissa and Paulette thought he was going to hurt Rascal. But Rascal started running around and Bear began chasing him. Then he tripped Rascal and sat on his haunches laughing. Then he took off running and Rascal chased him. This went on until Rascal was out of wind. "Okay, let Whiskey Jack loose."

The dog ran right in towards Bear and the chasing started all over again. This went on for a half hour before they each stopped and were out of breath.

Archer called Whiskey Jack back and hooked the leash. "Okay, it's time to leave."

"Goodbye, Bear." Bear followed behind them as far as the top of the knoll and he stopped and lay down.

"That is just unbelievable," Rita said. "I remember you telling me about a bear that played with Rascal and I didn't know whether to believe you or not. Now I've seen it."

"How long has this been going on, Mr. Ambrose?" Pearl asked.

"Please, just Rascal. It actually started soon after I returned from the first war in France. He chased Elmo Leaf and me for two and a half miles up the tracks right through the village. We were on a hand railcar." Then he had to tell them everything about Bear.

"How old do you think he is now?" Jarvis asked.

"Well, I first encountered him in 1919, twenty-eight years ago. He was maybe two or three hundred pounds then. He must be close to thirty."

* * * *

The next day, early, they all went fishing. Even Anita. Emma helped her into the middle of the canoe with her and Rascal. They were all going to work their way up to the head of the lake where they would cook trout over an open fire. Agent Butler went with the Cutlidges and Agent Dubois with the Kingsleys.

Rascal, Emma and Anita paddled right up to the inlet and started a fire and put on a pot of coffee to boil.

Even though there was a clear sky and it was warm, they managed to find some spring holes and caught enough brookies so they all had their fill.

"Rascal," Jarvis said, "you once told me you'd rather give me your wife than tell me where your special fish hole is. What is it going to be? Emma or your secret fish hole?"

Rascal looked at Emma. Everyone was looking at him. "You have me between a rock and a hard place. I'm not going to give you Em, so let's go fishing." Everyone laughed.

Rascal and Jarvis pushed off in the canoe. Everyone else stood on shore watching. Not really knowing what to expect. With ease and stealth he guided the canoe into the lily pads. Jarvis started to speak and Rascal sshed him. He brought the canoe to a stop and then he sat there waiting. Those on shore, all except Emma and Archer, were wondering what in heck he was doing.

After five minutes Rascal whispered, "Cast your line towards that white birch only about twelve feet or so and land your fly on top of a lily pad, then let it set there for a moment before you just ease the fly into the water. When you have a fish on don't let it dive or it will tangle up in the weeds."

Jarvis picked out a lily pad and worked enough line out and with his first attempt he landed the fly on the lily pad. And he waited like Rascal said and then he pulled the fly off and into the water and immediately a huge brookie took it and went airborne. Everyone on shore began shouting excitedly.

Jarvis had to pull it in quick like to keep it from diving. Rascal had his net ready and scooped it out of the lily pads and water. "Holy cow will you look at that!" Jarvis said. "That's the biggest brook trout that I have ever caught."

"It'll go five pounds or more."

"How much water is under the lily pads?"

"Not much, but you'd sink in the black mud up to your

neck." Jarvis knew what he was referring to and they both laughed.

They canoed back to the party and got out. "The only time you can catch big trout over there is when the sun is out bright. They like to hide in the shade under the lily pads." Both Kingsley and Cutlidge were impressed with Rascal's ability as a guide and his knowledge of the wilderness.

They stayed up at the head of the lake for hours. Butler and Dubois even caught the fishing fever and tried their luck in the lily pads, and they both caught a big trout.

They ate fish with biscuits and two pots of coffee. Archer and Paulette even went out fishing and when those were cooked they picked up and headed back for the lodge.

* * * *

Wednesday morning, Herschel, Perline and their daughter arrived. "We can only stay one night. I understand Hitchcock Company is coming back this summer."

"Yes, crews are out at the farm now building a new dormitory for more crews and then a new mill. They'll be taking the old equipment out of this one, for salvage.

"Your father, Perline, has made Hitchcock a good man."

"Thank you, Rascal."

Emma and Anita were so happy having everyone there. "It's just like a family reunion, Emma, isn't it?"

"Yes, Anita. It is a good feeling."

Even Butler and Dubois had loosened up and relaxed some and were joining in with conversations and the two would go out fishing by themselves.

And Rita knew her husband was in his glory. She could finally understand why he liked to come up to Whiskey Jack. It wasn't necessarily to catch a poacher as much as it was for the good fellowship that was here.

"I have an excellent idea," Emma said, "we are all family here and we always get together for Thanksgiving dinner on the old original date in November. That week we have no hunters. I would like to invite everyone to come and share that time with us. Mr. Butler and Mr. Dubois, you two have been here enough and we consider you family too. We hope you will come and bring your families. How about it?"

Of course they would love to come, and Butler and Dubois were almost in tears to think that they were now considered as part of the family and they could bring their families.

"The hunting will be good the last week of the season so come prepared," Rascal added.

In the evenings, they would sit out on the platform sipping wine and snacking on smoked trout. Sometimes until long after the sun had set.

Even though Paulette had only been there for a short time, she was considered as much a part of the family as anyone else. Archer, well he bewildered both Cutlidge and Kingsley with his interest in world affairs.

"When do you finish high school, Archer?" Kingsley asked.

"I graduated from the Beech Tree Academy the last of May."

"My, how old are you?"

"Seventeen."

"What are your plans now?" Cutlidge asked.

"I've been thinking a lot lately about the Navy. I'd like to see some of this world that I have been studying about."

"How are your grades, Archer?"

"Real good."

"How much math did you get, and science?"

"As much as I could. I like learning."

President Cutlidge looked at President Kingsley and without saying a word they both nodded their heads.

"Have you ever given any thought about the Naval Academy at Annapolis?"

"Once, but you have to have an appointment. You cannot

just apply by letter."

They both started laughing and then President Kingsley said, "Let's say you obtain an appointment, would you go?"

"You bet!" he replied excitedly.

"Well an appointment from two former Presidents should get you in the door," President Cutlidge said.

"The first year is the roughest. You won't have much time for sleep or anything else," President Kingsley said.

"You'd be pushed to your limit and at times even more," President Cutlidge said.

Archer was so excited and smiling. Rascal and Emma noticed and walked over. "Why are you so happy, Archer?" Emma asked.

He was too overcome with emotions to reply immediately.

President Cutlidge and President Kingsley stood up and said, "We have just agreed to give young Archer an appointment to the Annapolis Naval Academy.

The End

About the Author

Randall Probert lived and was raised in Strong, a small town in the western mountains of Maine. Six months after graduating from high school, he left the small town behind for Baltimore, Maryland, and a Marine Engineering school, situated downtown near what was then called "The Block." Because of bad weather, the flight from Portland to New York was canceled and this made him late for the connecting flight to Baltimore. A young kid, alone, from the backwoods of Maine, finally found his way to Washington, D.C., and boarded a bus from there to Baltimore. After leaving the Merchant Marines, he went to an aviation school in Lexington, Massachusetts.

During his interview for Maine Game Warden, he was asked, "You have gone from the high seas to the air. . .are you sure you want to be a game warden?"

Mr. Probert retired from Warden Service in 1997 and started writing historical novels about the history in the areas where he patrolled as a game warden, with his own experiences as a game warden as those of the wardens in his books. Mr. Probert has since expanded his purview and has written two science fiction books, *Paradigm* and *Paradigm II*, and has written two mystical adventures, *An Esoteric Journey*, and *Ekani's Journey*.

Made in the USA
Middletown, DE
28 March 2018